Darkness tinge~~d~~ with lightning . . .

. . . lurked in the tur~~bulence of~~ Kristian's dreams. It was a world she desperately wanted to escape, rife with multi-eyed aliens who stared at her from the sanctuary of their grubby abodes, watching, waiting in a frozen silence that set her teeth on edge.

Stealthy little noises crept in. She strained to separate and identify them, then felt herself jump slightly as an odd sense of reality took over from illusion. Odd because the differences were so subtle, virtually indistinguishable to her sleep-dulled mind.

Everything seemed foreign, all the shapes that were larger than life, swathed in mottled shadows, surrounding her, shifting, drawing closer—until finally one of them emerged from the darkness, taking on a more distinctive human form with each advancing step.

Or was it human? Kristian sat up and blinked her eyes. This dream had become a full-fledged nightmare. The approaching creature had a mouthful of sharp, pointy teeth that looked to be grinning at her, mocking her as she stared at it, unbelieving. Then, from out of the darkness, a hand came slowly into view, gloved and holding something white. . . .

ABOUT THE AUTHOR

As far back as she can remember, Jenna Ryan has been dreaming up stories, everything from fairy tales to romantic mysteries. She's read Harlequin Intrigue ever since the line was first introduced, and inspired by Anne Stuart's *Hand in Glove*, she set out to write one herself. A resident of Victoria, B.C., Jenna has been a model, an airline reservation agent, a tour escort, and a lingerie salesperson. She now writes full-time.

Books by Jenna Ryan

HARLEQUIN INTRIGUE

Southern Cross

Jenna Ryan

Harlequin Books

TORONTO • NEW YORK • LONDON
AMSTERDAM • PARIS • SYDNEY • HAMBURG
STOCKHOLM • ATHENS • TOKYO • MILAN

To Kathy

Harlequin Intrigue edition published September 1990

ISBN 0-373-22145-2

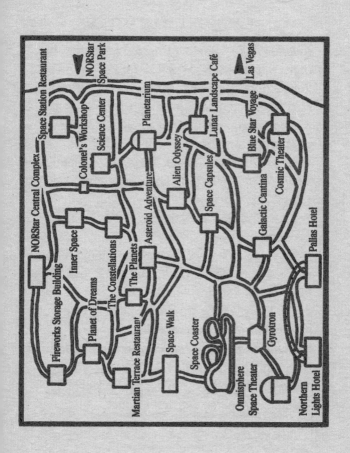

CAST OF CHARACTERS

Kristian Ellis—She'd witnessed a murder, but there was no body. Was it her imagination?

Tory Roberts—He believed Kristian, after she said the words "Southern Cross."

Morton Nash—A partner at NORStar space park who thought he was an "alien."

George Straker—Was he Tory's best friend?

Evan Odell—What did he know about Southern Cross?

June Atherton—Was she Kristian's loyal assistant?

Priscilla Warfield—Morton's goddaughter who worked at the space park. Did she know more than she was saying?

Lilith Lang—Why would the head of computer services hire a computer thief?

Nathan Brenda—He was called the "Colonel," the man who controlled the robots.

Simon Juniper—Was he really murdered?

Telestar—A person without a face.

Prologue

Simon Juniper moved quietly through the long, dark corridors of NORStar Center's main office complex. Like everything else in the sprawling Nevada space park, the building had a decidedly futuristic flavor, an air of galactic fantasy. It was a world of colorful planets and shining stars, of dreams and conjectures, of science and fiction and nebulous myths; a pleasant escape from the reality of the late twentieth century; a journey of sorts into the realm of a bright tomorrow.

There was nothing bright about Simon's tomorrow. He sensed that as he wound his way deeper into the eerily silent complex. He couldn't get in touch with the one man he knew he could trust, and he didn't dare waste precious time trying to locate him. Not after the unwholesome scene he'd just witnessed.

A trickle of cold sweat, which felt suspiciously like blood, slid down his back between his shoulder blades. It was a perfectly natural reaction under the circumstances, but he couldn't afford to dwell on it. He had to think, to act, to do something quickly before it was too late. Ex-Marines didn't panic, he reminded himself, and neither did space park security chiefs.

Unbidden, his mind turned back to another time and place. No more than a few fleeting months of his life, but perhaps something that would work should anything happen to him.

Eyes and ears alert for the slightest sound or movement, he changed direction, heading purposefully for the Saturn wing. A tiny mechanical whir distracted him momentarily as Crux and Carter, NORStar's two nomadic robots, passed each other in the star-studded hallway to his left. Beyond that, nothing stirred. Nothing would stir up here at 11:00 p.m. The park had closed an hour ago. He was alone on this level. He only prayed that situation would continue long enough for him to accomplish his task.

Leaving the door ajar, Simon slipped into one of the deserted offices and crossed the carpet to the elaborate computer console. A few uninterrupted minutes—that was all he'd need to carry out his hastily formed plan. Five minutes, a little bit of luck and a cool head.

"Don't think about it," he muttered as his deft fingers flew over the keyboard. "She's dead, you can't change that. The best you can do now is access the file she stole. And hope to hell you can hide it again."

Before his searching eyes, the information he sought flashed on the computer screen. He'd accessed it, all right, but even that major triumph couldn't override the chilling memory of the dead woman's face. The woman he'd seen murdered only a few short moments ago.

For more than forty-eight hours he'd been tracking her, scrutinizing her every move on his own time, following her everywhere she went, waiting to see where she would ultimately lead him. And lead him she had. Straight to her contact—and possibly far, far beyond.

She hadn't expected to die, he knew that. Mild surprise had changed to astonishment and finally to outright horror as the slender garrote had tightened about her neck.

Had she struggled? Simon couldn't remember, wasn't sure he wanted to. Had he been spotted? He didn't think so, but he couldn't be certain of that, either.

Agitated, he began striking the keys harder. Seconds stretched to minutes, passing in an arduous succession—until at last it was done.

With the back of his hand, he wiped his perspiring upper lip. He'd timed it perfectly. The information the woman had so cleverly buried had been moved, the file wiped clean. The odds were extremely slim that anyone would accidentally stumble across it. All that remained now was for him to get out of here in one unstrangled piece.

Controlling a tremor of revulsion, he reached over to switch the computer off. However, a soft whisper of movement in the outer corridor caused him to still the motion. There was nothing mechanical about this sound. Someone was out there, and heading straight for him.

Slowly he lifted his hand from the panel. With his other he felt for the edge of the desk. If he could slip through the connecting door, he still might have a chance to escape, to get to his own office and the extra gun he kept there. If he could just—

"Simon?" A woman's surprised voice greeted him from the doorway. "What are you doing here? I thought you were on vacation."

Kristian Ellis! Simon didn't know whether he spoke her name out loud or not. His heart was hammering so hard that it was the only thing he could hear.

He sucked in a deep steadying breath, willing himself to calm down. "I, uh, I had some work to finish up." A horrible thought occurred to him, and he frowned, glancing past her shoulder to the empty hallway. "Why are you here?" he demanded harshly, momentarily forgetting that she was in charge of the space park. "It's after eleven."

She tossed her leather valise onto the padded sofa, beneath an enormous lithograph of Orion, the hunter. "Morton decided to call a late-night meeting," she replied, with no rancor for his testy tone. "Something to do with the two new exhibits we're opening on Wednesday."

The NORStar acronym flashed instantly through Simon's head, along with the name of the four partners: Morton Nash, Evan Odell, Tory Roberts and George Straker.

Relief battled with fear in his brain. If Tory was planning to attend a meeting here tonight, perhaps there was still a chance.

He opened his mouth to speak, but the hopeful words died in his throat as his roving eyes suddenly caught sight of something in the smoked glass wall across from him. A barely perceptible glimmer that resembled a fading star. A gleam of metal that could only mean one thing....

Instinct took over from terror. In two rapid strides, Simon reached Kristian's side, grabbing her roughly by the shoulders and practically flinging her from the room.

"Get out of here!" he shouted, planting himself squarely in front of her. "Tell Tory—common ground."

In the back of his mind, he registered the startled expression on her face, heard the whiz of a silenced projectile launched from behind. But he had to finish, had to get it out. "Tell him," he hissed. "Remember Ibo!"

The words tumbled from his mouth in a rush. Then a blinding burst of pain sliced through the base of his skull. The world of planets and stars exploded. And all that remained for Simon Juniper was the vast emptiness of a black hole in space.

Chapter One

"Simon's what? He's where?"

Evan Odell grasped Kristian firmly by the arms, holding her steady while she endeavored to regain some semblance of coherent speech. It wasn't an easy thing to do. Not only had she just run the uphill equivalent to two city blocks, but she was positive she'd also just seen a man murdered. Shot from behind with a strange-looking gun.

"Kristian, what are you talking about?" Evan persisted with an aggravating lack of hysteria. "Simon can't be dead. He's not even in Nevada. He's somewhere in Rio, probably losing his shirt in a high-stakes poker game. He left Saturday morning—you know that."

Pulling herself free, Kristian treated him to a glare that was part anger, part impatience and part desperation. Evan was her boss, an uncommonly handsome male with long black hair, a full-lipped mouth and seductive brown eyes. Of the four men who were partners in the space park, he was the one she'd had the most contact with during the fifteen months she'd been there. More often than not, his cheerfully humorous nature made her job as park manager easier than it might otherwise have been. Unfortunately this wasn't one of those times.

"Simon's not losing his shirt in Rio or anywhere else," she stated with a violent shudder and a quick glance over her shoulder at the locked doors of the conference room. "He's downstairs in my office, and he's been shot."

She saw the flicker of uncertainty in Evan's dark eyes. Quite obviously he didn't know what to make of her shrill disclosure.

"Look," she tried again, this time in a slightly less frantic voice. "You don't have to take my word for it." Reaching out, she tugged at the sleeve of his navy blue jumpsuit, the uniform worn by the majority of the park's staff. "Call security, get some back-up, go down to my office and see for yourself. Simon's been shot. I was there when it happened. I saw the gun pointing at him."

"You saw a gun?"

"A gun and part of a NORStar uniform," she confirmed, still tugging urgently at his sleeve.

He didn't move, just stood there in the middle of the floor, staring at her as though she were an invader from Mars.

They were in the Andromeda wing, on the top level of the huge central complex. Overhead the enormous glass-domed ceiling revealed a sky liberally sprinkled with stars. The silvery light that bathed Evan's perfect Irish features gave him the appearance of a statue—one that didn't buy a word of her story.

He continued to stare at her, then finally shrugged his wiry shoulders. "All right," he relented, his tone frankly dubious. "I'll go look."

Kristian dug her fingernails into his arm. "Call security first," she warned, swallowing shakily. "I swear to you, Simon is here in this building, and someone just shot him."

To her own ears, the words now held a faint ring of absurdity. Somehow, standing in this room with Evan made the scene she'd witnessed seem like a snippet of a bad dream.

But she wasn't prone to fits of panic, and her dreams, though vivid, weren't usually this gruesome. What she'd seen had been real, as real as the disconnected message Simon had relayed before he'd forcibly ejected her from her office. Before she'd taken off at a dead run, certain that she was being chased by every murderous entity in the universe.

Her knees began to wobble with renewed fear. She clutched at the thick lucite table beside her, clinging to it as Evan strode over to the wall-mounted intercom and punched in the code that would alert the security staff in the basement.

She should have gone downstairs in the first place, she thought hazily. The night-duty officer would have acted instantly whether he'd believed her or not. She ran the park. He was obliged to follow her orders no matter how far-fetched they might seem.

But the lower levels were much harder to reach than the conference room. And since her sometime assistant, June Atherton, had been holed up with NORStar's senior partner, Morton Nash, for most of the day, she'd been running late for tonight's meeting. She'd known she would find someone up here. She only wished it had been one of her more serious-minded employers.

"Okay, security's sending someone up," Evan announced, giving the intercom a jaunty swat and Kristian a heavy-lidded look of skepticism.

She ignored it. "Who are they sending?"

"Hubie Bittman," Evan replied, and inwardly she groaned. Dear, hapless Hubie had the muscles of a well-developed ape and the IQ of an amoeba. Evan definitely wasn't taking any of this to heart.

For a moment, Kristian considered trying to contact the other three partners. While the reclusive Morton Nash seldom emerged from his hotel suite these days, she might be able to convince him of her sincerity. Or maybe she should wait for the other two men to show up. Surely one of them would listen to her.

Though it was the last thing she wanted to do, she forced herself to ask, "Where are George and Tory?"

Moving away from the wall, Evan caused the state-of-the-art sensory door to open with a delicate whoosh. To Kristian's relief no one had catapulted across the threshold. "George should be here any minute now. As for Tory—" he shrugged "—who knows?" A sly smile crept across his generous lips. "Do you want me to page him?"

No, she didn't want that at all. The less contact she had with Tory Roberts the better. But Simon's final message had been intended for him, not for the other three partners.

Reluctantly, Kristian nodded. "Maybe you'd better," she said with as much conviction as her numbed brain would allow. And forcing her muscles to comply, she accompanied Evan through the door into the opaque swirls of the Trifid Nebula corridor.

THEY CREPT through the silent complex like a pair of intrepid prowlers, although Kristian suspected that much of Evan's fearlessness stemmed from his total disregard of her story.

At least he'd taken the precaution of approaching her office in a roundabout fashion. He might not believe her, but he wasn't brash enough to go charging down the main ramp to the Saturn wing. No, Evan was a cautious man, particularly when it came to ensuring his own safety.

She saw him stop next to one of the storage closets and give the tiny cellular phone he always carried with him a disgruntled shake. "I can't get through to Tory," he said, punching a series of numbers for the third time. "Either he's out of range or this thing's busted."

"Try George," she suggested, not at all sure why she bothered. Neither man was likely to reach them before they arrived at her office.

"I already did. The signal must be jammed." He took her by the hand. "I guess that just leaves you and me."

"And Hubie Bittman," she added forlornly, peering past his arm into the hallway that stretched out like a starry wonderland before them.

Nothing stirred in the dim passage, not even the two robots that roamed the complex each night. For some strange reason, Kristian felt as though she were walking through the Milky Way when they started moving again. She didn't speak, hardly even dared to breathe as the constellations formed around her.

Evan's presence, while somewhat comforting, wasn't entirely reassuring. He talked a good game, but she had a feeling he'd be one of those people whose instinct for survival would far outweigh his desire to overwhelm any adversary. Not that she could really blame him, but it would have been a great deal easier on her nerves if she could have trusted him not to use her as a shield should they happen to run into the person who'd shot Simon.

Slowing her footsteps, Kristian gestured to the light spilling from her office. "He's lying right inside the door."

Evan looked over at her, his expression dubious, yet tinged with...something. Whatever that something was, though, it vanished before she could decipher it, and his features assumed their usual jocular cast.

"Come on," he said, keeping a firm hold on her hand. "We might as well get this over with."

Kristian wasn't sure how she did it, but she managed to take the final few steps into the pool of light that bathed the corridor. A picture of Simon's terrified face flashed sharply through her head. She could still see the desperate look in his eyes, still hear the words he'd shouted at her. And no matter how hard she tried not to, she could still recall the sight of him dropping to the floor less than five feet from her office door.

Drawing a shaky breath, she forced her gaze down to the carpet where he'd fallen. The memory was so strong, so indelibly etched in her mind that she had to choke back a sob of remembered panic.

Fingers wrapped around the door frame, she stared at the floor, her vision clearing as the reality of the situation slowly dawned on her, as confusion took over from fear. Her valise was sitting on the sofa exactly where she'd left it ten minutes ago. In fact, everything was precisely as it had been when Simon had shoved her into the hall. Everything except for one significant detail.

Simon's body had disappeared!

Chapter Two

"Welcome to the Theater of the Cosmos," a velvety soft voice intoned as Tory Roberts wandered aimlessly into one of NORStar's two soon-to-be-unveiled exhibits.

He'd been outside for the past ten minutes waiting for George Straker to show up. They were supposed to be at some meeting that Morton had evidently called moments before the park closed, a meeting Tory hadn't heard about until he'd received George's message half an hour ago, one he wouldn't have bothered attending if George hadn't cut him off before he could object.

"I'm on my way to the park now," his friend had told him over the fuzzy phone line. "I'll catch up with you at the Cosmic Theater. We can take a quick look around, then drive across to the main complex together."

"Late as usual, George," Tory remarked, passing unconcernedly through an infrared light shield.

Two security guards immediately materialized around the corner of the galactic labyrinth. "Is that you, Tory?" one of them called out.

"No, it's a burglar," he muttered, lifting a half-empty bottle of Lowenbrau to his lips. He raised his voice and called back an easy "Yeah, it's me. Have you seen George anywhere?"

The older of the men joined him in the purple light of a glassed-in Venusian waterfall. "Not since this afternoon,"

he said. "The only people I've seen in this building are
Priscilla and the Colonel. They're tinkering around in the
control room."

So what else was new, Tory wondered, finishing off his
beer. Nathan Brenda, the Colonel, as he was better known,
was NORStar's resident toy maker, though his talents certainly didn't end there. He spent every working hour tinkering with something in the park—if not a control panel or
an imperfect hologram, then one of his computerized creations. And, naturally, as head of maintenance, Morton
Nash's goddaughter, Priscilla Warfield, couldn't allow him
to do any of those things alone. Not without risking a mi-
graine when one of the Colonel's experiments backfired as
they occasionally did.

Leaving the guards to complete their rounds, Tory headed
for the theater's workroom. George labelled it the Oz
chamber. The place where ultramodern technology reigned
supreme.

Wearily, he punched the necessary entry code, a little
surprised that he could still remember it. He hadn't really
intended to consume anything stronger than coffee when
he'd gone into the on-site cantina. Actually, he hadn't even
meant to be on the grounds at this time of night. But the
bartender was an old friend of his father's and he'd started
reminiscing the moment Tory had drifted through the door,
making a drink an absolute necessity.

Grimacing, Tory tried to blot the man's words from his
mind. Three months after the funeral, and it still felt like
yesterday. His father, a retired Air Force colonel from Las
Vegas, was dead, the victim of a massive stroke that had hit
him while he watched a nightclub floor show. The doctors
said he probably hadn't felt much of anything, but that
didn't alter the fact that the last member of Tory's once-
large family was gone. Only Lydia, his ex-stepmother, was
alive, and she was off in Europe these days, probably re-
decorating the *schloss* of some impoverished German baron.

The door in front of him opened with a stuttering clunk, which didn't sound entirely healthy. He spared it no more than a cursory sideways look. Priscilla was a mechanical genius. A few reconnected wires, a good kick or two, and she'd have the bugs out of the system in no time flat.

The control room of the elaborate Cosmic Theater looked like something straight out of a sci-fi movie. An array of computerized panels, screens and projectors housed behind a thick Plexiglas wall was backed by even more gadgets behind yet another transparent wall. At the far, far end of the long chamber, Tory spied both Priscilla and the Colonel. The technician and the inventor, hard at work as usual, hovering around a gigantic console that looked even less healthy than the outer door.

"If you're planning on going in, don't waste your time," a voice remarked to the right of Tory's shoulder. "The whole electrical system seems to be out of whack. We're locked out but good."

Tory glanced at the security officer he'd spoken to moments before. "What's the problem?"

The man grinned. "Can't say, but whatever it is must be a real brainteaser. Priscilla and the Colonel have been in there since the park closed down an hour ago. Frankly I'm surprised George isn't with them. This theater's his baby. I don't see him taking kindly to the idea of delaying the grand opening of his new exhibit."

Tory gave the intercom buttons an experimental flip, receiving nothing for his efforts except a few dull clicks. He could have banged on the Plexiglas and maybe caught Priscilla's attention, but there seemed little point in interrupting her. He wasn't in the mood to deal with whatever glitches she and the Colonel were attempting to correct. Besides, George would be here any minute, and his friend knew a lot more about this particular exhibit than he did.

They'd all brought something to the space park, he recalled, letting his mind drift back five years in time. Morton had come through with the bulk of the capital, George

possessed the technical expertise, Evan the organizational
skills and Tory the creative insight. They'd met in the Air
Force, four individuals hooked on Flash Gordon and flying
saucers, each wanting to expand on his galactic fantasies. At
least that's what they'd claimed. He wasn't sure he believed
it. More likely they'd been attempting to compensate for
some deficiency in their lives.

Tory halted on that thought, a personally painful one he'd
been dwelling on far too much lately. He should be inured
to his losses by now. His sister and two brothers had
drowned in a boating accident twenty-five years ago; his
mother in her grief had taken a fatal overdose of tranquil-
izers six months later. An eleven-year-old child might have
a hard time accepting all that, especially when that child's
father had responded by burying himself in his work, but at
thirty-six, Tory knew he should be able to control his feelings, if not always his memories.

Control. The word brought a vastly different set of
thoughts to mind. Memories of the time he'd spent in the
Air Force in Baden-Baden, West Germany. George's suggestion that they spend their days off in Heidelberg. The
blond-haired, green-eyed beauty he'd met in the outdoor
beer garden, the same one he'd fallen in love with, the one
who'd claimed to love him, but who'd ultimately accused
him of trying to control her life and in a fit of temper ended
their relationship less than a year after it had begun.

A strident beep cut sharply through the hum of machinery in the room, bringing a frown to his lips and an end to
his errant musings. He knew he was late for the meeting, but
that was nothing new. Maybe it was George trying to reach
him again.

Removing the tiny black box, one of the Colonel's hand-
ier inventions, from his belt, he pressed the Receive button.
"I'm here. What's up?"

"You sound like you're a hundred miles away." Evan's
voice greeted him with a static-filled crackle. "Where's
here?"

Tory resisted the urge to snarl his response. Talents aside, Evan Odell had an irritating tendency to forget that he was the junior partner in the space park. Despite the placement of the *O* from his surname in the NORStar acronym, he'd been the final man to join up, replacing his older brother who'd decided at the last minute to extend his military career by another four years.

"The Cosmic Theater," Tory replied, his tone deceptively mild.

"Is George with you?"

"No."

An unintelligible flap erupted over the garbled line, ending with an impatient "I know, I know, I'm getting to it," from Evan, followed by a sigh and a world-weary, "Look, Tory, I'm over at the main complex with Kristian. She thinks something's happened to Simon."

Tory refused to react to the mention of Kristian Ellis's name. It was past history between them—or so he'd half-convinced himself since she'd been hired to manage the park. Their relationship had started and ended eleven years ago in Heidelberg. Any contact they had these days was invariably business related, and even those encounters were limited.

He lifted the communication box to his mouth. "Something's happened to Simon, where? In Rio?"

Another loud crackle blasted back at him, overriding most of whatever Evan was attempting to say. He caught the words, "Kristian insists..." and "...shot in her office," before the static took over completely.

"Shot?" the security guard repeated doubtfully while Tory smacked the recalcitrant box with the heel of his hand. "Is that what he said? Shot?"

"That's what it sounded like."

"But how is that possible? Simon's not even in the country."

"He's not supposed to be." Tory whacked the box against the Plexiglas and tried again. "Evan, can you hear me?"

"Must be something interfering with the signal," the guard surmised as the static grew louder. "You want me to head over to the center and see what's going on?"

"We'll both go." Tory took a quick look at Priscilla and the Colonel who were still fiddling with the dead computer console, oblivious to everything except the blank monitor before them. "Tell your partner to keep an eye open for George."

Aware that he was in no condition to drive, Tory let the security guard navigate his Jeep through the intricate twists and turns of NORStar's blessedly deserted thoroughfares. Even though their course was unhampered by pedestrians, it took them more than ten minutes to forge a path between the maze of buildings in the huge space park. Naturally the Cosmic Theater was situated as far from the central complex as it could possibly be, and when they finally arrived at the multisectioned center, Tory couldn't remember which seven-number entry code was being used that day.

"Sorry, this isn't my sector," the guard apologized. "I only patrol the red zone. Maybe you could hot-wire the panel." His eyes sparkled. "I heard you were good at things like that back in your Air Force Academy days."

"The rumors of my erstwhile abilities have been greatly exaggerated," Tory informed him without reproach. "Don't take everything George tells you to heart. In his own subtle way, he was the biggest troublemaker of us all."

"Now who's spreading rumors?" a good-natured voice remarked from the shadows of a steel girder. Smiling, George Straker strolled into the tremulous white light, reached around Tory's arm and punched in the ever-changing code. "Sorry I was held up. I take it you got a summons from Evan, too."

"If you can call it that."

"Garbled?"

"Yup."

"He said something about Simon getting shot," the guard put in, scratching his balding head. "At least I think he did."

George's dark brows came together in a puzzled frown. "That's more than I heard. Of course I was outside the gates changing a flat tire at the time. Did he say anything else?"

Tory started through the door. "He mentioned Kristian's office. I don't know, though—it could be that Simon phoned her from Rio and told her he'd shot his entire vacation wad at the blackjack table."

George shrugged. "More likely Evan wanted to be sure we'd both show up for tonight's meeting."

Almost any other time Tory would have bought the latter explanation, but some nagging inner instinct warned him not to jump to any convenient conclusions. Maybe it was the fact that Evan had mentioned Kristian's name. If he'd simply wanted all the partners represented at tonight's meeting, he would have yelled fire, not, Simon's been shot. And he certainly wouldn't have used Kristian Ellis as bait to lure them here.

"Look, people, this is getting out of hand," Tory heard Evan declare the moment the elevator doors slid open near the Saturn wing. "I think we can all agree that there's no one here, dead or otherwise, except us. Now I don't know what you saw, or thought you saw, Kristian, but it couldn't have been Simon."

Tory made it to her office just in time to glimpse the smoldering glare Kristian directed at Evan's spine. In his peripheral vision he also spotted June Atherton, Morton Nash's liaison and Kristian's assistant, crawling around on her hands and knees on the plush carpet. She was a vibrant woman, fifty or better, though she refused to be pinned down to a specific year. A mop of wispy brown curls more or less clipped into submission framed a set of cheerful gamin features and warm hazel eyes that seldom stopped twinkling.

"I could have listened to my horoscope and spent a nice quiet evening at home," she was grumbling with no real antagonism. "But no, like a fool I agreed to come to tonight's meeting. And what happens? I stop by my office to pick up a few files, and I wind up crawling around on the floor—finding nothing except plush fuzzballs, I might add." She continued to separate and examine the carpet's thick, gray fibers. "Sorry, Kristian, there's simply no blood here."

"And no body, either," Evan tacked on emphatically. "Hello, Tory, George. It's about time you showed up. Will one of you please tell Kristian that Simon is not lying on the floor with a bullet in his neck? She refuses to listen to me."

Tory ignored him and gave his full attention to the striking golden-haired woman who was standing mutinously by her desk. Someone had once referred to her as hell's original angel, and he'd never argued the point. She had a quick tongue, a hot temper and a stubborn streak no mule could hope to match. He should know. He'd been on the receiving end of all three.

"What's going on, Kristian?" he asked, vaguely conscious that George had squatted down beside June on the carpet. "What did you see?"

"I saw Simon get shot," she replied, and he knew her teeth were clenched.

"When?"

"Twenty minutes ago."

George raised his thoughtful eyes to her face. "June's right, there's no blood. Are you sure you saw him get shot?"

"I'm sure."

"Oh, for God's sake," Evan moaned. "Will you stop and listen to yourself? There's no body, no blood and no damned way that Simon could possibly be within five hundred miles of this place. You know what he's like. Dangle a pair of dice in front of his nose, and he'll follow you anywhere. He's living it up in Brazil and will be for the next three weeks."

Standing, George stuffed his hands into the pockets of his pants. "Did Simon say anything to you?" he inquired gently.

Kristian hesitated, not for more than the time it took to blink. Tory had known her too well and for too long to be fooled by any mask she chose to don. Simon had said something, all right, but whether she'd admit it remained to be seen.

"No, he didn't," she said with a subtly spiteful look at Evan. "Someone shot him from the connecting door between my office and June's. He pushed me into the hall; he fell, and I ran."

"Corpses do not get up and leave the scene of a crime," Evan insisted.

She speared him with her frosty green eyes. "I didn't say he was dead, I said he was shot."

Tory shook his head, temporarily disregarding her earlier pause and the lie he knew had followed. "This is getting us nowhere," he muttered. He motioned to Hubie Bittman, who, in spite of his pumped-up muscles and six-foot-four-inch frame, had somehow managed to blend into Kristian's enormous mosaic of Pegasus. "Round up some of the people from downstairs," he instructed the bewildered-looking man. Then he glanced at the red-zone security guard beside him. "You'd better go along, too. Search the building and the grounds outside. If you find anything, let me know."

Evan threw up his hands. "Okay, that does it," he surrendered. "This one's all yours, Tory. I'm going home. We can reschedule the meeting sometime tomorrow."

"Fine with me," June agreed, rising nimbly from her knees and giving her tousled brown hair a perfunctory pat. "I'll check in with Morton at the hotel, then head for my own hacienda and the latest episode of 'Lost in Space.' I think they're blasting off for Earth tonight."

"How unspeakably exciting."

Yet another voice entered the fray, this one belonging to Lilith Lang, the woman in charge of programming NOR-Star's extensive computer network. As always her thick black hair was pulled straight back from her face in a severe knot that emphasized her perpetually gloomy expression. She moved into the office with all the grace of a poorly constructed android, a white lab coat drawn over her flight suit, a pair of horn-rimmed glasses planted securely on top of her head.

"Might I be so bold as to inquire why I wasn't informed that the meeting had been moved down here?" she asked in the same stilted monotone she employed regardless of her mood. "I've been sitting in the conference room alone for the past eight and a half minutes."

The woman was precise to a fault, Tory thought, glancing at her. She'd probably ticked off each of those minutes in her semimechanical brain before switching her muscles back on and venturing down to this level.

"It's a long story, Lilith," George inserted, catching her arm and bringing her around in a neat little half circle that had her exiting the office at his side. "I'll fill you in on it while I walk you to your car."

"By this am I to assume we're not having a meeting tonight?" she queried woodenly.

"Nope, we've gone beyond that, kiddo," June piped up. "We're hot on the trail of a dead body. You didn't happen to bump into one in your travels, did you?"

"You're asking a corpse if she's seen a corpse?" Evan grumbled under his breath. "That's it. I'm out of here." He ushered June through the door behind George and Lilith, pausing only long enough to murmur a fervent "Good luck, pal," to Tory before he left.

Tory didn't say a word but kept his eyes on Kristian, who was busy tapping the keys on her computer.

"There's nothing here," she stated, sounding perplexed. "But it's switched on. He must have been in my office for a reason."

Tory frowned. "Who? Simon?"

"Yes, Simon." She flipped the computer off, took a quick look at the empty corridor, then lifted her gaze to his. "I'm not lying, Tory. I know what I saw."

He held his ground near the entranceway, making no attempt to bridge the gap between them. "You saw someone shoot him," he repeated, wishing he'd passed on the cantina, wishing a lot of things that had little bearing on the present situation.

Her eyes didn't waver from his. "Yes."

"But you didn't see who it was."

"Not the person, no. All I saw was an arm, a gloved hand holding a gun and part of a park uniform."

"You're sure it was a park uniform?"

"I'm positive." Heaving a weary sigh, she moved to stand in front of the door that connected her office with June's. "It was one of our jumpsuits. The sleeve had the NORStar logo sewn onto it."

Tory lowered his lashes. He didn't want to believe her. Common sense told him he shouldn't. There wasn't a shred of evidence to support her wild story. And yet, the gnawing in his stomach told him there was something. Something she'd omitted when George had questioned her earlier.

"What did Simon say to you, Kristian?" he asked, certain he wouldn't want to hear her answer.

She hesitated again, casting an apprehensive look into the colorful corridor beyond her office. With his foot, he kicked the door closed.

"We're alone," he told her. "As much as we might both like to ignore that fact, there's no one here but you and me. Now, I know you trust me to a certain extent or you wouldn't have agreed to work at the park. Tell me, what did Simon say to you before he was shot?"

She hunched her shoulders, a move so uncharacteristically defensive that Tory had trouble keeping his features evenly set.

"He said to tell you—common ground."

Tory's eyes darkened in confusion. "Common ground? Is that all?"

"No." She bit her lower lip. "Before he fell, he told me to tell you to remember Ibo."

He wasn't sure how he did it, but Tory managed not to react to a name that hit him like a stunning blow. A name she couldn't possibly have pulled out of thin air or likely even heard before tonight. "You're absolutely sure about this?"

"Yes."

Wordlessly, Tory lowered his gaze to the spotless carpet. No blood, no body, no sign of an intruder. Just a message that only Simon Juniper could have left.

He looked up and straight into the beautiful green eyes across from him. "I believe you."

"I KNEW IT," the woman growled, giving the computer keyboard in front of her a furious swat. "Simon changed the code word. And God knows what he changed it to." She shoved her chair back, right over the toe of the man behind her. It was after midnight. She'd been hunched over the console for more than fifteen minutes. She didn't dare remain there any longer. "Meddlesome fool," she snarled. "I should have realized he'd do something like this."

Her partner moved out of range, his eyes shimmering eerily in the greenish light of the computer screen. "The file's there," he said softly. "It's still there. He buried it in another program, that's all."

"Brilliant deduction," she retorted with heavy sarcasm. "Of course he buried it, you idiot. The question is, where? We've entered every word he shouted at Kristian forward, backward and sideways and come up empty. As it is, we're pushing our luck by stopping here. Tory's got security combing the park. We can't afford to waste any more time searching blindly."

An enigmatic smile pulled at the corners of the man's mouth. "It was a message," he murmured in a tone that made her skin crawl.

She hated it when he turned creepy on her, although she wasn't sure why. If anything, he was more manageable when he got this way. Still, she should probably be grateful for his weird lapses. In the end they'd undoubtedly work to her advantage.

"A message to Tory?" she deduced, tempted to run her chair over his foot again in an effort to bring him back from Alpha Centauri or whatever distant star his mind was currently orbiting.

"It's possible," he said, flicking an invisible speck from his sleeve. "Simon is a gambler. Maybe he's gambling on his friendship with Tory."

"Simon *was* a gambler," the woman corrected. "Past tense. In the present, he's nothing more than a problem, one of two we have to dispose of tonight. I've done the hard part by hiding the body. It's up to you to handle the next phase." She snapped her fingers in front of his face. "I trust you remember the whole plan?"

He nodded, his eyes clearing with an almost frightening suddenness. "Have I let you down so far?" he challenged, and she shrugged.

"Not yet, no, but there's a first time for everything. And I'm not overly fond of loose ends. Kristian could easily have run in the opposite direction. She could have tried for the service elevator and spotted one or both of us."

"She could have, but she didn't," the man said with a faint smile. "Our timing was perfect. Close but perfect. She doesn't know a thing—including how Simon's body managed to vanish from the floor of her office."

"She knows what he said to her."

"True, but only Tory will hear about that."

"Then Tory becomes a problem, too, doesn't he?" his partner countered sweetly. "However, that's in the future. It's past midnight and we still have a lot of work to do, both on the grounds and off. When the time is right, I'll dispose of our first victim's body while you get Simon out of here."

"What about Kristian?" he inquired, and despite the awkward situation, she couldn't resist a nasty chuckle.

"I believe I'll let our hired help tend to her. She's of absolutely no use to us alive. On the other hand, her death might be worth a great deal."

"I don't understand."

"You don't have to understand," the woman snapped. "Just make sure you don't forget any of my instructions. It's imperative that you carry them out step by step."

"I always do," he assured her.

A chilling smile grazed her lips. "I hope so," she said coldly. "For your sake, I certainly hope so."

Chapter Three

He'd done it to her again!

Kristian stared broodingly out the window of NORStar Center's lavish 430-room Pallas Hotel. The glittering night lights of the space park shone like cosmic jewels against the desert sky. It was a stunning sight that brought back memories of science fiction movies, rocket ships and moon landings. But it wasn't a sight she should have been beholding at twelve forty-five on a Tuesday morning.

"Damn him," she swore under her breath. She shouldn't have let him bring her here. Wasn't it bad enough that Simon had been shot in her office, then disappeared into thin air? Did she have to make matters worse by allowing Tory Roberts to walk back into her life and strip her of her control as he'd come so perilously close to doing eleven years ago in Germany?

"Did you say something, Kristian?"

June tore her riveted gaze away from the television screen where Dr. Smith was skulking around the bridge of the Space Family Robinson's flying saucer. Thank God for small favors. Her assistant, with her impeccable sense of timing, had shown up at the door ten minutes ago, mere moments after Tory had done his usual thorough job of messing up her perfectly ordered existence.

Kristian sulked at the memory. "Humor me, and stay at the hotel tonight," he'd entreated her, the order ill-masked by his coaxing tone. "You'll be a lot safer there than in your own home. Whoever shot Simon has to know you're a witness. You could be in more danger than you realize."

Comforting words, Kristian thought bitterly. So comforting that she'd offered little more than a frustrated grunt of protest as he'd whisked her out of the park and up to the luxurious fifteenth-floor hotel suite.

It was exactly the way her spit-and-polish military father would have handled the situation. Of course, she was the youngest of four children, the only one who'd been in a position to balk at his autocratic orders. By the time she'd been born, he'd already spawned three regimented offsprings, and his career was thriving. He'd had little time to mold her, so he'd settled for trying to run her life. From base to base they'd moved, and with each new post had come more prestige, more responsibility. By the time Kristian was fifteen, he'd taken to leaving memos inside her schoolbooks, tedious rosters that opened with sit-ups at 0700 and closed with lights out at precisely 2200 hours.

"You must learn to follow orders...."

The statement shot through Kristian's head. Those six little words typified her father's attitude toward her. To a certain extent, those same words also summed up Tory's attitude, although perhaps not in quite such a rigid fashion.

Against her better judgment, she stole a glance through the open door to the hall where Tory was currently talking to Hubie Bittman and two of the hotel's in-house security people. Not that she paid much attention to the threesome. How could she with Tory standing there in faded jeans and a rumpled red-and-black-checked shirt, looking like every woman's sexual fantasy?

His dark brown hair was wavy and much, much longer than it had been eleven years ago. He'd always seemed taller than five feet eleven inches, but she suspected the added height was an illusion that had to do with his sleek, athletic build and supple muscles. Even in her most cynical moments, Kristian couldn't deny his sensual appeal, that irritatingly elusive quality that set him worlds apart from the legion of male beauties she'd encountered in Las Vegas.

"I said, maybe I should phone Morton and tell him what I saw." She dragged her gaze from the hallway, responding to June's earlier question with little thought of what she was saying. Certainly, she didn't need to call Morton. As always, Tory was in complete control of the situation, even if he stubbornly refused to give her any details about it.

Her assistant glanced up at the ceiling. "Better save that call till tomorrow," she advised, her expression cheerful but firm. "I just came from the penthouse. Morton's already locked himself in for the night."

Eager for any distraction, Kristian left the window and went to perch on the arm of the sofa. "Tell me," she invited. "Does Morton ever come out?"

"Of his bedroom?"

"No, I mean does he ever leave his suite? I've been working at the center for over a year, and I've never once gotten a good look at his face."

"You probably never will, either." June's features lit up with an impish smile. "To paraphrase a well-known song: he wears his sunglasses at night. He also wears them during the day—although in that dungeon of a penthouse he calls home, believe me, it's very hard to make the distinction between twelve noon and twelve midnight."

"Doesn't he like daylight?"

"He can't stand it." Tory supplied the answer as he strolled into the suite behind a trolley-bearing waiter. With a grin and a flick of his hand, he indicated a pot of coffee, three covered plates and a variety of condiments. "I thought you might be hungry."

Kristian's head shot up. Midnight food raids were part of their past. He couldn't have forgotten that. Nothing showed in his expression, however, no glimmer of taunting humor, not even a mocking tilt of his dark brow. Maybe she was overreacting. Heaven knew, she had good reason.

Taking a deep breath, she forced herself to meet his disconcerting gaze, a difficult task at the best of times. Tory Roberts had been blessed with the most beautiful eyes she'd ever seen. Fringed by long, black lashes and colored the deepest shade of aquamarine imaginable, they could mesmerize, hypnotize and enchant with a single stare. She should know. She'd let him do all those things to her once.

With an effort, she pulled her mind back to the present and Tory's comment about NORStar's senior partner. "I know Morton's considered a recluse," she said, her curiosity unfeigned, "but isn't living in a black hole day in and day out a bit extreme?"

Tory shrugged. "Not for him." He regarded the departing waiter, nodded at Hubie, who was hovering on the threshold, then wandered over to the trolley and lifted one of the covered plates. "Do you want a hot dog?"

Kristian clenched her fists, glaring at him. No, she didn't want a hot dog. She wanted to go home. She wanted answers and information he flatly refused to give her. She wanted him to turn that impossibly sexy body of his around and get out of her temporary jail cell.

Ignoring her cutting stare, Tory rooted through the bowls of mustard and relish and chili peppers. "To answer your question," he said at length, "there's something wrong with Morton's optic nerve." Taking a huge bite of his loaded bun, he settled onto the sofa arm she'd recently vacated. "The problem wasn't so bad a year ago, but these days almost any kind of light drives him crazy."

"He's photosensitive?" Kristian asked, sidetracked in spite of herself. She'd always thought the man was simply an aging eccentric, who, with the exception of June and his goddaughter Priscilla, preferred to keep his distance from the park's staff.

"Supersensitive," June confirmed, eyes still glued to the flickering television. "And more than a little reclusive. Not that he doesn't like people, you understand. It's just that he's grown rather—"

"Mysterious?" Kristian offered diplomatically.

"Peculiar," June clarified. "A shadow dweller, if you will. Last time I got a halfway good look at him myself was back before Christmas. Now he's a little more than a voice in the dark, even to Priscilla and me. Oh, every once in a while I catch a glimpse of a bony white hand and maybe a flash of teeth in the corner, but that's the extent of it."

Kristian poured herself a cup of black coffee. "He sounds like a vampire," she muttered.

"A space vampire?" June laughed. "You know, I think I saw something like that once, in a sci-fi movie. Only this particular vampire fed on energy rather than blood."

In which case, she'd be safe from his ravenous clutches, Kristian thought wearily. She felt drained, as though she were living on the last of her energy reserves. It didn't help that Tory was perched only a few short feet away from her, calmly munching on a late-night snack and looking appealingly indolent as only he could. He gave the impression of being completely detached from the situation, but Kristian knew him better than that.

She waited until June had turned her attention back to the TV, then, using the trolley as a barrier, sent him an accusing stare. "Are you planning to tell me what's going on?"

He paused before taking another bite of his hot dog, lifting his eyes but not his head. "There's nothing to tell," he said, and she was tempted to hit him for thinking she'd swallow that lie.

"Nothing?" she challenged, her voice a hiss.

A barely perceptible nod in June's direction reminded her that this was not an appropriate time to be discussing Simon's final message. Maybe there never would be a good time, she reflected, taking her coffee with her to the window.

Behind her, she noted a brief flash of movement. A second later, Tory's low voice reached her ears. "Much as I hate to, Kristian, I have to leave. Are you going to be all right?"

She looked back in some surprise. Not for a second did she doubt her ability to recover from the events of this night. "I'll be fine," she said, aware that he was pulling a set of car keys from his jeans pocket, more aware of the dull ache in her heart that was impossible to ignore. "Are you going back to the center?"

"For a while." His entrancing eyes caught and held hers. "You'll be safe enough here. I've got security camped out on this floor. They won't let anyone get past them."

"Tory, that's really not—"

"It's necessary," he interrupted, grazing her chin ever so lightly with his knuckles, causing the ache in her heart to double. How easy it would be to slip into the past, to let her feelings take over, to let Tory take over....

She leaned calmly against the windowsill. At least she could fake an unaffected attitude. "Have it your way," she agreed, and couldn't resist adding a quietly determined "but only this one time."

She saw the ironic smile that quirked the corners of his mouth as he tossed his crumpled napkin onto the cart, and felt her muscles constrict. Despite the glimmer of amusement there was an intensity about him that reminded her of the stories she'd heard from more than a few of his air force buddies. He was a known risk taker. Not crazy, just mercurial under certain circumstances. It was a vaguely frightening side of him that Kristian had glimpsed often enough to be concerned.

As he started to turn away, she brushed her fingers over his sleeve, not quite trusting herself to touch him. "Tory?"

He glanced at her, his strikingly handsome features unreadable. "What?"

She fought a regretful sigh. "You aren't going to do anything reckless, are you?"

A wicked smile she didn't need to see crossed his mouth. Reaching out, he cupped her cheek in his warm, slightly callused palm. "I already did that when I let George talk me into hiring you."

With difficulty, she managed not to react to his touch. "That isn't what I meant."

A spark of humor lighted his eyes. "I know."

"Damn you, Tory," she snapped, giving in and batting his hand away. "All I want is a straight answer."

"No."

She lowered her lashes in suspicion. "No, what?"

"No, I'm not going to do anything reckless."

"You might have said so in the first place," she muttered, exasperated. For a moment, she considered adding a sweetly sarcastic parting comment, but she bit it back at the last second and summoned a more deferential "Thank you, Tory. For everything."

His smile widened as if he sensed her restraint. "You're welcome. I'll see you tomorrow. Come on, June. I'll walk you to your car."

Kristian watched him cross the floor with mixed emotions and a sudden attack of exhaustion. Why, she wondered distantly, did she always wind up being involved with this man?

She squeezed her eyes closed, aware that the answer in this case was painfully simple. She'd accepted the job as manager of NORStar knowing that Tory was a partner. Any involvement between them now was more her doing than his.

Murmuring a distracted goodbye to the departing pair, Kristian waited until the door had clicked shut, then turned her longing eyes to the shiny silver telephone. There were any number of people she could call and talk to. Friends in nearby Las Vegas, her sister in Tucson, her brother, Sean, at Nellis Air Force Base.

No, not him. Sean and Tory had known each other for years. They'd gone through the academy together. They'd even flown together in the Atlantic. All Sean would do was tell her to trust Tory's judgment—which meant she'd receive no solace from that familial quarter.

Closing her eyes, she dropped back onto the plush white sofa. Pictures of Simon's face, his final words, his crumpled body, ricocheted through her head, mingling discordantly with a far different set of images. Visions of her and Tory and German beer gardens and too damned many nights when they'd broken every rule in every imaginable book.

She shouldn't even have been in Heidelberg the weekend she'd met Tory. If her father had found out, he would have locked her in her room for a year. But she'd been driven by desperation to get off the base for a few days. After all, how was she supposed to meet men when she was never allowed to come in contact with anyone except her classmates and a scattering of bookish males, all of whom had been approved by her father and none of whom she'd found appealing?

Tory hadn't been bookish. Nor had he been the type of man her father would have wanted her to date. The moment she'd spotted him, Kristian had known that. He was gorgeous and sexy—and dangerous in every conceivable sense of the word. But he was also strong-willed and self-reliant, unreachable on a number of emotional levels. Deliberately so, as she'd come to learn during the next several months.

Four members of his family had died when he was very young, and though he couldn't control the past, he'd been determined to control the present. That dominating attitude applied to his personal relationships as well as to his career. However, after eighteen years of being ordered about by her father, Kristian wasn't prepared to let another man start dictating her life to her.

So it had ended in the very city where it had begun. Two months later, Tory and George had been reassigned to a base in the South Pacific. Kristian had gone off to the university in Vienna and after traveling through Europe had eventually wound up living and working in her mother's native Las Vegas. It was Tory's native Las Vegas, too. If she was honest with herself, she'd admit that somewhere deep in her soul she'd always known their paths were bound to cross again at some point in time.

Pushing the truth aside, she thought of her subsequent four-year marriage to a California market analyst that had ended with a proverbial whimper and a polite peck on the cheek. She thought of Tory's three-year marriage to a Las Vegas reporter that had ended with a heated bang. She thought of every natural disaster she could drum up, and then she thought of Simon. Not in Rio where he should have been burning up the blackjack tables, but here at the park, in her office, lying in a motionless heap on the floor.

"Remember Ibo," he'd said. Tell Tory to remember Ibo. But what had he meant?

The only thing she knew for certain was that Simon had been a Marine, stationed somewhere in Polynesia for much of his time in the service. Hadn't he also met Tory and George in that region of the world? She seemed to recall hearing that somewhere. But she'd never heard of anyone called Ibo, and she couldn't begin to imagine what "common ground" might be. Knowing Simon, probably some seedy, rat-infested casino.

Too tired and shell-shocked to think straight, Kristian crawled off the sofa and began making her way to the enormous king-size bed. Even her reflection in the closet mirror didn't have the power to jolt her out of her trance-like state. So what if she looked half dead, if her normally wavy blond hair hung in long, limp tendrils about her face, if her cheeks and lips were pale, her green eyes shadowy and dull? She was still breathing, wasn't she? It was more than she could say for Simon.

Shivering at the memory, she stripped off her jumpsuit, turned out the lights, climbed between the cool cotton sheets—and promptly fell into a fitful slumber, brimming with dreams of stars and guns, disappearing bodies and murder in the deep, empty reaches of space....

THE DESERT NIGHT was cool, the air blowing in the windows strangely rejuvenating as the vehicle bumped and lurched along the isolated road. The terrain had grown rougher, steeper, more desolate with each passing mile. This wasn't a traveled route. It was the optimum spot. A body might never be discovered in such a remote place.

"Just a bit farther," the woman in the car announced without inflection to the dead female beside her. "Then we can part company for good."

She glanced at her watch. One-thirty a.m. Funny, it didn't feel that late. Of course, two murders were bound to make for a short night. Especially when one had to make plans on the go.

Lips set in a thin line, she pumped hard on the car's worn brakes, stopping on the rim of a jagged cliff that dropped sharply into a barren canyon.

"Okay, your turn to drive," she informed the dead female body in the passenger seat. "Slide on over and take the wheel."

Artfully, she draped two flaccid arms of the dead woman over the steering wheel. She positioned the right foot resting lightly on the brake pedal, head up, eyes open. Skid marks were intact—perfect.

Smiling clinically, she reached through the open window and released the groaning emergency brake. Then she stood back and watched as the car, already teetering precariously over the edge of the cliff, began its inexorable descent to the rocky canyon floor.

"So long, problem number one," she muttered, dusting off her gloved hands.

Taking one last stoical look into the darkened canyon, she turned and caught the flicker of headlights coming toward her. So far, so good. With an icy chuckle, she stood back to wait, completely at ease with the thought that there would undoubtedly be more bodies to dispose of before she departed the cosmic world of NORStar Center.

"REMEMBER IBO? That's what he said to her?" George's narrow face registered complete bewilderment. "What was he trying to tell you?"

Tory regarded the starry night sky beyond his kitchen window. He'd been staring at it absently, identifying the myriad constellations, since his old friend had shown up at the ranch half an hour ago with the news that the security staff had found nothing unusual in or around NORStar's main complex. Running the side of his hand across his upper lip, he shook his head. "I don't know. Maybe Simon thought the people who killed Ibo were after him."

"That'd be a good trick, seeing as they're both rotting in some roach-infested Polynesian jail."

Tory slumped back in his chair. "Common ground," he muttered out loud.

"Ibo's bar in Raratonga?" George suggested.

"Could be. That's where we first crossed paths with Simon." Tory pushed his fingers through his long, brown hair. "Dammit, George, what was Simon doing at the park? And why would anyone want to shoot him?"

"Maybe he was in to a loan shark for more than he could handle. He's been known to do that before."

Tory shook his head. "No, if he needed money, he'd have come to one of us for it. Hell, he owed me thousands, and he probably owed you more. He knew the well hadn't run dry yet. Besides, what does Ibo Quan have to do with a gambling debt?"

"Nothing, as far as I can tell." George's dark eyes took on a speculative glint. "Maybe we have to approach this from a different angle. Don't forget, Ibo's partner and his girlfriend turned on him. They squandered most of the profits from the bar, then killed him to keep him from reporting them to the authorities."

Tory's curse was low and succinct. George had a knack for saying things he'd rather not hear, usually things he was thinking without realizing it. "I trust Morton and Evan," he maintained flatly.

"That's because you're a trusting person at heart. We both are. But if it happened to Ibo, it could happen to us. Just because someone's your partner doesn't necessarily mean he won't betray the trust you've placed in him."

"We're talking about murder," Tory reminded him. "Cold-blooded and deliberate."

"That's right."

"Dammit, George, I can't accept that. I won't accept it."

Shoving his chair back, he stood and crossed to the kitchen window. A ridge of hills beyond the house blocked his view of the distant space park, but he didn't have to see it to picture it in his mind. He'd helped design the place. It was his concept, his dream. The only one he could govern outright. He refused to believe that dream might be crumbling to pieces at his feet.

"You don't have to accept it." George lit a cigar and regarded his friend shrewdly. "But you do have to consider the possibility."

"What, that we might be in partnership with a killer?"

"If you believe Kristian, which I think we both do at this point, yes. What else could Simon's message have meant?"

"I don't know." Tory rubbed the aching muscles at the back of his neck. "Maybe I don't want to know. Until we do some checking, or find Simon's body, our hands are tied. We can't bring in the authorities, and we just can't let this slide."

Thoughtfully, George studied the glowing tip of his cigar. "Do you have someone watching her?" he asked at last.

A slow grin tugged at Tory's lips. He knew Kristian resented his suggestion that she stay at the hotel tonight. No doubt she would have slugged him if he'd given in to temptation and ordered security to trail her around the park until this mess was resolved. "The best I could do was put a guard on her room," he said, reaching into the cupboard for whatever edible matter came to hand.

The package of month-old pretzels he dug out would satisfy part of his hunger, but only a very small part, he noted dryly, ripping the cellophane with his teeth and wishing he could shed his desire for Kristian as easily. Still, if he hadn't managed to do it by now, it was unlikely he ever would. Not only was she the strongest, most independent woman he knew, but she was also absolutely stunning, a green-eyed, blond-haired, long-limbed beauty who'd managed to steal—and break—his heart a long time ago.

Shaking the hurtful memory aside, he focused his mind on the present and his eyes on the stars that shone like ancient diamonds in the summer sky. A feeling of restless frustration pulled at him, a need to do something, anything, no matter how rash. "Any suggestions?" he asked over his shoulder as he bit into a handful of stale, broken pretzels.

George came up behind him, his expression a blend of calm reassurance and determination. "The usual. Think, ask questions, conduct a quiet but thorough search of the grounds." He clamped a firm hand down on Tory's shoulder. "Whatever's going on, we'll figure it out. We've been through a lot, you and me. We'll get through this, too, just like we always do."

Would they? Tory offered no response, but his doubts ran deep on this one. Deeper than they ever had before. He shifted his gaze in the direction of the Pallas Hotel, and hoped to hell he was wrong.

DARKNESS TINGED with lightning streaks of purple and red lurked in the turbulent dimensions of Kristian's dreams. It was a world she desperately wanted to escape, rife with multi-eyed aliens who stared at her from the sanctuary of their grubby abodes, watching, waiting in a frozen silence that set her teeth on edge.

Stealthy little noises crept in. She strained to separate and identify them, then felt herself jump slightly as an odd sense of reality took over from illusion. Odd because the differences were so subtle, virtually indistinguishable to her sleep-dulled mind.

She hated to think what kind of monsters loomed beyond the curtain of black mist that pressed in on her. She couldn't see them; only their catlike footsteps on the carpet betrayed their presence. Everything seemed foreign, all the shapes that were larger than life, swathed in mottled shadows, surrounding her, shifting, drawing closer—until finally one of them emerged from the darkness, taking on a more distinctive human form with each advancing step.

Or was it human? It looked that way from the neck down, even if it was clad in a shapeless one-piece garment. But the head was all wrong. It was too large, with bulging eyes, a huge, blue-veined cranium, pointed ears that stood straight up on the occipital lobe and a pair of antennae that dangled in a loose arc over the creature's broad forehead.

Kristian felt the terrified pounding of her heart as the hideous being continued its lumbering trek toward the bed. She was dreaming. She had to be. But if that were the case, why did everything seem so real?

She sat up and blinked her eyes. One thing was certain: this dream had become a full-fledged nightmare. The approaching creature had a mouthful of sharp, pointy teeth that looked to be grinning at her, mocking her as she stared at it, unbelieving. Then, from out of the darkness, a hand came slowly into view, gloved and holding something white.

"Don't fight me, Kristian," a man's rusty voice mumbled. "You'll only make things worse for yourself."

There was a thick, uncultivated edge to the voice, and even though there could be no doubt that she was caught in some horrible nighttime hallucination, Kristian felt herself inching across the mattress, over smooth cotton sheets to the far side of the bed.

A light film of perspiration broke out on her skin; her breathing was shallow, her heart racing a mile a minute. Wake up, she ordered herself, lowering her lashes and fighting the blades of panic that stabbed at her. Why couldn't she wake up?

Something clawed at her wrist, and her eyes flew open—to the darkness and a blue-skinned face no human had ever possessed. A scream rushed from her throat, changing swiftly to a yelp of pain as the fingers on her wrist dug in deeper, squeezing just enough to hurt while the other hand slammed a white cloth over her mouth and nose.

Legions of extraterrestrials promptly began to swim in her head. The grip on her wrist slackened, the mumbled voice became a guttural grunt she couldn't understand. A sweet, chemical odor assailed her, dulling her senses as she twisted and squirmed in an effort to repel it. Bulging eyes bored into hers, the body beneath them bending over her struggling form in a distinctly menacing fashion.

Jerking one hand free, she hammered at the barrel chest above her, fighting with every scrap of her rapidly dissipating strength. She could feel the ruthless assault on her muscles as a smoky, white cloud engulfed her, sapping her energy. It had to be a combination of perversity and unqualified fright that gave her the force she needed to knock the smothering white cloth away with a furious swat. Indignation spiked through her, trailed by growing alarm, but they were torpid, unfocused emotions, blunted by the blue-gray haze that threatened to overwhelm her.

She battled the dizzying sensations, as well as the creature. This couldn't be a dream, her frantic brain croaked.

Garbled words, some of them remarkably obscene, fell from the alien's black-painted mouth as it attempted—and succeeded in—pinning her flailing wrists on either side of her head. Awake or asleep, however, Kristian had no intention of succumbing to a show of brute force. She thrashed around on the bed, butting at the massive body, ignoring the bestial grunts. Again she screamed, and this time the sound wasn't cut off. At least not completely. For an instant, the toothy monster hesitated, lifting its head and tightening its cruel grip on her wrists.

Still thrashing wildly, Kristian took advantage of the lapse and fought to wriggle out from beneath the restraining knee that was pressed across her legs. Miraculously, the creature didn't react, and a second later she was free. With a spiteful growl she rolled away and brought her foot up hard, landing a solid, satisfying blow to the most vulnerable part of her attacker's obviously human anatomy.

The bluish mist spiraled in again, but not before the alien sprang back, antennae bobbing, staggering drunkenly as it tumbled from the large bed. Razor-sharp teeth flashed in the pearly half light that showered the room. Teeth that could undoubtedly slash her to ribbons.

The room began to spin in crazy circles. The creature's anemic features loomed in front of her. The nightmare shadows deepened as Kristian made a last-ditch effort to combat the darkness that threatened to claim her.

It was a losing battle, over before it really started. She felt herself floating away. Through a smoky brume, she also saw the hands that reached for her. Hands that looked large and strong and very, very real. Human fingers poised to strangle. Moving closer and closer to her unprotected throat....

Chapter Four

"Ms. Ellis? Can you hear me?"

A gravelly female voice penetrated the outer fringes of Kristian's sleep. She surfaced slowly, with a low groan and a blurry recollection of someone trying to choke her.

"Ms. Ellis?" From a great distance, she felt the hands on her shoulders, shaking her roughly while the voice continued to punch holes in her restless slumber. "Are you all right?"

Forcing her heavy eyelids open, Kristian brought the woman's features into focus. Thin lips, broad cheekbones, muddy brown eyes and a cap of hacked-off black hair greeted her. Her name was Hildy something, Kristian thought groggily. She was in charge of hotel security and about as approachable as a coiled snake. But at least she didn't have any antennae.

The nightmare crowded in with a jolt that brought her fully awake. Instinctively, Kristian jerked away from Hildy's strong hands, surging up and shoving the damp hair off her cheeks only to find two sets of startled human eyes staring down at her.

"We, uh, heard you scream and thought you might be hurt." It was the second person who spoke, the male half of the hotel security team Tory had stationed in the hall outside her suite.

Still too uncertain to think straight, she regarded the twosome before her, suspicion darkening her eyes. "I thought there was someone here with me. Did either of you see anything when you came in?"

Hildy drew back, her severe expression not lightening a bit. "Nothing unusual," she said in a brusque tone that would have done a drill sergeant proud. "You must have been dreaming."

"Maybe." Kristian wasn't sure whether she believed that simple explanation. She peered past the guards into the sitting room. "Where's Hubie?"

The man, whose name escaped her, grinned, but he sobered quickly when his partner shot him a stony glare. "We—that is, I sent him to the kitchen for coffee and cheesecake. The night crew wouldn't dare kick up a fuss, not with those biceps of his."

Almost on cue, Hubie Bittman plodded into the suite, calling out a puzzled "Hey, what's going on here? Where is everyone?" and holding tight to a tray loaded with coffee, half a cheesecake, a bag of Oreos and a carton of milk. He blinked at Kristian, who couldn't quite shed the notion that this man wasn't as dull as he looked. "You hungry, too?" he asked.

She declined the offer, studying him. "Did you see anyone in the corridor, Hubie?" she queried cautiously. "Man, woman, child . . . alien?"

"Alien?" he echoed. "You mean like E.T. or Mr. Spock?"

The male guard laughed. "I think she means an illegal alien, Hubie." He hesitated and slanted Kristian a quizzical glance. "Er, that is what you're talking about, isn't it?"

She could, probably should, have told them the truth, but right then she wasn't exactly sure what that would entail. Nor was she sure she wanted to pursue the subject. Maybe it had been a nightmare. If she was smart, she'd write the whole episode off as a delayed reaction, a belated bout of hysteria that had played itself out in her dreams.

"I don't know what I'm talking about," she admitted tiredly, falling back against the pillows. "I never make much sense when I first wake up."

"Would you like some coffee?" the stern-featured Hildy asked.

Yes, she would, Kristian thought, but did she really want to stay awake for the rest of the night? She snuck a look at the digital bedside clock: 3:42 a.m. Groaning inwardly, she shrugged, plastering a dispassionate expression on her face and murmuring a polite, "You can leave me a cup, but at this point I think I'd rather get some sleep."

With a curt nod, Hildy plucked a cup from the tray, motioned to Hubie and her partner and turned for the door. Both men followed dutifully on her heels, though Kristian thought she detected a tiny break in Hubie's stride.

If she could have found the strength, she would have held him back and cross-examined him. As it was, she could barely scrape up the energy to stagger around the suite in her peach teddy, checking the windows and doors.

Two doors, she noted, grimacing as she snapped the dead bolt in place on the one that led to a sparsely trafficked corridor near the fire stairs.

"It was a dream," she stated aloud, leaving the bathroom light on and curling up on the upholstered window seat with her pillow and coffee. "It had to be a dream."

No trail of steam rose from the coffee cup, she noticed instantly. It was tepid and much too watery, and Kristian's suspicious mind immediately started working overtime, speculating on the possible reasons why. It certainly would have been easy enough for Hubie to leave his pilfered tray of food and beverages on the fire stairs while he donned a mask, slipped in here and tried to...

No! She'd been dreaming. No one had broken into her room. No man, woman, child or alien. If her head was throbbing, it was a perfectly natural reaction to the events of the night. And if her wrist still tingled, well, that didn't necessarily mean anyone had grabbed her. There were no marks or bruises of any kind on her skin.

Hunching her shoulders, she turned determined eyes toward the flickering lights of the space park. She wouldn't dwell on this. She was still alive, and, for the time being, well enough. Not like ex-Marine Simon Juniper who'd had the good fortune to meet Tory and George in some raunchy South Seas port eight years ago—and the misfortune to be gunned down in her office tonight.

Kristian squinted at the faraway central complex, unable to bring it into focus, then looked at her bedside clock: 4:00 a.m. Simon had been shot just under five hours ago. She knew for a fact that was no dream.

And so did the reptile who'd shot him.

THE MAN'S FEET felt like pieces of lead as he trudged into the deserted Space Walk exhibit. No, not deserted, he amended, slogging across the soft, misty blue surface of the Neptune chamber. He'd never be that lucky.

He lifted apprehensive eyes to the arced ceiling. Where spiky ice thorns would normally be somersaulting lazily overhead, there was nothing except a wall of darkness and a silence so thick it was almost deafening. Suffocating. He'd been dreading this trip for the past two hours, sweating out the seconds, the minutes. Afraid to show up; even more afraid not to.

She scared him in a way no one else could. He wasn't sure how or why; he only knew she was as cold and mean and unforgiving as the crystalline fury bolts that forked through the poisonous Neptune atmosphere each day.

He slowed his pace to a shuffle, head swinging every which way, panicked eyes combing the starless, planetary shadows. Maybe her partner would come instead. He was much less frightening than she was. He'd understand. Anyone could make a little mistake.

"You're five minutes late."

Her quiet statement slammed down on him like a giant sledgehammer. "I—I had a problem," he blurted self-consciously.

"So it would seem."

He took a gawky backward step. It was cowardly, and he knew it. If she had a gun, she wasn't waving it around. Anyway, she wouldn't kill him for one tiny blunder. Would she?

He tried to puff up his biceps along with his courage. "I did what you said," he defended. "But Kristian's real quick. And loud. She screamed before I could put her out."

"I see."

The glacial smile on her lips didn't waver. He kept his feet rooted to the crater-pocked floor, hoping against hope that the blue Neptune mist would rush in and hide him from her. It didn't and her smile widened as if she could read his mind.

Before he realized what was happening, she'd closed the gap between them. One delicate finger skimmed across his quivering Adam's apple, and he could see clearly the shark-like cruelty in her eyes.

"This is your lucky night, my friend," she practically purred. "It just so happens that I'm feeling uncommonly charitable." Her fingernail slid to the base of his throat. "Still, you'd do well to remember that I'm not likely to be in such a good mood again, should you ever have occasion to test me." She regarded him through emotionless eyes. "I trust I'm making myself clear."

He held himself very still, relief, revulsion and shock chasing one another through his mind. "Perfectly," he croaked.

She'd kill him in a minute; he knew that now. And swiftly, silently, he uttered a desperate prayer for his soul.

THIS WAS so unworthy of her, Kristian mourned as she crept through the space park early Tuesday morning. Here she was in a top-level management position, and she was darting around between pavilions like an escaped felon, trying desperately not to attract the attention of the ever-present security people who were busy running their preopening check of the grounds.

She couldn't help it. After what she'd been through last night, she was suspicious of any and everyone wearing a NORStar uniform, and that included those people hired to sniff out trouble in the park.

Sunglasses perched on her nose and dressed in a pair of nondescript olive-drab pants, a matching shirt and sneakers, she ducked out of the Planet of Dreams exhibit, smiling absently at Lilith, who was slumping along en route to the central complex. "Good morning," she murmured without stopping.

Lilith shrugged, turning unenthusiastic eyes toward the cloudless blue sky. "If you say so," she replied in a dreary tone that matched the expression on her face.

She offered nothing more, and Kristian couldn't summon the energy to strike up a conversation. It would have been one-sided, anyway. Lilith could only deal with computers, not people.

The sun beat down relentlessly as Kristian slipped through the door of the popular Martian Terrace Restaurant. Although the day promised to be a scorcher, the immense, glass-walled dining room was blissfully cool. To her relief, it was also devoid of humanity. Only George's holograms, beyond the walls, were up and about, and they were too busy cavorting across the rough Martian terrain to bother with her.

Even in her preoccupied state, she couldn't resist pausing to watch the aliens play. The Martian Terrace was exactly what its name implied: a glassed-in room with a magnificent, if rather fanciful, view of the planet Mars. Whether any life-forms of the type that were currently flitting across the pock-marked ground had ever really existed was doubtful, but that didn't make the three-dimensional show one bit less spectacular.

A fascinating array of multilimbed creatures, some walking, some crawling, some floating over the rusty, windblown soil, entertained the visiting masses daily. It was a feast for the senses, a riveting display, complete with tiny meteors that streaked intermittently through the Martian heavens, illuminating the crimson sky with a bright silvery glow. Not surprisingly, the delicious Mexican fare offered by NORStar's renowned Southwestern chefs frequently wound up taking a back seat to the unique holographic images outside the Plexiglas walls.

The aroma of freshly brewed coffee intruded on Kristian's surveillance of a knock-kneed dust rooter as it endeavored to bury itself in a mound of dirt. Tugging off her sunglasses, she zigzagged between the tables and snatched the steaming pot from its hot plate.

A quick glance at her watch told her it was almost eight-thirty. An hour and a half until the park opened.

Wonderful, she thought with a sigh. That left only ninety minutes for her to dredge up the courage she'd need to venture into her office.

She wondered briefly if she'd be able to do it, then decided she probably would. Already she'd managed to sneak out of the hotel, drive to her suburban Las Vegas apartment, shower, change and drive back to the park. She'd even worked up the nerve to check out the costume storage area in the Planet of Dreams exhibit. It came as no great surprise that the black-lipped mask she'd seen, or thought she'd seen, last night was locked up in its usual cupboard. It also didn't prove a thing when she got right down to it.

At least no one, human or extraterrestrial, had tried to attack her this morning. Still moving covertly, she slid into a corner booth with the coffeepot, a clean mug and a big black cloud of doubt and suspicion weighing heavily on her mind.

She didn't like what she was thinking one little bit. Simon had been shot by a person wearing a NORStar jumpsuit. That had to mean the crime had been committed by someone working at the park. No one except an employee at the space park could possibly have gained access to the central complex last night.

Picking up her cup, she settled deeper into the booth, not at all comforted by that thought. With a frustrated sigh, she took a drink of coffee—then almost spat it out when something stirred behind her.

"Did anyone ever tell you that you drive like a maniac?" a voice close to her ear inquired.

Forcing herself not to jump, Kristian responded to Tory's mocking comment with a sweet "Did anyone ever tell you that people who hang around in restaurant shadows making nasty cracks run the risk of having hot coffee thrown in their faces?"

"To anyone who happened to be on the freeway with you this morning, that wouldn't have sounded like a nasty crack."

She heard the lazy taunt in his tone and would have taken the bait if she hadn't suddenly realized what his remarks implied. "You followed me to the city," she accused, swinging around to glare at him.

He didn't deny it. Pushing himself from the back of the high booth, he grinned and slid with his customary animal grace onto the padded seat. "Let's say I tried," he drawled. "I'd have to have been a Grand Prix driver to keep you in sight." A dark brow was lifted in her direction. "You do know where the brake pedal is, I assume?"

Kristian counted to ten and at the same time directed her body to stay put. He was too close, too sexy and much too disturbing, but she wouldn't allow herself to sidle away from him. Ignoring the humorous gibe, she calmly raised the coffee mug to her lips. "And here I thought all you flyboys had nerves of steel."

"Another myth bites the dust, huh?"

"Don't flatter yourself, Tory. I saw through most of those macho military myths a long time ago." She set her cup down carefully, highly conscious of the soft shadows that played across his face and the way he was half sprawled, half sitting in the booth. "Why did you follow me?"

He shrugged, but a trace of amusement still lurked in his beautiful eyes. "I'd have thought the answer would be obvious."

Curiosity and some other emotion Kristian chose not to acknowledge tugged at her. "It is. What I want to know is why you followed me instead of sending Hubie—" she masked a delicate shudder "—or one of his brawny cohorts in your place."

She shouldn't have pushed the matter. It never paid off with Tory. Smiling silkily, he reached out and grazed the soft skin of her throat with his fingers, sending an instant alarm signal to her brain. "And trust the safety of this lovely neck to someone else? Not a chance, Kristian."

A hot shiver swept across her skin. Controlling it, she swallowed though she couldn't stop herself from trembling slightly. "I don't like being followed," she told him and meant it. "I can take care of myself."

"So you've always insisted," he murmured. Never one to be easily discouraged, Tory shifted his attention to the hair at her temple, brushing it away with a lazy stroke of his thumb. "Hildy tells me you were having nightmares about E.T."

Kristian swore under her breath. It figured Hildy would turn out to be one of Tory's stool pigeons. "Actually," she retorted coolly, "it was a minion of the Beldam Dracona from the Planet of Dreams. And I'm not altogether sure I was having a nightmare."

"You think one of Dracona's minions paid you a visit?"

As absurd as the question sounded, there was no amusement in Tory's tone. Kristian almost wished he would find something humorous in all this. Maybe then it would seem less real. Less pernicious. "I honestly don't know," she admitted, lowering her eyes to her hands. "I thought he grabbed me, but I can't be sure."

Tory took her hand, turning it over and examining the tender skin of her inner wrist. "I don't see any bruises."

She resisted the urge to withdraw from his warm touch and the strange surge of emotion that accompanied it. "I know. Like I said, I'm not sure if anything really happened." With more than a passing regret, she watched his hand fall slowly away from hers. Straightening in her seat, she searched for a new topic, settling quickly on the one that had plagued her for much of the night. "Uh, Tory, what did Simon's message mean? Who's Ibo?"

"Someone we both knew." He regarded her through his lashes, a shutter falling over his eyes. "You're sure it was one of Dracona's minions?"

Inwardly she groaned. This was like pulling teeth. "Positive," she said, wishing she'd held her tongue, wishing he'd cooperate for once in his life. "Why did Simon want me to tell you to remember Ibo? And what's 'common ground'?"

Whether he intended to answer or sidestep her questions was hard to say. Their conversation was interrupted when one of the space park's little robots zoomed noisily into the restaurant.

"Slow down, Crater," a throaty voice shouted after him. "You can't clank around the central complex all day with a defective wheel."

An out-of-breath Priscilla Warfield stalked through the door behind the robot, nabbing him before he could roll out of range. She flicked the power button on his barrel chest then pushed him over to the corner table.

"If you two are trying to blend into the Martian landscape, it won't work," the maintenance woman told them, grunting as she dropped to her knees on the gleaming floor. "Evan saw you come into the park, Tory. He sent me over to tell you the meeting's been rescheduled for ten-thirty this morning."

Tory cast her an ironic sideways glance. "Evan's here already?"

"Bouncing around like a rubber ball," Priscilla confirmed. "Oh, by the way, George is looking for you. Says it's important, bordering on urgent. He's over at the Space Walk exhibit."

Kristian let out a relieved breath at that bit of information. Being in Tory's company for prolonged periods of time was much more difficult than she'd anticipated.

He slid easily from the booth, pausing just long enough to send her a level stare. "Don't take any chances today, Kristian," he warned, and she nodded mutely, for once not feeling the urge to snap at his authoritative tone.

She kept her mouth closed until his back had faded from sight, then looked questioningly at Priscilla. "Is the meeting in the conference room?"

"Nope, over at the Cosmic Theater. Not that Evan bothered to thank me, but the Colonel and I finally got the bulk of the new systems back on line. I want you to know, I'm putting in for overtime on this one, Kristian. Eighteen-hour workdays are definitely not on my list of pleasant experiences, especially when they keep me out of the action mainstream." She glanced behind her. "I hear there was quite an uproar over on this side of the park last night."

Kristian stifled a sigh, leaning forward and propping her elbows up on the table. "Does everyone know?"

"About Simon?" Shrugging, Priscilla sat back on her heels and swept her unruly mane of red-brown hair over one shoulder. "I doubt it. George was very explicit in his warning that those who do know should make a point of keeping their mouths shut."

"George believes me?" Somehow she hadn't expected that.

"I guess so." Priscilla pawed through her leather tool belt for a wrench. "All I know is he subjected me to an interrogation that would have made the FBI boys look like a bunch of bumbling Inspector Clouseaus."

"Why did he question you?"

"He was probably hoping I'd seen something. A reasonable enough assumption considering I didn't get out of the park until almost three a.m."

Kristian regarded her with a morsel of hope. "And did you see anything?"

"Plenty, but nothing George considered significant." Priscilla gave Crater's cockeyed wheel a sharp rap with her wrench. "I'm afraid there wasn't a whole lot happening out at the Cosmic Theater. Anyway if Simon really was around here last night—which, I'm sorry, Kristian, I find very hard to believe—I guarantee he'd have had more sense than to get within shouting distance of me. He hit me up for three hundred dollars two weeks ago, and like a fool I loaned it to him. He's made a point of avoiding me ever since."

"Sounds like you're getting soft," Kristian noted dryly. "A few years ago when we were both working at the Casa Grande Resort in Las Vegas, you would have laughed at anyone who made such a request."

Priscilla grinned. "Must be my mother's more tolerant side of the family coming out in me. Either that or it's this glamorous lifestyle I've adopted." With her work boot, she directed a well-aimed kick at the robot's left wheel. "Dealing blackjack to a pack of leering wolves in Vegas was hard work. Fixing broken down machinery, that's a piece of cake. Still, I haven't gotten so soft that I'd let a three-hundred-dollar loan go by the board without a fight."

Vintage Priscilla, Kristian reflected, draining her cup. Tough on the surface, but beneath her unwieldy locks and wordly-wise demeanor, she was a full-fledged cream puff. Very much like a certain male about whom Kristian flatly refused to think.

Forcing a smile, she stood and reactivated the robot. "I'll make sure Crater gets over to the main complex before we open. Since the meeting is taking place at the Cosmic Theater, I think it might be a good idea if you were there. The Colonel, too, if he's around."

"He's probably in his workshop," Priscilla said. She stuck her wrench into her tool belt. "I don't know exactly what you saw yesterday, but you sure got the boss men hopping. I haven't seen Evan up this early for months, and I've never seen George acting so intense or Tory so concerned."

Possibly because they'd never had to deal with such a bizarre set of circumstances, Kristian thought distastefully.

Shivering, she followed Crater into the brilliant morning sunshine. She just had to figure out what Simon had been doing at the space park yesterday. Somehow, she had to discover why he'd been shot. And by whom.

Chapter Five

"So how goes it, Kristian? Does the complex feel like home sweet home again?" Without knocking, June strode buoyantly through the connecting door from her office and perched on the corner of Kristian's overflowing desk. "Afternoon, Crux," she greeted Crater's twin. "You're right on schedule, I see."

Kristian smiled as the little robot circled the room, then made a beeline for the corridor and the next stop on his programmed route.

"Home never felt quite like this," she confessed. "But if you're asking how I'm coping, the answer is, adequately. It's been one problem after another since the meeting this morning."

"In other words, it's business as usual." Chuckling, June shook out a folded piece of paper. "Well, let me just add to that list of problems you're having." She slid a pair of bifocals onto her nose. "Now, where shall I start? Ah, yes, here we go."

"Is this a long list?" Kristian interrupted, stealing a quick look at her watch. It was already past three and she'd been hoping to slip away from the space park early. She wanted to do some digging into the last few days of Simon's life, and she couldn't do that from behind her desk.

"Long yes. Dull no. First off," June began, "shuttle chamber number five evidently took a young couple where no man had gone before. Picture it, Kristian. There they were zooming through our computerized cosmic realm en route to the Rigel system, when suddenly their controls went dead. Before they knew it they'd slammed right smack into a passing asteroid. And if that wasn't enough of a jolt, they soon discovered they were locked in their ship. Now, I'll grant you, they're not complaining at all since an ailing shuttle beats the tunnel of love any day, but I thought you might want to do something special for them. It took Priscilla's people more than an hour to jimmy the chamber's hatch."

Kristian couldn't resist a smile. "Are they staying at one of the hotels?"

"The Northern Lights."

"Okay, leave me their names and room number. I'll get in touch with them. Next."

"Next I'm supposed to tell you that one of our wandering extraterrestrials tripped and sprained his ankle. He claims the eyes on his mask are out of alignment. As you might imagine, the Colonel's contesting that one, but you'd better check it out, anyway. You know how touchy the old dear can be when it comes to his costumes."

Kristian took another unobtrusive look at her watch. "I'll speak to him before he leaves the park."

"You can speak to him now if you'd like, kiddo. He's in his workshop with Tory and Evan."

"Terrific."

June peered over the top of her glasses. "I beg your pardon?"

"Nothing. Go on."

It took a full twenty minutes for June to rattle off the remaining items on her list. She finished with a tentative "Oh, and I talked to Morton after this morning's meeting. You know, about Simon."

Kristian compressed her lips but kept her voice level. "He doesn't believe me, does he?"

"Let's say he's skeptical. After all, there's no body and no indication whatsoever of foul play."

Yes there was, Kristian thought, controlling her expression. "It's all right," she lied. "I don't really expect people to believe me. Anyway, I've contacted a private investigator to trace Simon's movements this past weekend. Not that I think he'll find much, but I'm willing to try anything at this point." Shoving back her chair, she plucked a bright pink memo from the pile of computer printouts on her desk. "I'll be leaving the park in a few minutes. If you can find the time, I'd like you to contact personnel for me. Apparently one of the programmers in Lilith's department didn't report for work today."

June blinked. "So why should something like that concern us?"

"Ordinarily it wouldn't, but I gather they're having some problem locating her. Just look into it for me as soon as you can. The woman's name is Anita Brace, and her file shows a Las Vegas address. Personnel will give you the rest of the details."

"If you say so." June tucked the memo into the pocket of her jumpsuit. "I'll call down right after my coffee break."

She breezed through the door with her customary light tread, but not before sneaking a surreptitious look at the carpet she'd been crawling on last night. At the very spot where Simon had fallen.

Kristian couldn't bring herself to follow her assistant's curious gaze. Instead she wandered over and poured a cup of Brazilian coffee from the sleek machine near the window that spanned one entire wall of her office. With a sigh, she dropped into her padded chair, unable to force her mind back to the clutter on her normally tidy desk.

For once the mess didn't bother her. Neither did burning her tongue on the scalding coffee. Even the persistent beep of the computer at her desk did little more than scratch the surface of her muddied thoughts.

She should contact Jaime Alverez, the assistant manager at the Northern Lights, and have him arrange a special dinner for the couple who'd gotten caught in the Blue Star Voyage shuttle chamber. She should leave word with security to send Hubie Bittman upstairs when he came on duty. She should take a preliminary stroll through the new Planets exhibits and the Cosmic Theater. Most of all, though, she should look for Simon.

"Damn," she muttered softly, reaching for the telephone. She was sorely tempted to march over to the galactic cantina and drown her sorrows in a bottle of schnapps. If she tried hard enough, she might eventually acquire a taste for the stuff, but she doubted it. Her tastes ran more to Dr. Pepper then the grainy flavor of alcohol.

Swiveling her chair around, she began punching Jaime's number, only vaguely aware of the computer still beeping shrilly in front of her. She paused uncertainly, her finger poised on one of the touch tone buttons. Beeping?

Her eyes fastened on the trembling screen, on the columns of figures that were vanishing a row at a time as if by magic. Had she leaned on the keyboard, she wondered, frowning. Spilled coffee on it and caused some kind of mysterious short circuit? Both seemed improbable, but something must have happened. To the best of her knowledge, NORStar's computers, sophisticated and temperamental though they might be, hadn't yet developed minds of their own.

She lowered the telephone slowly, unwilling to recognize the presentiment of dread that stirred inside her. The beeping ceased abruptly as the last set of figures blinked out, leaving the screen blank and sending a tiny trickle of alarm through her bloodstream.

She was overreacting, Kristian told herself firmly, not quite ready to trust the now-silent collection of circuits and microchips. Machines broke down all the time around here. If this had happened yesterday, she wouldn't have given it a second thought.

Shaking aside the worst of her apprehension, she took a discreet stab at the keyboard, then held her breath as the monitor began to flash. Within seconds the menu was in place and Kristian was falling back in her chair, certain her nerves had never before undergone such a ruthless pounding. What she needed to do was clear up any pressing matters on her desk and get away from the center as quickly as possible.

Decision made, she picked up the phone with one hand and the latest park expense reports with the other. She had Jaime's private number half dialed when a demanding little chirp to her right stopped her.

She didn't want to look, that much she knew. She definitely didn't want to lift her eyes and find Dracona's pointy-eared, black-lipped minion glowering at her.

Steeling herself, she inched her gaze upward, prepared to confront her nightmarish nemesis. But it wasn't a masked alien she encountered. It wasn't Crux or Crater or even a crazed killer wearing a NORStar uniform. It was a shrieking mass of complex machinery, throwing a tantrum, sounding conspicuously like a spoiled child.

The sullen cheeping continued as once again the computer screen went blank. If she hadn't known better, she would have said it was about to explode. And actually, when she got right down to it, Kristian couldn't be at all sure it wasn't going to do just that. She certainly didn't want to wait around and find out the hard way. But neither did she intend to let a malfunctioning piece of office equipment turn her into a quaking coward.

In front of her, the computer whirred and hiccuped and suddenly fell silent. Kristian stared at it, distrust changing slowly to a startled horror that kept her rooted to the spot despite several frantic directives from her brain to run.

The beeping had stopped. The office was quiet, unnaturally hushed, still except for the glowing amber words that appeared one by one in the center of the monitor. Haunting words that brought a knot of fear to her chest and a wintry chill to her skin.

In the seeming paradox of our dreams,
are life and death mere illusions—
or the only certainties
this boundless universe has to offer?

"YOU SEE, my boy? There's no vision problem. None at all." Nathan Brenda, affectionately known as the Colonel, a title carried over from his days in Britain's Royal Air Force, skirted a collection of furry Mercury fire-kittens and sailed serenely across the room. "Why I could get three fingers through each of those sockets. That young lad didn't sprain his ankle because of this mask." He glided to a halt at Tory's side, a starched white apron covering the dress shirt, vest and tweed Savile Row trousers he habitually wore. "Why don't you try it? Tell me what you think."

Tory grinned. "Thanks, but I'll pass. Don't worry about it, Colonel. My spies tell me the kid's a hustler from way back. Legal won't have any problem handling this."

"Good thing, too," Evan added, his head appearing over the top of a large flying saucer. "If Kristian has her way, legal will have its collective hands full sorting out Simon's job-related affairs. By the time he gets back from Brazil, his obituary will be old news."

Inwardly, Tory grimaced, but not by the flicker of an eyelash did he react to Evan's sarcastic remarks.

The Colonel, a tall, reed-thin man, with a head of gray-white hair, a clipped white mustache and the stately bearing of a perfect English butler, adjusted his tortoise-shell glasses and set the rubber mask aside. "This story about Simon, Tory," he said in his usual tactful fashion. "Is there any chance that it could be true?"

"No." It was Evan who negated the possibility.

"Maybe," Tory countered, offsetting his partner's flat denial.

Evan rolled his eyes. "You know, don't you, that even Morton doesn't believe it?"

The Colonel shook his elegant head. "I'm afraid that doesn't mean a thing," he said. "Morton believes only what he chooses to believe. This park is a reflection of his hope for the world of tomorrow, not for the reality of today. He's an idealist, that man, though, I must concede, not without good cause. His parents were killed during the Second World War, shot by Nazi troops occupying France. Is it any wonder that he should prefer to believe in life over death?"

"Hey, you're talking to the wrong person here, Colonel," Evan reminded him. "I happen to agree with the guy."

No surprise there, Tory thought, picking a careful path through the toy-filled room. Evan invariably chose the line of least resistance. No complications, no questions asked, nothing but a perfectly normal love of money and the prestige that came from owning one-quarter of a growing space park.

"Tory?" The Colonel hailed him before he could exit the overflowing workshop. "I meant to tell you earlier; that new space toy I've been working on is ready now."

"What—you mean Norres, the space dragon?"

"I attached his wings yesterday," the Colonel confirmed, rolling up his crisp white sleeves as he moved back behind the orderly work bench.

Evan rubbed his hands together. "Now this I've gotta see. A new life-form for the Planet of Dreams exhibit. It's about time we had a fresh product to market. No matter what George says, there's not half as much money to be made on holograms as there is on toys."

The Colonel chuckled gently. "I think you're underestimating George's talent just a trifle, Evan. The holograms are a major attraction in and of themselves. In any event, I enjoy working with him."

Evan's answering shrug was noncommittal. "You could be right," he allowed. "But I still think we need the toys. Kids can't cuddle up to projections at night."

Spoken like a true pragmatist, Tory reflected as the Colonel glided off in the direction of the huge storeroom. Perhaps not the worst quality in the world, but irritating at times.

"I have to go," he told his partner who now seemed engrossed in making a miniature space ship whiz about the room. "Tell Priscilla to run one last check on the systems in both the Planets exhibit and the Cosmic Theater."

"Already done," Evan returned. "We're pretty well set for the grand opening tomorrow." He took his eyes off the streaking saucer. "Where are you going?"

Tory paused and dug his car keys from the pocket of his black jeans. "Into the city. I have some business to take care of."

He left without a backward glance, but he knew Evan wasn't a fool. He'd have little trouble figuring out exactly what that business was.

No matter, Tory told himself with a shrug. He trusted his partners, all three of them. They'd had no part in the shooting Kristian had witnessed. And they hadn't attacked her in the hotel last night.

Someone had, though, he was sure of it. Maybe searching Simon's apartment would tell him who that someone was, but it certainly couldn't hurt to have a look. There might even be an answer or two waiting to be found. And one little answer might be all that was needed to nail Simon's killer.

THE WOMAN tore through Simon's dumpy Las Vegas apartment like a blazing comet. No need to straighten up behind herself, she thought with a disgusted sneer. The late Simon Juniper had been an absolute slob.

A slob whose packed suitcases still resided next to his unmade bed. Now those would definitely have to go, she decided, hauling them over to the door. At some point in time either Kristian or Tory were bound to get the bright idea of breaking in and further ransacking the place. It simply wouldn't do for them to trip over such an obvious piece of evidence.

Kristian or Tory... The names left a sour taste in her mouth. She wanted them dead, Kristian more than Tory at this point in time. Unfortunately, her hired muscle had failed her in that respect.

"Do you really think it's, er, wise to eliminate Kristian?" her partner had asked this morning. "I mean, won't that look awfully suspicious?"

Hesitant questions, the woman recalled with a disdainful sniff, but valid enough when reasoned out. While Kristian might be an enormous pain right now, she also possessed the tenacity of a bull terrier, a quality that could prove advantageous under the circumstances. With luck and a threat or two, she'd almost certainly give Tory the nudge he needed to focus his mental energies on solving the riddle of Simon's final message. It was worth a shot, the woman conceded. Not her personal preference, but acceptable for the time being.

Straightening, she caught a glimpse of her reflection in the dresser mirror and couldn't resist a self-satisfied chuckle. She hid her true nature well. No one would ever suspect her of murder. Her partner perhaps, eventually, but that was unimportant. If they caught him, she'd kill him. If they didn't, well, it would be all the same in the end.

She could have used him this afternoon. Too bad it hadn't been feasible to bring him along, but Tory had been all over the park today. Her absence, if it was even noticed, could be explained. Hers and his together would have been much tougher to get around.

Her sharp eyes circled the messy bedroom. She ignored the dirty dishes, open hampers and rumpled sheets, then smiled and tossed Simon's NORStar uniform, the one she'd help strip from him last night, over her shoulder. It landed in a shapeless heap beside the closet.

Yes, she thought, giving herself a congratulatory pat on the back, she hadn't missed a trick. Simon had been wearing his uniform when he'd died. Dear, observant Kristian would never forget a detail like that. Now, here it was in his apartment, right where he would have left it if he had indeed taken off for South America on Saturday morning, another misleading tidbit for the unflappable Ms. Ellis to ponder.

She continued to prowl the room. Within minutes, she had Simon's passport, his airline tickets and his itinerary tucked safely in her pocket. She'd even had the presence of mind to have her partner phone the hotel in Rio, but of course, Simon had already canceled his reservation there.

"You thought you were onto something big, didn't you, Simon?" she mocked him. "You followed your female suspect right into my trap, listened to her talk, saw her die and pieced together the rest of my scheme from there. You almost panicked, too, didn't you? But you held on long enough to change the computer entry code. Long enough to give Kristian a message. Well, you blew it, pal. You not only ended your life, but quite likely several others, as well."

A tiny sound from the living room interrupted her caustic mutterings. She ran for the bedroom door, stuck her head out and strained to locate the source of the intrusive sound.

The lock! Dammit, someone was plying the lock on the apartment door, and doing it with aggravating ease.

She swore a blue streak in her mind as she searched desperately for a place to hide. How could she have been so stupid? She hadn't brought a weapon with her, and she wasn't foolish enough to believe that she could overpower anyone other than a member of her own sex unaided.

Beads of sticky perspiration broke out along her hairline. She hated being caught off guard like this. Advance planning, that was her forte. When the situation warranted it, as it had yesterday, she could even make plans on the

move. But this was different. She was trapped in a stifling
cage with no air conditioning, no means of escape and no
idea who was about to come bursting across her one and
only threshold to freedom.

Lips compressed to a grim, colorless slash, she clicked the
bedroom door closed behind her and made a dash for the
kitchen. A sinkful of poorly rinsed dishes greeted her, but
perhaps they would work to her advantage. The accordion
doors above them were open a crack. If she used the
scorched pots as a shield, she might be able to get a look at
her adversary.

The intruder entered the apartment with inordinate
stealth. That let out the lumbering landlord she'd eluded
earlier. Maybe it was Kristian!

The woman's palms began to sweat under her gloves, a
sure sign that she was letting her nerves get to her. Think,
she ordered herself angrily. *Use your wits. That's it.
Breathe. Breathe....*

A cold calm settled over her, diminishing the fiery adrenaline flow to her limbs. She inched upward from her crouch,
peering between plates and pot handles. The intruder was
visible now, still moving stealthily about the living room
floor, but at least she could identify him.

Long, dark brown hair, smooth graceful stride, athletic
body. Damn, it was Tory. She was in deep, deep trouble.

She sank back behind the counter. Overpowering him was
out of the question. He was thirty-six and in excellent shape.
He also knew how to fight. While he wasn't prone to striking women, she suspected he'd be quite willing to make an
exception in the case of a murderer.

Rubbing her gloved hand on her knee, she looked up at
the sink. Her brain worked feverishly fast. Something hard
and weighty, that was what she needed. Something she could
swing.

Her fingers wrapped around the edge of the counter and
tugged. Tory was sifting through a bunch of papers near the
window. Though it wasn't open, she knew the traffic noises

on the street outside would be sufficient to mask any small sound she might make. This was her chance. Perhaps her only chance to get away.

She waited until every muscle in her body was firmly under control, then drew Simon's cast-iron skillet from the top of the stove. A frosty smile pulled on her lips, and she relaxed a little more.

Slowly, her brain instructed. Keep down. *Don't let him hear you. He's quick and he's agile.*

She stopped breathing halfway to the window, ducking behind the couch for shelter. Tory had squatted down and was in the process of digging through the wastebasket. Papers crinkled, slot machines from the hotel next door clanked, tires squealed and her palms began to sweat again. Not from fear, but from her sudden desire to launch a reckless attack. To lunge at him full force.

No. Lunging was out of the question. She couldn't afford to be reckless. Everything hinged on her ability to maintain control. Of herself, of the situation, of the problems plaguing her.

She steeled her muscles, took three measured steps, then swung the skillet with all her strength.

The impact was full, flat—and entirely effective. Tory fell as Simon had fallen, as the woman before Simon had fallen. But unlike his predecessors he wasn't dead. Not even close from what she could see.

She released her pent-up breath in a rush, backing up a pace and leaning on the wall for support. It had been a very close call, one she would truly prefer not to repeat. Still, she knew she didn't dare kill him now. Disposing of his body would be next to impossible, and leaving him here would only complicate matters further.

With a scowl, she returned the skillet to the stove. For the moment, she'd done all she could. She'd have to think things through before she took care of this particular problem for good. With any luck at all, it shouldn't prove too difficult a task to carry out. Even the great Tory Roberts wasn't indestructible. He was a man just like Simon.

And just like Simon, he could die.

Chapter Six

he could do this, Kristian told herself as she trudged up the
airs to Simon's fourth floor apartment. She didn't like
eing threatened by obscure little messages that popped up
n her computer screen, then vanished as if they'd never
xisted. For what it was worth she now knew the attack on
er last night had been frighteningly real, but the knowl-
dge was poor consolation for the feelings of terror that
ere fast becoming her constant companion.

A vanishing body, an alien attacker, a cryptic message...
his was getting out of hand. For Simon's sake and her own
eace of mind, she had to overcome her misgivings about
e legality of breaking into another person's home. That
oing so would fly in the face of every scruple her father had
tempted to drum into her head during her twenty-nine-
ar lifetime was immaterial. All that mattered right now
as finding some scrap of evidence to support her claim that
mon had not left the country Saturday morning.

Forcing herself not to skulk like a common criminal, she
ipped past an open apartment door on the third floor. To
er relief, the pot-bellied man inside didn't bother to turn his
aze from the TV. Gratefully, Kristian continued climbing
e stuffy staircase to Simons' fourth-floor walk-up.

It had to be at least ninety-five degrees in the old build-
g. There was no air conditioning that she could detect. For
at matter, there was very little air circulating at all. The

entire place smelled of sweat and cigar smoke, refried beans and chili peppers. If she hadn't had such a strong stomach she would have abandoned her quest and sought out the blessed cool of her own apartment.

Her sneakers made only a faint noise on the threadbare carpet. The hall was dark and dingy, the wallpaper stained and badly faded in spots. The lone ray of sunlight that somehow managed to find its way in through the window at the end of the corridor revealed a wall of floating dust particles and a cracked ceiling that was sorely in need of repair.

To call the place a dump would have been generous. To think that Simon Juniper, NORStar's chief security officer, had actually lived here was virtually incomprehensible. But Kristian knew that Simon's gambling addiction had been strong. This was probably the best he could afford, she thought as she neared his door.

Reaching into her pocket, she pulled out a bobby pin. Good intentions aside, she despised the fact that she was capable of doing what she was about to do. Worse still, she was more than capable, she was damned near an expert. Thanks to her youthfully reckless passion for Tory, her father's stern but ineffective attempts to keep her in line and her penchant for losing keys, she'd spent many a night breaking into her family's overseas living quarters. An armored truck might be beyond her talents, but Simon's paper-thin door was its single twist lock was definitely no match for her trusty bobby pin.

She felt the knob turn beneath her fingers. It grated loudly in the latch, and hastily she snatched her head up to look around.

No curious eyes peered at her from the neighboring apartments. No alarms rang out to herald her illegal entry. All was quiet and still except for the clang of several abused slot machines in the hotel across the alley.

It must be her conscience that was making her feel so guilty. It was one thing to break into her own home, and ther thing entirely to be contemplating snooping about a friend's place.

A *dead* friend's place, she prodded herself, giving the door a determined inward shove. There was a difference.

Cautiously, she stepped into the apartment, stopping just aside the door and letting her eyes travel over the tacky furniture.

The living room was a mess, from the sagging sofa with is crumpled collection of McDonald's bags to the window-ll that was lined with empty beer and soda cans. Crooked enetian blinds rode halfway up the glass, blocking what-ver tiny slivers of sunlight might have been able to get past the side of the hotel. There was a potted cactus on the floor, a gargantuan punching bag hanging from the ceiling, a yel-owed poster of Humphrey Bogart plastered to the wall and two decks of well-used playing cards strewn across the cof-e table.

Squaring her shoulders, Kristian started for what ap-peared to be Simon's bedroom. Although there wasn't any good reason for it, she felt her nerves begin to tingle as she skirted a large fan in the middle of floor. Twisting her head round, she tried to identify the source of her sudden uneasiness. Of course any fear she felt right now was bound to be self-induced.

Search the place and get out, she ordered herself, nudg-ng the bedroom door open. *You owe it to Simon and to ourself.*

A tight knot formed in her stomach as her gaze swept the untidy room, coming to rest on a blob of navy blue cloth that sat in a heap beside the poorly-hung closet door. She took a step forward, unbelieving. It couldn't be! Simon's uniform? Here, in his apartment?

With her toe she probed the material, then dropped to her knees and began hunting for the logo sewn on the sleeve.

NORStar Space Park. She found the tag instantly, along with Simon's security badge. This was the suit he'd been

wearing last night. It had to be. She knew for a fact it wa
the only one he owned. What in God's name was going on'

A spurt of useless anger had her flinging the uniform
against the nearest wall. Whoever was behind all this had a
very sick sense of humor. Either that or a sadistic streak.

Pushing herself to her feet, she made her way to the bed
room door, lost in thought but perceptive enough to rec
ognize the errant tremor that suddenly slid along he
backbone.

Her eyes skimmed the furnishings once again, suspi
ciously this time. Despite her best effort to bat it down, th
message she'd received on her computer flashed darkl
through her head. Maybe coming here today hadn't bee
such a bright idea, after all. True, it was broad daylight, bu
she had a sinking feeling that time didn't concern murder
ers nearly as much as opportunity. And what better oppor
tunity to get rid of a witness than in such tawdr
surroundings as these?

She halted on the threshold, acutely aware of every muf
fled bang and screech from the lower levels. The buildin
was swarming with people and probably a few other un
speakably vile occupants, as well. Surely, though, she ha
nothing to fear from any of them.

But what about Simon's killer? She had plenty to fea
from that person. Only a fool would break into a dea
man's apartment. What if the murderer had counted on he
showing up here? What if this was a trap?

Her resolve faltered, then deserted her totally when on
of the shadows in the hallway to her right shifted. It mad
no sound, but there wasn't any question in her mind that i
moved.

Choking on a hastily drawn breath, she spun around an
made a dash for the door. The shadow could have bee
anything. Maybe even her own. Whatever the case, sh
didn't intend to find out. Simon was dead, she was sure o
it, and joining him in that state was not a prospect she care

contemplate. Without looking back, she raced past the
an and curled her fingers around the pitted doorknob.

Her heart pounded in her chest, her vision blurred, blood
urged through her veins—but to her complete horror, the
oor refused to open.

She tugged on it frantically, begging the warped wood to
ooperate. It didn't. And suddenly she realized that she
asn't alone. There was someone in the apartment with her.
omeone who surely had no more right to be here that she
id.

From behind she heard a softly muttered curse. At the
ame instant, she felt a strong arm clamp itself around her
aist and with a sick feeling of dread spied the hand that
as pressed against the door, preventing it from opening.

Several possible escape tactics sprang to mind. Scream-
ng, kicking, scratching, biting. Yet even as a cry for help
ormed on her lips, the hand that had been pressed against
ne door came down firmly over her mouth, stifling the
hriek that was now lodged uselessly in her throat.

"Knock it off, Kristian," a man's all-too-familiar voice
nurmured in her ear. "I'm not in the mood for a wrestling
natch."

Tory! His name rocketed through her terrified brain. Only
y exerting every ounce of her self-control was she able to
top herself from sinking her teeth into the hand that still
overed her mouth. She ripped it away instead and pushed
t the arm wrapped around her waist.

"Let me go," she rasped, unable to infuse more than a
veak note of indignation into her tone. Heaven help her, she
vasn't really sure she wanted him to comply, which made it
ll the more imperative that he do just that.

She knew only a moment's regret when he let his arm drop
o his side. Squashing it, she turned to regard him, to rail at
im for almost giving her a heart attack. Then she spied the
lood on his cheek and heard herself emit a startled gasp.

"My God, what happened?" she whispered, concern
viping out her anger.

He moved one shoulder. "I was blindsided."

She stared at him, struggling with her emotions. "By whom?"

"If I knew that, Kristian, Simon's murderer would be well on the way to jail."

She swallowed her fear and reached up to touch his forehead. "Simon's murderer was here?" It was more of a statement than a question as she recalled the uniform she'd found in the bedroom. The one that must have been planted there.

"Either that or my search was interrupted by a burglar with exceptionally low standards."

His search? A renewed shaft of terror and determination raced along her spine. Tory could have been killed, and she still had no idea why.

Reluctantly, she removed her hand. He wouldn't appreciate being made to feel vulnerable in any way. "Ibo," she said aloud, picking up a relatively clean towel from the sofa and handing it to him. "That's it, isn't it? Ibo's name is the key to this whole thing."

"Maybe." He wiped the blood from his temple, then tossed the towel aside. "Come on, let's get out of here."

She took another apprehensive glance around the messy living room. "What were you trying to find?"

For an answer, he yanked open the door and propelled her into the hall. "Same thing as you. Proof of whatever it was that kept Simon from boarding his flight to Brazil. Something neither of us is likely to uncover at this point." Curling his fingers warmly around her wrist, he drew her toward the staircase. "Whoever killed Simon last night went through this place with a fine-tooth comb."

Kristian shook her head in confusion. "I don't understand. Are you saying that Simon was killed by a professional?"

Tory nodded but didn't elaborate. Typical of him, she thought, mild annoyance momentarily overriding her concern for his injury. He probably had no intention of telling

1er any more than he already had. It seemed to be an un-
spoken law among those people who'd served in the mili-
:ary. Never divulge a detail that wasn't absolutely necessary.
And never, ever volunteer information.

Well, that was fine where the security of the nation was
concerned. But it wouldn't work here.

She waited until they were outside, then, ignoring the
stubborn set of his jaw, pried her wrist free of his hand,
1alting on the pavement to look up at him. "Tory, I know
you don't want to explain what's going on, but I have a right
:o hear it. I'm the one who saw Simon get shot, and I'm the
one who gave you his message."

Without turning his head from the busy street, he sent her
a tolerant sideways glance. "And if you'd shown up here
hirty minutes earlier, you'd have also been the one who got
knocked out."

He really did have a knack for unsettling her. Reluc-
antly, Kristian raised her eyes to the bruise on his temple.
t had to hurt, but he'd never admit that, any more than
1e'd admit anything else he chose not to. "Can't you at least
ell me who Ibo is?"

He shifted his gaze to her. "Ibo owned a bar called the
Southern Cross in the South Pacific," he revealed at length.

"Owned?" she echoed.

Tory's eyes narrowed. "Ibo's dead, Kristian. He was
murdered eight years ago. By his partner."

Kristian felt as though someone had jammed a fist into
1er stomach. The hum of traffic and pedestrians faded.
Waves of heat rose from the sun-baked pavement, blurring
1er vision, adding to the confused tangle of emotions that
assailed her. Shock won out, followed closely by a bur-
geoning sense of dread as the ramifications of Tory's state-
nent sank in.

"Are you telling me that one of your partners shot Simon?" Even as she uttered the words, she found herself re-
ecting—no, resisting—the possibility. And judging from

the implacable look on his face, she knew Tory felt the same way.

His restless eyes scanned the crowded street. "No" was all he said before taking her by the arm and steering her toward her bright red car, parked beside the curb half a block away.

"Well then, what—?"

"I don't know." He'd cut her off shortly. "But not that."

He sounded irritable, his tone falling just short of a snarl. Kristian knew better than to take it personally. She also knew better than to push him right now. Patience was a virtue Tory possessed in abundance, except on those rare occasions when his strongest personal convictions were challenged. Doubtless Simon's message had done just that.

A chill crawled over her skin, leaving her cold despite the blistering heat of late afternoon. Somehow she held her curiosity in check, managing not to utter a sound—until they reached her car.

"Wait a minute, what are you doing?" She eyed Tory warily as he withdrew a set of keys from his pocket.

He nodded at his dust-covered car on the far side of the street. "I'm going to follow you back to the park."

The quiet note of authority was clear enough, but this time Kristian was having none of it. "You can't drive," she insisted firmly.

A small grin crossed his lips. "Neither can you, but that minor oversight hasn't stopped you yet."

"Very funny, Tory," she retorted dryly. "Look, I realize you hotshot flyers think you're above serious injury, but had it occurred to you that you might have a concussion?"

He moved closer, his grin widening, and Kristian fervently wished she'd kept her mouth shut. More physical contact between them, no matter how brief, was not in her best interests. "And I thought you didn't care," he murmured, resting his hands on the roof of her car, effectively trapping her with his gorgeous body.

A faint ripple of surprise shot through her. Could it be he'd changed? "I thought you didn't want me to care," she said softly.

"Maybe we both thought wrong," Tory replied, his expression unreadable, though not as remote as usual. To her bemusement, he let one arm drop away, returning the keys to his jeans pocket. "Okay, you win. If I survived the Autobahn with you behind the wheel, I guess I can live through a flight down Route 15."

Eyes locked on his impassive features, she pulled the door open. This wasn't like him at all, which either meant he was hurt worse than he'd let on or he wasn't as indomitable as he'd once tried to make her believe.

The latter was a ponderous notion and more than a little difficult to accept. Fortunately their conversation subsided as she joined the heavy afternoon traffic flow, giving her a moment to collect her scattered thoughts. Contrary to Tory's belief, she was an adequate driver. A bit lead-footed perhaps, but nowhere near the crazed demon he liked to paint her as being.

She slid her gaze to his face. Even at a glance, she could see that his mind wasn't on her driving skills. Nor was it on the person who'd attacked him. He was thinking about Simon's message.

Lucky for him he only had one message to contemplate, she thought, trembling slightly. Maybe now would be a good time to mention the threat that had appeared on her computer. Tory was nothing if not calm during a crisis.

On impulse, she cut away from the Interstate, heading for one of the less traveled back roads instead. A hot, dusty breeze blew in the open windows, carrying with it the scent of sun-baked sand and earth—and the shattering wail of a police siren.

It had to be guilt that made her snatch her foot from the gas pedal, her eyes snap up to search the rearview mirror for a glimpse of the flashing red and blue lights behind her.

Tory's wry grin didn't help matters. Neither would a display of temper, she cautioned herself. Suppressing a fatalistic sigh, she slowed the car, easing it onto the shoulder as far as she dared and waiting for the long arm of the law to do the same.

Strangely, it didn't. The vehicle that whizzed past in a frenetic burst of light and sound showed no sign of stopping. In fact, it barely slowed down enough to negotiate one of the road's numerous hairpin turns.

"Must be your lucky day," Tory noted in lazy amusement, still slouched negligently in his seat. "You want to keep it that way and let me drive?"

She eased back in gear and pushed the hair away from her face. "I think you're missing the point of this shared excursion." She smiled a little, glancing at the cut on his forehead, glad to see the bleeding had stopped. "You're supposed to be grateful, not sarcastic."

"I'm your employer. I'm allowed to be sarcastic."

"Not when I'm behind the wheel."

"Fair enough. However, you might consider keeping the speedometer below warp one until we get past the state troopers."

Kristian caught sight of the spinning lights through a cloud of dust kicked up by the tires of no less than eight police cars and two mammoth-size motorcycles. Khaki-clad bodies of every conceivable size and shape had converged near the rim of a particularly treacherous canyon. The guardrail, a mediocre barricade at best, showed signs of recent demolition. There was a tow truck parked next to the broken rail and behind that a trio of emergency vehicles barely visible through the swirls of sand and dirt.

Tory squinted at the official circle. "Pull over," he instructed her, and Kristian, in the process of tugging on the emergency brake, frowned at him. His reaction time was definitely down. Funny how that didn't please her.

"Tory, are you..." she began, then realized she was talking to an empty seat. He was already on the road, calling something she probably didn't want to hear over his shoulder. So much for her misguided concern.

A blast of hot air washed across her face, blowing gritty dust and sand particles into her eyes as she slid from the car. More on instinct than by sight, she made her way to the crowded lip of the canyon.

"It was a young trucker who spotted the wreckage," a twangy-voiced trooper was explaining when she came up behind Tory's broad back. "Near as we can figure, the driver must have lost her brakes and crashed through the guard rail." Familiar sun-crinkled eyes acknowledged Kristian's presence. "Afternoon, Kristie-Ann." Sergeant Jon Hayes offered his usual teasing mispronunciation of her name. His daughter worked at NORStar, making Jon and his family frequent visitors to the space park and long-standing acquaintances of both owners and management. "I gotta say, you two picked one hell of a time to show up."

Kristian peered deep into the rocky canyon where the crumpled shell of a blue-and-white car sat like a squashed bug. "Were there any survivors?" she asked doubtfully, inching closer to the edge of the cliff.

"Nope." The man nodded toward the ambulance. "There was only one person in the car. We just brought her up. I've seen messier sights, that's for sure, but dead's dead no matter how you look at it."

Without appearing to move, Tory hooked two strong fingers through Kristian's belt loop, preventing her from straying too close to the precipice. "When did it happen?"

"Last night, I reckon. Probably quite late. My guess is she was on her way home from the space park." He nodded through the boiling dust to a black body bag that was currently being loaded into the ambulance. "The ID we found indicates she worked there."

Kristian turned her head away sharply. "She was one of our employees?"

"Well, she wasn't wearing a uniform, but there was a NORStar pass in the glove box with her name and picture on it."

Tory's expression remained impassive. Deceptively so, Kristian knew. For all his faults, he placed a high value on life. "What was her name?" he asked without inflection.

"Brace," Jon replied, signaling to another officer with his hand. "Anita Brace. Ring any bells?"

"Yes!" Startled, Kristian spun to face Tory. "I know her. At least I know of her. Personnel called me earlier today. They tried to phone her when she didn't report for work this morning. Apparently the number she'd given them wasn't in service."

"Makes sense to me." A second blond-haired trooper sauntered over, taking silent stock of the cut on Tory's temple. "I think you might want to change the name on that report of yours, Sarge."

"Change it to what, Lars?" Tory asked, and in a distant part of her mind Kristian found herself wondering just how many of Nevada's finest he knew. Probably half the combined force. His father had been good friends with the Las Vegas police commissioner. His late father, she remembered on a gentler note.

Lars swatted lazily at a fly on the back of his neck. "You remember Willard Barrows?"

"The computer thief?" Tory nodded, retaining his hold on Kristian's belt loop. "He died two or three years ago, didn't he?"

"Three, and it was murder. We figure he was killed by our old friend Telstar, but that's another story. To keep this one short and sweet, the woman we just hauled up from the bottom of the canyon was Barrows's daughter, Annette."

"Annette?" Kristian repeated, suddenly wary. What happened to Anita?

Tory swore through clenched teeth. "Annette Barrows." His hooded eyes flicked to the wrecked car below. "Lars has a photographic memory for faces. He pulled her father over for speeding one night and wound up arresting him for a computer heist he'd pulled nine months earlier.''

This was getting worse instead of better. ''Was his daughter involved in the crime?''

''Not that we know of,'' Lars supplied. ''She was at his trial, though. No record of her own, but I'll lay you eight to five odds that she was following in her daddy's footsteps.''

The trooper's inauspicious words echoed in Kristian's head along with a dozen other unwelcome thoughts. Security Chief Simon Juniper had been shot last night at the space park. Now the daughter of a known computer thief, a woman who'd obviously been working at NORStar Center under an assumed name, was dead, the victim of an auto accident. But had it been an accident, Kristian wondered uneasily? Or was there a connection between this woman and Simon? The notion made her skin crawl, and she took an involuntary step closer to Tory.

''I don't like it,'' Jon was saying in a troubled tone. ''No sir, it's too easy, too convenient.''

Beside her, Kristian felt Tory shift, his inscrutable eyes come to rest on her face. ''What did Anita Brace do at the park?'' he asked. ''Which department did she work in?''

It took all of Kristian's self-control not to groan out loud. ''Lilith's,'' she murmured, then met his gaze. ''Anita Brace was one of our computer programmers.''

Chapter Seven

"Disappearing bodies," Tory muttered under his breath. "Computer thieves, computer threats." He punched the button, propelling Kristian out of the elevator and into the lunar-landscaped corridor of the central complex's third floor. "Why didn't you tell me be about this 'message' you received earlier?"

Her delicate jaw was set in a stubborn line. "Maybe because I was too busy trying to find out what Simon's message meant. Besides, it was more like a philosophical statement than a direct threat."

As she spoke, Tory felt her attempt to disengage her fingers from his firm grasp. A tiny smile pulled at the corners of his mouth. He could have let her go now that they were safely inside the Center. Could have but wasn't about to, he reflected dryly, turning for the personnel offices located at the far end of the Bay of Rainbows passageway. A decision he might well regret before this mess was resolved.

Right now he had other problems to deal with, the biggest being a gargantuan headache that was getting worse by the minute. And then there was Telstar to consider. He hadn't heard that name, or rather code name, since before the space park opened more than a year ago. Like any chain, though, one link invariably connected to another. Of course, if the rumors he'd heard had even a grain of truth to them, Telstar was as dead as Willard Barrows and his daughter Annette—whose personnel file was bound to be as phony as the alias she'd been using.

With his free hand, Tory massaged his sore temple. Guilt and a latent sense of obligation gnawed at him. The first thing he should do was get Kristian out of the space park, possibly out of the state, for as long as it took to unravel this deadly puzzle. But did he really want to do that? Or was he just sick enough to consider using Simon's disappearance as an excuse to spend more time with her?

No. His mind rejected the idea outright. He couldn't have sunk that low. And he couldn't send Kristian away. It would be a wasted effort, in any event. Her conscience, her curiosity, her desire to balk at his orders—all those things would hold her here, even if it meant working in close quarters with him.

Tempting though the prospect was, Tory recognized the drawbacks. On the one hand, if he told her what he knew, which at this point wasn't much, he ran the risk of further endangering her life. On the other, the more he put her off, the more determined she'd be to get to the truth.

He glanced down at her, amused in spite of the pounding in his head and a situation that was beginning to look positively grim. They really did bring out the worst in each other. The worst and, strangely enough, the best. Sometimes the contradiction amazed him.

"Stop struggling," he murmured as they neared the end of the hall. "This is supposed to be a casual walk-through."

"The people here keep office hours, Tory," she reminded him, still fighting his grip, though not as vigorously as she could have. "Even if they didn't, I'd hardly call having you drag me through the Sea of Rains casual."

"Bay of Rainbows," he corrected, pushing open the smoked-glass door in front of them. Out of nowhere a metallic body shot past him into the twilight-blue records room. That couldn't be right. The robots weren't supposed to be running loose on this level. "What's Crater doing here?" he asked, frowning at Kristian.

"Visiting friends?" she suggested, and while it wasn't an answer, he was glad to hear the hint of humor in her voice. She looked around his arm, regarding the bank of silent computers without much enthusiasm. "Do you want me to access Anita Brace's file?"

Tory negated the offer, releasing her hand and noting abstractly the flash of disappointment that passed through her green eyes. If his head hadn't felt as if it was about to explode, he might have stopped to wonder about her reaction. "See if you can access a bottle of aspirin," he told her instead. "I'll find the file."

After the subtle battle she'd waged in the outer corridor, the last thing he expected her to do was reach up and push the hair from his forehead. "You really got whacked, didn't you?" she said softly.

He didn't move, didn't say a word. He simply let her inspect the wound and waited for the latent sense of loss to close in on him as it invariably did whenever she strayed too close.

"Maybe you should let someone in medical services take a look at you."

Her voice slid through him like warm brandy. Damn, but she could get to him. He sensed the warmth of her body even with the gap between them, felt the cool touch of her fingers on his bruised skin and the stirrings of a desire too strong to ignore, too intense to combat—and too untimely to act on.

Lowering his lashes, he murmured a deceptively bland, "It's not as bad as it looks. All I need is an aspirin."

"Liar." She ran the back of her hand over his cheek. "You look terrible."

Which was nothing compared to the way he felt. But to admit that was to admit he could be hurt. And that wasn't something he was ready to do, not even to Kristian. Not yet. He dropped into a padded chair with an indifferent, "Fortunately, I can't see myself."

"I could bring you a mirror?" she offered sweetly.

"I'd settle for something to dull the pain."

A cloud he couldn't interpret passed through her eyes. "I'll see what I can find."

She was gone before Tory had a chance to reconsider his dispassionate stance. It was better left this way between them, he maintained, flipping on the nearest computer and punching in his clearance code.

An uncharacteristic irritability settled over him as he set about locating Anita Brace's employment record. Anita, Annette, Willard... Telstar. The code name kept slamming through his brain. Why Telstar? Surely there was no connection between Annette Barrows and a mysterious, hopefully deceased, professional middleman.

"Who or what is Telstar?"

The question came from directly behind him, from Kristian, who was placing two tablets and a water-filled cup in his hand. He tossed the pills into his mouth, ignoring the tepid water and the enticing scent of Lutèce that washed over him. "Nobody special," he lied. "Why do you ask?"

"Because that trooper, Lars, mentioned the name, and you just growled it out again a second ago."

"Did I?" Tory was only mildly surprised. "Whatever, it doesn't really matter. Whoever Telstar was, he or she has been presumed dead for the past two years."

"You're not sure?"

"Not one hundred percent. Telstar's a code name. No one was ever able to positively identify the person behind it."

"So this person might very well be alive."

Tory fingered the cut on his temple. "I doubt it. I hope not. Telstar was, for lack of a better description, a seller of secrets. Government, corporate, personal—if the telling paid, Telstar told."

"Who bought these secrets?"

"Anyone interested in what he'd obtained. Usually the highest bidder."

Kristian's smooth brow furrowed. "Exactly how does one go about obtaining corporate and government secrets?"

"By hiring experts to do the dirty work."

"Like hacking into a computer." Crater had rolled silently up to Tory's elbow. Kristian moved the robot aside and sat on the computer desk. "Tell me, why did Telstar kill Willard Barrows?"

Tory turned his distracted gaze to the flashing computer screen. "To be honest, I don't know. A lot of people in Air Force Intelligence believe that Barrows was working with Telstar on a project that went sour. Barrows naturally became the sacrificial lamb, though it probably wouldn't have made much difference if things had gone as planned. Telstar was notorious for getting rid of so-called 'partners.'"

"Terrific," Kristian sighed, sliding from the desk. "So what you're saying is that Willard Barrows worked with some code-named seller of secrets who might or might not be dead. Annette Barrows, alias Anita Brace, who is very definitely dead, worked at NORStar as a computer programmer—a situation that could lead to any number of horrible conclusions. Simon's gone, and the private investigator I hired to trace him hasn't turned up even a scrap of useful information. We have no idea what this mess is all about and nothing to go on except a message that doesn't exactly inspire a feeling of security. I don't see how this can get any more complicated."

Tory leaned back in his chair, eyes fastened on the trembling screen. "You will in a minute," he said, reaching for her hand. "Take a look at Anita Brace's employment file."

Expression guarded, Kristian studied the monitor over his shoulder "'Application submitted six months ago,'" she read aloud. "'Position: computer programmer. Third-grade security clearance. Previous employment record: computer programmer at Triton Corps of Nevada, Panorama and Casa Grande Resorts, Las Vegas. Reference check...suspended?'" She halted on that point, incredulous. "All references have to be checked. It's part of the screening process. Who authorized that?"

Obligingly Tory moved the cursor lower on the screen, until he reached the appropriate line:

"Application approved by Lilith Lang."

SHE STOOD in the indigo shadows, breathing deeply, steadily, forcing herself to remain calm. Watching as Kristian and Tory exited the Lunar level for points unknown.

When they were gone, she stepped into the pearly blue light. Shoulders rigid, she clutched a thick wad of papers to her chest and marched over to the still-warm computer. Within seconds, the file they'd been viewing was gliding across the screen.

Not a trace of emotion showed on her taut features. Nothing to betray a single one of the feelings that simmered inside her. She stared at the information, then slowly cleared the monitor and switched the computer off.

"They know," she said to the alert little robot beside her. "I didn't get here in time."

Tipping her head back, she relaxed the tension-knotted muscles in her neck. This wasn't good, but it could be handled. The sooner the better, a tiny voice in her brain supplemented.

From her pocket, she withdrew a sleek remote-control unit. "Come along, Crater," she instructed, pushing the manual override switch. "We have a lot of work to do."

And shoving back the sleeves of her uniform, she pushed the robot out of the records room.

"SCRAM, CRUX. I've got a ton of work to do. I don't need you racing around behind me like some wired robo-dog." Priscilla crawled out from under an open control panel in the new Planets exhibit, covered with grease and looking as grumpy as she sounded. She viewed Kristian from a cross-legged position on the floor. "Pretty outfit," she said, wiping her hands on her pant legs. "Black's good on you. Perfect for the occasion. So did you ditch Auntie Griselda and her troop of professional pickpockets, or are they hitting on a higher power?''

Kristian gave her an absent smile. "You're a cynic, you know that?''

"Actually, I'm buzzard bait. Those society matrons would've eaten me for lunch instead of their dainty finger sandwiches. Still, you look like you fared all right.''

All things considered, Kristian acknowledged inwardly. Between the barrage of police and FBI agents who'd descended on her first thing this morning with the confirmation that Anita Brace was indeed Annette Barrows, and the bevy of socialites with whom she'd been obliged to have lunch, she was mentally and emotionally tapped out. "Griselda Payne's motives are pure enough,'' she said, shrugging the matter aside. "She's just a little pushy.''

"A little pushy!'' Priscilla snorted in disgust. "She'd push that Milquetoast husband of hers right out of the mayor's seat if she thought she could claim it for herself. What did she demand today? Money, time, free tickets to the grand opening of our new exhibits?''

"All of the above. How are the repairs on the air-conditioning system coming?''

"Take your pick. Desert hot or arctic cold. It's the best we can do without Crater.''

Kristian peered into the access shaft, careful not to smear grease on her black silk dress. "Can't you use Crux instead?'' she asked, not encouraged by the battery of disconnected wires that were sticking out at all angles.

Priscilla shook her head. "Crux isn't programmed for this kind of repair work. I'm not even sure he's equipped for it.''

"Well where's Crater?''

"Last I saw, Evan was whisking him off to the science center. He says the crowds love watching a robot do whatever it is he makes the robot do.''

"Would you like me to have security round him up?''

"Who? Evan or Crater?''

Kristian hid a smile. "Take your pick.''

"I'm not fussy," Priscilla said, climbing to her feet. "By the way, have you seen George or the Colonel around anywhere? Someone who knows the holograms should take a trip through this display."

"Kristian and I can do it."

Oh, no, Kristian moaned silently, closing her eyes. Not Tory. Not now when her emotional defences were so low. Not after the two miserable days she'd just suffered through and the sleepless nights that had preceded them.

While the latter had been free of alien attacks, it hadn't done a thing to soothe her tattered nerves. Knowing that Tory was residing in the adjoining hotel room with nothing but an unlocked door between them was not conducive to a peaceful slumber.

Her eyes snapped open as the significance of his statement suddenly sank in. Kristian and I can do it? She felt the heat of his body behind her and schooled her features accordingly before turning to face him. "*Kristian* has a lot of work to do, Tory," she informed him calmly, firmly. "Besides, I'm not a hologram expert."

"Then it's time you had a lesson." He took a dangerous step closer, all hot and sweaty and dirt streaked, his eyes on hers. It shocked her a little that he was almost as grimy as Priscilla. In a pair of old jeans, a smudged white T-shirt and a Dodgers baseball cap, he looked more like a construction worker than the part owner of a multimillion-dollar space park. And very, very sexy.

Damn him, he would do this to her, she thought, only vaguely startled by the familiar tightness that invaded her chest under his compelling stare. She slapped down an urge to run her fingers over the healing cut on his forehead. He didn't need or want her concern. He was fine. He wouldn't allow himself to be anything less.

"I don't have time for this, Tory," she protested as Priscilla was pulled aside by one of her assistants. "You know very well you don't need my help."

He shrugged, not moving. "No, but I'd like it."

Her first impulse was to ignore his low, sexy tone and get as far away from him as possible. Her second was to hesitate and look up at his beautiful black-lashed eyes. He'd like her help? In all the time she'd known him, he'd never said that to her. Maybe he'd never said it to any woman. Had he in fact changed, or was it just wishful thinking on her part? "Will it take long?" she inquired carefully.

"It shouldn't." With his thumb, he brushed a strand of blond hair from her cheek, tucking it neatly into the sedate chignon at the nape of her neck. "You look tired. Didn't you sleep last night?"

"I was watching for marauding aliens," she lied, unable to shake the strangely mesmerizing feeling that swept over her. "We'd better go," she managed faintly. "I have to get back to the central complex before Lilith does."

Priscilla strolled over then, with Crux trailing along behind her. "Don't hold your breath on that one, Kristian," she advised. "I heard Lilith's lecturing in the city today."

Tory's hand fell away, and Kristian drew a steadying breath. "She is, but she's due back at the park by six. I checked her calender."

"Checked her programming, you mean. Robots are more spontaneous than that woman. Speaking of which—" she shoved Crux at Kristian and the remote control at Tory "—this one's all yours."

It was foolish, Kristian knew, but she was grateful for Crux's lively presence in the domed shuttle that would transport them through the solar system. Preferably at the speed of light, though after taking a furtive look around the tiny glass car she would have settled for more space.

The hatch snapped shut behind them and Kristian stiffened, curling her fingers around the support rail. How could she possibly hope to keep her jumbled emotions under control in such a confined space? Without turning, she asked. "Do you know what we're looking for?"

"Snags in the shuttle mechanism, defective images."

"Air," she added as he moved up on her. "Tory, it's way too hot in here."

"It's hot everywhere." There was a hint of amusement in his voice now. "We had a power surge while you were pretending to be polite to Griselda Payne. I'm surprised you didn't see the lights flare."

Kristian felt his breath in her ear, his fingers trail a teasing path around her waist. "It must have happened when Griselda found a black thread on her blouse and thought it was a spider." She pressed herself against the rail. This wasn't what she wanted, she told herself, but the lie was clear even if she chose to brush it aside. "Is that why you're so dirty?"

"Uh-huh." His hands slid across her ribs. "Priscilla's people were all busy. Someone had to crawl under the Gyrotron and replace the scorched wires. Why don't you loosen your dress if you're hot?"

She swallowed, willing herself not to respond to his touch. She even managed a semi-defiant, "I wouldn't be this hot if I didn't have a human blanket draped all over me. Back up."

"I can't. Crux is behind me."

"Then switch places with him."

"If I do that, I won't be able to see the exhibit."

"Fine, you stand here and I'll switch places with him."

"Why don't you just stay where you are and enjoy the scenery?" Tory suggested.

She heard the lazy humor in his tone, felt the heat of his body along her spine and had to fight the crazy impulse to press herself against him. Or was it crazy?

She wasn't sure what to think anymore. About Tory, about herself. About time and experience and all the things that could change in a universe where flow and motion were two of only a very few constant concepts.

Was he a different person now, she wondered. Was she? The answers weren't there, only more questions, none of which she could concentrate on with Tory so close behind her. The least she could do was make a show of slapping his wandering hands from her waist before they did something she might regret.

She opened her mouth to say something, but the words didn't come as her eyes suddenly locked on the cosmic spectacle unfolding around her.

The domed capsule appeared to be gliding through a panoply of shimmering stars, riding a slender specter of light that drew it down to skim the crater-covered surface of Mercury. One crater in particular drew Kristian's attention. It was huge, with high, rough edges and hundreds of delicate white spears that radiated from the center like a sprinkling of powdered sugar. On the horizon, silent volcanoes sent up a spray of rubble and rock that fanned out in a soft arc to dust the surrounding landscape.

"Looks real, doesn't it?" Tory remarked, his mouth next to her ear, his hands still subtly exploring the wrap-style front of her dress.

"Very," she agreed, swatting at his arm as the capsule continued toward its next destination.

He wasn't diverted, and Kristian knew she was starting to weaken badly. Tory could be incredibly persistent, not to mention persuasive. His breath on her neck was warm, the touch of his lips too disturbing to ignore. It wasn't easy to work up a credible protest.

"I hope you realize that your behavior could be deemed sexual harassment," she pointed out, pleased with the coolness of her tone.

Undaunted, he shifted his attention to her ear. "Maybe, but I'll risk it. If I were really harassing you, I'd have three broken ribs by now and probably a few more unpleasant injuries, as well." With his hand, he tipped her head to one side, and she felt a fiery tremor slide through her as his lips nuzzled the sensitive skin below her earlobe.

"I could lie," she murmured.

"You won't."

A wistful sigh escaped her. "I know."

The yellow mists of Venus came swirling into sight. Holographic illusion slowed the motion around them. Molten lakes bubbled and seethed and occasionally shot up an explosive curl of red lava while, overhead, brilliant streaks of lightning crackled across a pitch-black sky.

Thunderstorms in space, Kristian thought as a low, sonic rumble shook the car. Computer simulated and amazing, but like all the other special effects in the park, spawned by a human brain.

Her own brain began to spin. The heat, the feel of Tory's strong, lean body behind her, the tantalizing touch of his lips along her jaw, the scent of his skin, the brush of his hair across her cheek—all those things contributed to her growing confusion. How could she be expected to make sense of such a muddled situation when it was all she could do to keep her knees from buckling beneath her?

They'd settled into a low orbit around Earth. Constellations glittered in a black-velvet sky, star groups never seen above the Equator. Corvus, the Raven; Hydra, the Water Serpent; *Corona Australis*, the Southern Crown; *Crux Australis*, the Southern Cross...

"*Crux.*" The generic name fell from her lips, and Tory lifted his head, momentarily diverted.

His hold on her didn't slacken as he followed her gaze to the four stars of the celestial cross, but at least his mouth was no longer sliding down her neck, stirring up feelings too dangerous to explore.

"Ibo named his bar for that constellation," he told her as the shuttle moved on.

"Ibo. Common ground. Simon's message. It has to mean something." Kristian shivered despite the heat, allowing herself to relax for the first time since entering the capsule. "Tory, why did Ibo's partner murder him? Was it for money?"

"In a way. Lee Dong, his partner, wanted to...expand their operation, offer their patrons something other than alcohol."

She caught the meaningful tone of his voice. "In other words, he wanted to sell sex as well as alcohol?"

Tory shrugged. "He felt it would be a profitable addition to their business. Ibo disagreed, so Lee Dong and his girlfriend decided to get rid of him."

"How did they do it?"

"Trust me, you don't want to know."

"That bad?"

"Uh-huh."

"But you don't think anything like that could happen to you?"

"I won't let anything like that happen to me. Or to you."

Before she could object he plucked two bobby pins from her chignon, loosening her hair with his fingers and arranging it in a silken cloud about her shoulders. She wanted to scream at him, to push him over Crux and right out of the capsule into Jupiter's fiery Red Spot. Of course, it didn't help that she also longed to shove aside all the dictates of her adult mind and indulge in one final reckless fantasy. Sort of a farewell fling to banish the last vestiges of her youthful passion for the one man she couldn't seem to resist. Wasn't sure she wanted to resist.

Lightning superbolts snaked through a layer of ice clouds and were quickly swallowed up in the caldron of boiling gases on the planet's surface. Bright, unmixed colors danced before her eyes as Tory threaded his fingers through her hair. It was too hot to breathe, much too hot to move. Well, maybe she could move a bit. Enough to establish that she wasn't the only person in the capsule with sybaritic tendencies.

She swallowed a groan. It was madness, pure and simple, a doomed attraction she couldn't understand or combat. Her head throbbed just thinking about it. Either that or she was suffering from some bizarre form of holographic space sickness.

Somehow she found her voice and with it a measure of compunction. "You know, we shouldn't be here, Tory

Anyone could have checked this exhibit. We should be out on the grounds looking for answers."

"I've been doing that for the better part of the day," he returned, moving his hands up her arms and massaging her shoulders with his thumbs. "What little I learned isn't exactly encouraging."

Kristian worked herself around to face him. A mistake, admittedly, but it was too late for second thoughts. "Is it something about Simon?"

"Not exactly," he murmured, touching her cheek. "Jon Hayes paid me an official police visit late this morning."

"And told you that the coroner confirmed Annette Barrows's identity. I already heard that."

"I know you did. But what you haven't heard is the official cause of death."

The muscles in Kristian's throat constricted. "Obviously not in a car accident."

"No, not that way. There were bruises on her neck. Not many but enough to convince the coroner that Annette Barrows was strangled. She was dead before her car went over the cliff."

Chapter Eight

"I'm telling you, Tory believes her," June announced to Lilith and Priscilla, seated at her table in the central complex's colorful Io Cafeteria. "He's convinced that Simon is dead. You know what that means." She gave her companions a smugly confident nod. "Trouble with a capital T."

"It also means I'm out three hundred dollars," Priscilla grumbled, dipping into a bowl of coconut ice cream. Her mouth turned down at the corners. "Working overtime, every piece of machinery in the miniuniverse breaking down around me—and now I find out that Simon's probably dead. This hasn't been my week."

"Yes, well, evidently it hasn't been Anita's, either," June told her.

"Anita who?" Priscilla demanded, poking at her ice cream.

June leaned forward, planting her elbows on the table. "Anita Brace, alleged computer thief," she revealed in a conspiratorial tone. "Now, mind you, I didn't quite catch the whole story, but I did manage to slide past George a time or two when he was chatting with the police this morning. It appears that one of our computer programmers took a nosedive over a cliff a few nights ago. Only it turns out that this particular programmer was using an alias. Anita Brace is, or rather was, none other than Annette Barrows."

"Is that bad?"

"Turn up the volume, Priscilla. I said she might be a computer thief. At least that's the general consensus. Odd that you don't recognize her name. Word is she worked at the Casa Grande Resort."

Priscilla rolled her eyes. "For God's sake. Do you think I had nothing better to do than run around memorizing names and faces at the annual Christmas party? Big deal she worked at the Casa Grande. So did Kristian and five thousand other people over the years. Where do you get this stuff, anyway?"

"I told you. I overheard George talking to the police. And for your information, Anita Brace, a.k.a. Annette Barrows, just happens to be the daughter of a most unsavory man whose dubious talents are believed by many to have been passed on to his now-deceased offspring."

Priscilla shrugged, unimpressed. "So?"

June arched an exasperated brow. "So," she repeated. "We might very well have had a computer thief on staff. Things like that aren't supposed to happen at NORStar Center. Someone around here screwed up. Badly. Needless to say, Kristian's not very happy."

"Is anyone?" Lilith inquired woodenly.

"Probably not," Priscilla said with a smirk. "But at least some of us don't have the misfortune of being on the boss's verbal hit list." Lashes lowered, she calmly licked her spoon. "Don't look now, but you're about to come under fire—and not from one of Io's holographic volcanoes."

Lilith's head jerked to the left as Kristian, her facial expression and body language deceptively serene, began threading her way through the crowded cafeteria, heading unerringly toward the table where the three women sat.

"I want to talk to you, Lilith," she stated without preamble.

Lilith regarded her from behind the thick lenses of her glasses. "Can it wait? I'm in the middle of my dinner." As if to prove that statement, she shoved a piece of the fried rattlesnake few people could even look at, let alone eat, into her mouth.

Kristian managed not to flinch. "It's important."

June nudged Priscilla's arm. "Maybe we should leave."

"Translated, that means we should make a polite show of moving to another table at which point we'll make an even more polite show of not listening to every word being spoken here." Priscilla scraped her bowl clean. "*Très* discreet, June."

Unchastened, June fluffed her brown curls. "Everyone knows I'm a very discreet person. Do you want us to go, Kristian?"

"There's no need," Lilith said, her tone flat. "I don't have any secrets."

"None at all?" Kristian challenged.

"I believe I said that."

Kristian kept her expression impassive. "In that case, you won't mind telling me about Annette Barrows."

Lilith blinked. "Should I recognize the name?"

"Hell, even I recognize that name," Priscilla declared. "Annette Barrows, alias Anita Brace, alleged computer thief and former NORStar employee. What do you do, Lilith? Close your ears when other people talk?"

"I told them about our little problem," June inserted for Kristian's benefit. Then she frowned. "Did you know her, Lilith?"

Lilith's spine stiffened. "We were acquaintances."

"Is that why you bypassed the security check and approved her employment application?" Kristian inquired.

"I needed someone with ability." Lilith's answer was stony, almost mechanical. "Anita was available, and her credentials appeared to be in order. I saw no need to waste time with a security check."

"Did you know her as Anita or Annette?"

"Anita. We met at a computer show in the city last fall. November thirteenth, to be precise."

"You weren't aware of her father's criminal record?"

"Not when I hired her, no."

"But you found out."

"Yes."

"When?"

"I don't remember." A disbelieving snort from Priscilla underscored Lilith's tight-lipped "Does it matter?"

Kristian shrugged. "Seeing as the woman was murdered, yes, I'd say it matters."

June's brows shot up. "Murdered? But I thought her car went over a cliff in the hills. What's going on, Kristian? When did all this happen?"

"The same night that Simon was shot."

"Sounds like a busy night," Priscilla noted dryly.

And Kristian didn't think she imagined the flash of anger that passed through Lilith's black eyes.

TORY DIDN'T FIND Kristian until eight-thirty that evening. She was sprawled on her office couch, a cold washcloth covering her eyes, a diet soda clutched in her hand, listening to the *Star Wars* overture on compact disk and paying no attention whatsoever to Crux who was zooming through on his way to June's office.

"I don't care who you are or what you want, just go away and leave me alone," she ordered, not moving a muscle. "I'm off duty."

"And out of sorts," Tory remarked from his lounging stance in the doorway. "Time to wake up, Sleeping Beauty. We have work to do."

She still didn't move. "You do it. I have a headache."

He refused to be sympathetic. "So do I." Eyes glinting, he came into the room and wrapped his fingers around her wrist, tugging her gently to a sitting position. "I know it goes against the grain, but you might try faking a little respect."

She pushed the hair from her cheeks. "You're my boss, not my father. You only get respect during working hours."

"The park's still open," he reminded her. "Technically these are working hours."

"Not for me," she repeated crossly, throwing the damp cloth at him. "I've had a lousy day. I don't need to make it worse by going fifteen unproductive rounds with you."

She looked tired and cranky, maybe a little flushed, but then the air-conditioning system wasn't up to full operating capacity yet. Of course, he'd prefer to believe that there was another reason for the heightened color in her cheeks. The same reason that made his muscles tighten to a painful knot.

With a vaguely ironic grin, he gave her wrist a tug. "Sounds like you finally had your chat with Lilith."

"If you can call it that." She eyed his fingers consideringly. "I've had more enlightening chats with Crux and Crater."

Given her present mood, Tory knew she'd probably bite him in a minute. Even so, he wasn't prepared to release her just yet. Maybe he didn't want to let her go at all. Maybe it was time to forget the past and move forward.

Did he love her, he wondered, then quickly shunned the thought. To love was to hurt, and he'd been hurt enough already. One way or another, the people he cared about most wound up leaving him.

Blocking the unpleasant memories, Tory pulled her to her feet, noting in a dangerous aside that she hadn't changed her clothes. Black silk still clung to the delightfully slender curves of her body, a lethal addition to her shimmering green eyes and the spun-gold hair that tumbled over her shoulders in a mass of loose waves and curls.

With more gentleness than force he removed the soda can from between her fingers, flipped off the stereo and urged her toward the door. "You can tell me all about your conversation with Lilith on the way to the city," he said, not letting her teeth get anywhere near his hand.

"The city!" She'd allowed him to pull her forward a few steps. Now she dug in her heels and stared at him. "I don't want to go to the city."

He turned patient eyes to her mutinous face. "You don't want to sleep in your own bed tonight?"

"No...yes." Suspicion undermined her defiance. "I thought you said we had work to do."

"We do. I need you to drive me into Las Vegas to pick up my car." His lips twitched. "Correction, I'll drive, but I still need you there."

"What you need is a lesson in civilian courtesy," she grumbled, sending him a sarcastic look as she snatched her purse off the arm of the sofa.

"That, too," he agreed, and was glad to see the annoyance in her eyes fade. "Let's go."

"You know, anyone could do this, Tory," she pointed out as they neared the elevators. "Why don't you take George? Then you can spend all night drinking beer and reminiscing about the good old days."

He let go of her fingers, setting his hands firmly on her shoulders and meeting her challenging gaze. "I don't want to take George, and in spite of what you think I'm not dying to take a trip down memory lane. This might surprise you, Kristian, but I don't live in my glory days of the past. I don't even think about them all that much." Except when he was with her, a voice in his head prodded, and even then his recollections had little or nothing to do with any erstwhile military exploits. "All we're doing is driving to the city together." He grinned. "If it'll make you feel better, I promise to stay on my own side of the car."

She stared at him for a long mistrustful minute. "We'll only talk about the present?" she asked in a cautious tone.

He punched the elevator call button. "With all that's happened, it shouldn't be hard to stay on-topic."

"One wouldn't think so."

The humor in her voice was evident and suddenly Tory felt rejuvenated, despite a nagging headache and a lingering soreness in his body that even a hot shower hadn't been able to erase. Maybe a clash of wills was exactly what he needed to shake off the uncustomary apathy that had been plaguing him for the past several months. Then again, he mused, maybe the answer was even more basic than that.

"What are you smiling about?" Kristian's question cut through his reflections and he flicked faintly amused eyes to her face.

"If I told you, you wouldn't get in the car with me."

"Right. Take George."

Spinning on her heel, she started to walk away, but he caught her before she could slip out of his range. "Nice try," he murmured, ushering her unceremoniously into the elevator.

She lifted her chin, but made no attempt to shake off his hand. "You have a mean streak in you, Tory."

A distant smile crossed his lips. "No," he said calmly, "I don't." Reckless perhaps. High-handed, probably. Guilty of exercising bad judgment, undeniably. But he didn't have a mean bone in his body, and Kristian knew it.

To his amazement, she sent him a grudging look. "No, I guess you really don't," she admitted with a tired sigh and the tiniest hint of a smile. "After all, you did let George hire me."

Tory arched a dark brow. "Does that mean you're finished arguing with me?"

"Never."

"I figured as much." The elevator doors slid silently open. "Shall we go?" he asked, holding out his hand to her.

She seemed to consider the matter for a moment. Then, without a word, she placed her hand in his.

It was a start.

SOMETIMES LIFE could be incredibly confusing, Kristian decided as she made her way along one of NORStar's crowded thoroughfares toward the Colonel's workshop. She should be fighting Tory's orders, not strolling along at his side like some besotted Air Force groupie.

She couldn't even be bothered asking him why they were making this little detour. Her head hurt, her eyes felt gritty and sore, and she was in a bad mood. Admittedly, not as bad a mood as she'd been in before Tory had teased her out of it, but she still didn't feel like driving to the city. Why then, she wondered, hadn't she just said no?

The answer, while obvious enough, was much too complex to explore, and Kristian immediately turned her mind to another topic. Murder was, if nothing else, a concrete concept. It was also terrifying and confusing. Maybe she should try her hand at transcendental meditation. If she could mentally zap herself into a semidivine state of consciousness, she wouldn't have to think about Tory, Simon, Annette Barrows or Telstar.

Or the totally bizarre sight that greeted her as she entered the Colonel's workshop.

"George?" Tory pushed aside a black curtain, leading Kristian into an area of the shop that was, for lack of a better term, George Straker's playroom. "Wait here with the little green men," he said when no answer was forthcoming. "I want to talk to George. I'll only be a couple of minutes."

Kristian's mute compliance had more to do with a childish sense of awe than either fatigue or obedience. There were aliens everywhere, some familiar, some not, but all having a wonderful time as they bounced, flew, tumbled and spun about the room. The scene had all the earmarks of an intergalactic Mardi Gras, a wild cosmic festival set to Rossini's *"Barber of Seville."*

She took a step backward, trying for a better view of the creature spectacle—and found herself thumping solidly into Tory's chest.

"On second thought, maybe we should stay together," he murmured, his breath warm on her neck.

She battled a tremor of awareness and glanced at the door in the background. "Your faith in me is staggering. I'm not a delinquent child, Tory. I don't intend to run and hide the first chance I get."

"I know," he said with a vague half smile. "It's my insecurity surfacing. Humor me."

Disbelief momentarily robbed Kristian of speech. Had he really said that? She didn't utter a sound as they forged a path through the colorful holograms. She was so shocked by Tory's uncharacteristic admission that she almost missed seeing George, who stood quietly among the three-dimensional images, surveying the antics of his multi-limbed creations.

Ignoring his friend, Tory continued on toward the rear of the workshop. "I thought you wanted to talk to George," Kristian said, tugging on his sleeve.

He looked down at her. "I do. Why?"

"Well, isn't he . . . ?" She stopped suddenly, frowning as George's eyes met hers. Or did they? Moving closer, she passed her hand through his shoulder. "It's a hologram!" she exclaimed. "But it looks so real."

"Not real enough to suit its creator, I'm afraid." In his usual formal fashion, the Colonel glided out from behind a computerized projector. "George insists he can do better, though in what way I've yet to determine."

Kristian bit back a smile. The Colonel was so refined, like an old English manservant. Tall and elegant, yet always with a sparkle lurking deep in his faded-blue eyes, he was polite to a fault and completely devoted to his toys. Almost as devoted as George was to his holograms.

"What are you doing here, Tory?" On cue, George emerged from the mandibles of a pink Tritonian snow crab. "Evan told me you and Kristian were going into the city."

Tory shrugged. "We're on our way. I just wanted to let you know that Jon Hayes and a handful of FBI people will be making the rounds tonight."

"Feds, huh? I bet that's an intense group. How long were you tied up with them?"

"Three hours."

"Not bad. What about you, Kristian?"

She shook her head. "I was busy with the mayor's wife for most of the day."

George grinned. "I think I'd rather face the Feds. Colonel?"

"Well, I've talked to Jon, of course, but no one else. I can't imagine what I could tell them, in any event. I was in the Cosmic Theater all night. The only people I saw were Priscilla and—" He clamped his elegant mouth shut and summoned a polite smile. "Well, Priscilla, at any rate. As to the other, perhaps my eyes are beginning to play tricks on me."

Kristian knit her brow. "What other, Colonel?" she asked, her fingers tightening on Tory's arm.

"Oh, it won't be of any use to you or to the FBI," he assured them. "At best you'll all think I've been spending too much time with my toys."

Tory ran a hand through his long hair, wearily flexing his shoulders. "Don't count on it," he drawled. "What or who did you see?"

"You won't believe me."

"I'd believe Bugs Bunny at this point."

The Colonel adjusted his tortoiseshell glasses. "Would you also believe Darth Vader?" His speculative gaze embraced the startled threesome before him. "No, I thought not. As I said, my eyes were probably playing tricks on me. I haven't had them examined for several years now."

Kristian found her voice first. "Did Priscilla see this person, as well?"

"I'm afraid not. I did mention it to her, but she felt certain it must have been one of the security guards."

"Dressed up like Darth Vader?" George turned dubious eyes to Tory. "Is it my imagination, or is this situation getting completely out of hand?"

He didn't know the half of it, Kristian reflected, her nails now gouging holes in Tory's arm. Unless Tory had told him about the creature that had attacked her in her hotel suite two nights ago, which, of course, he probably had. George was the very last person Tory would suspect of treachery.

With a start, Kristian realized she wasn't quite as loyal. George was, after all, one of Tory's partners. But was he capable of betraying a friend? Possibly. There was still Evan to consider. And Morton, whom she'd never seen, had seldom even spoken to.

"Very odd," she murmured, then realized three pairs of eyes were staring at her. More if she counted the frolicking aliens. "Colonel, where did you see this, uh, thing you saw?"

The Colonel patted her hand. "Your tact is greatly appreciated, my dear. I saw it in the Cosmic Theater."

"What time?" Tory asked.

"Oh, after one in the morning I should think. Too late for any of our extraterrestrials to be wandering about. Not that we have a Darth Vader on staff."

Kristian sighed. "At least I'm sure Simon wasn't shot by a *Star Wars* character."

"It's enough that Simon was shot at all," Tory said, prying her nails from his forearm and holding up her wrist to look at her slim watch. "We'd better get going. It'll be dark soon."

"Save time and take the back roads," George advised as Kristian stepped cautiously around a three-dimensional projection of the same blue-skinned, pointy-eared minion that had attacked her two nights before. "I hear there's a seven car pileup on the freeway."

"Six cars, one produce truck," the Colonel corrected, his eyes twinkling. "Tomatoes everywhere, they say."

"Attack of the Killer Tomatoes," Kristian mumbled as she and Tory exited the colorful workshop. "This is a bad omen. Why don't we wait till tomorrow?"

"Because you don't really believe in omens, I'd like my car back and I also want to take a look at the accident site tonight."

"Naturally."

"No sarcasm, Kristian."

"I'm too tired to be sarcastic. What is it you're hoping to find? We already know that Annette Barrows was murdered before her car went over the cliff."

"She was strangled," Tory said, steering her toward the employees' parking lot.

"By the same person who shot Simon?"

"That'd be my guess."

Kristian regarded him suspiciously. "What is it you're not telling me?"

For once he didn't put her off, though in her beleaguered condition, she almost wished he had. "I decided to do a little research," he told her. "Willard Barrows was strangled, too."

She stifled a groan. "By Telstar?"

He took her hand firmly in his. "By Telstar."

DARKNESS FELL SLOWLY over the Nevada desert, floating in on the heels of a glorious orange-and-purple-and-red sunset. Under any other circumstances, Kristian would have been mesmerized by the delicate play of color and light on the western horizon. It wasn't at all like the sunsets on the Rhine. For one thing there weren't any castles in the desert.

She dragged her gaze from the bristly terrain and the indigo shadows that deepened to midnight blue as Tory turned her car toward the hills. No, she told herself firmly. She had to keep her mind on the present. Not that thinking about the present was any less disruptive.

She stole an unobtrusive sideways glance at Tory's enigmatic profile. His beautiful, aquamarine eyes swept the road before them, taking in every detail of the rough terrain. Did he ever look at her that way?

Biting her lip, she huddled deeper into her seat and stared at the winding road ahead of them. "I still don't understand what you expect to find," she said, amazed at the blandness of her tone. "Aren't the police usually quite thorough in these matters?"

"Not always," he said.

Kristian cast him a droll look. "Could you be a little more specific?"

"No, the police aren't always as thorough as they could be in these matters."

He was being stubborn, but in that area Kristian knew she could match him. "Why not?"

He shrugged. "For one thing, they don't have all the pertinent details."

"One of those 'details' being Simon's death, I suppose?"

"Alleged death."

"Semantics, Tory," she said, sighing. "Don't you think withholding information like that is a little unethical?"

"Not especially."

When he didn't elaborate, she opted for a more direct approach. "Let me rephrase that. Since you seem to feel that Simon and Annette were connected in some way, mightn't it be a good idea to tell the police everything we know?"

Without removing his eyes form the road, Tory arched a dark brow. "And just what do we know?"

"We know Simon was shot."

"True, but we can't prove it. For all intents and purposes, Simon's on vacation."

"We know my private investigator can't track him down."

"It's not enough, Kristian. The point is, technically Simon's on his own time and not accountable to anyone."

"Ergo, he can't officially be considered a missing person yet," Kristian translated. The injustice of the situation infuriated her. She folded her arms across her chest, partly out of frustration, partly to combat the chilly night air. "I hate a mandarin mentality," she grumbled. Her eyes slid to his face. "Just out of curiosity, why didn't the FBI agents come looking for me today?"

Reaching into the back seat, Tory retrieved the black bomber jacket he'd thrown there and handed it to her. "You had enough on your mind. Besides, they'll catch up with you sooner or later."

"You know, you might try giving me a little more credit," she muttered, tugging on the jacket. "I've dealt with plenty of highbrow government types in my life and survived. I've even dealt with you and lived to tell about it."

A grin she couldn't comprehend curved his lips. "Nice try, but I don't believe you."

That was nothing new. She wondered if she should punch him now for his highhandedness or wait until they got to the city. A glance into the abyss that fell away from the driver's side of her freshly serviced car made the choice simple. "Believe it," she said, removing a tape from the glove box and sliding it into the cassette deck. "My life didn't end when I left you that night in Heidelberg."

His grin grew slightly mocking. "That's not quite what I meant. You might have dealt with me and lived, but you didn't tell anyone about it."

She lifted ingenuous eyes to his face. "Oh? You're sure of that, are you?"

"Uh-huh. I know you, Kristian. You're not the kiss-and-tell type. It isn't your style."

Maybe not, but shoving a certain arrogant male out of her car suddenly seemed very appealing. Of course, the way this day had gone, Tory would doubtlessly ricochet off a cactus and land in a nice soft patch of white sage, while she sailed out over the cliff and dropped like a stone to the canyon floor.

She settled for sending him a defiant glare, then sat back and gave a full one-quarter of her attention to Animotion's latest release.

The problem with Tory was twofold. Threefold, if she included her own chaotic emotions, something she wouldn't be able to avoid much longer. He knew her too damned well, knew her flaws and faults, her likes and dislikes. And yet he

didn't know her well enough to understand why she'd left
him. Lately she wasn't sure of the reasons herself. Maybe
they'd figure it all out someday, maybe they wouldn't. Right
now it was a moot point, one Kristian's instinct for survival
cautioned her not to dwell on.

Luckily, she didn't have time to wage any heavy emotional battles. They were approaching the spot where Annette Barrows's car had crashed through the guardrail. Or
been pushed through. One way or another, the end result
was the same. The woman was dead, killed by what her
murderer undoubtedly hoped would look like an accident.

Through the windshield, Kristian spied her first and favorite night star: Venus, glittering brightly in a blue-black
sky. On impulse, she lowered her lashes to make a wish, but
snapped them up again when a pair of glaring headlights
suddenly appeared on the road in front of them. They were
blinding in their intensity and much, much larger than they
had any right to be. They were also coming closer.

She stiffened her spine, wrapping her fingers convul-
sively around the edge of her seat. "Tory, it's a truck," she
whispered, her voice inaudible above the loud rock music.
She didn't add that it was an enormous truck, eighteen
wheels or better, and bearing down on them at a frightening speed. He could see that for himself.

For a long, horrible moment, she was sure the two vehicles were going to collide. It seemed inevitable. There
couldn't possibly be enough room for both of them on this
narrow strip of road. And they certainly weren't going to get
any help from the splintered guardrail.

She sank her teeth into her lower lip, her fingernails into
the upholstery. In that same split second, her terrified eyes
found Tory's face, composed as always during an emergency, illuminated by the headlights that were all but on top
of them now.

With a succinct "Hold on" to her, he swerved sharply to
the left, throwing the car onto the gravel shoulder at the exact spot where Annette's car had plunged into the canyon.

Squeezing her eyes closed, Kristian prayed for a miracle. Around her, the world seemed to spin out of control. Or was it the car that was spinning? She saw wild flashes of light, heard the thunder of drums and the blood that pounded a matching beat in her ears, felt the tires slide, then grab, then bounce sideways. Away from the oncoming truck. And closer to the rim of the deadly precipice....

Chapter Nine

Tory wouldn't let her die.

For reasons that made no sense at all, Kristian clung to that irrational thought, believed it. He was an excellent pilot, a first-rate driver and the one, the only, person she would ever allow herself to depend on in a crisis.

The car continued to skid. Loose stones, sand and clumps of sun-baked earth pelted the underside. Dust swirled thickly about the partially open windows. Too scared to breathe, she dug her heels into the floorboards and braced for whatever impact might follow.

An eternity ticked by before she realized that they were slowing. That they had stopped. They weren't going to shoot over the edge of the cliff, after all.

A weak feeling of relief trickled through her. In a dim corner of her mind, she realized Tory's arm was pressed across her shoulders, pinning her upright every bit as securely as her seatbelt.

"Are you all right, Kristian?" She heard his voice through a fog. "Did you hit your head?"

Particles of dust floated before her eyes, stinging them, but aside from that and a parched rawness in her throat she was uninjured. Shakily, she pried her fingers from the seat. "I'm okay," she managed so tremulously that she could scarcely hear the words. "What...where are we?" Her head suddenly cleared, and she found herself groping for him. "You're not hurt, are you?"

"No, but we're hanging by a thread, so don't make any jerky moves."

Hanging? Her eyes widened as she stared into the darkness straight ahead of her. Darkness and certain death. That wasn't the road out there! She was looking down into the canyon from a car that hadn't stopping moving at all. It was poised on the rim of the cliff, dipping and swaying like a rocking horse caught in the wind. And with a sinking feeling of horror, Kristian recalled just how fickle the wind in these hills could be.

"Oh, God," she breathed, immobilized with terror and some other emotion that felt perilously close to hysteria. No! She wouldn't panic, she told herself furiously. She'd save that till later when her feet were safely back on solid ground.

Moistening her dry lips, she ventured a thready "What are we going to do?"

"First off, we're going to stay calm." Tory's voice was a low, soothing sound in the pitchy night air. "Next, you're going to unfasten your seatbelt very carefully. Then you're going to lower your seat and slide into the back of the car."

He expected her to move? She swallowed hard over the lump in her throat. "Tory, I can't—"

"Yes, you can," he promised in the same soothing tone as before. "Just do it, Kristian. Take your seatbelt off first. I won't let you fall forward."

She couldn't be a coward about this. Eyes glued to the inky black gorge, she fumbled with the release mechanism, forcing her strained muscles to follow Tory's instructions. "It's stuck," she croaked, then caught back a painful breath as the car's front end tipped toward the canyon at a precarious angle.

"Keep going," Tory coaxed, his arm strong about her shoulders, his voice reassuring and warm in her ear. "Don't look down. Just close your eyes and trust me."

"Trust you?" She sent him a feeble glare that neverthe
less bolstered her courage. "I'd rather trust a snake."

"Liar," he accused, pushing the now-loosened strap
away. Briefly he grazed her cheek with his knuckles. "Now
find the lever and lower your seat. I'll be right behind you."

Although it felt like several hours, it took only a few sec
onds to locate the spring-loaded bar. In the gusty breeze, the
car continued to seesaw back and forth, never quite losing
its tenuous grip on the ledge. Kristian heard the ominou
moans of fatigued metal against rock, the terrified banging
of her heart in her chest, the blood that hammered loudly in
her ears. But most of all she heard Tory's voice, so calm and
steady, so completely under control that she could almos
believe her fears were groundless.

Behind her, the seat fell away, the car tilted back then
forward and her stomach gave a panicky lurch. So much for
her fleeting illusion of safety.

Palms damp with perspiration, she pushed herself back
ward, unable to see anything except the wall of darknes
visible through the windshield. *Look at the stars,* a smal
voice in her head commanded. *Look at Tory. Don't look
down; don't think. Just keep going.*

That was easier said than done. Her entire body felt lead
weighted. And frozen stiff. Even her fingers refused to work
properly. She tugged on the door handle, silently thanking
her brother for insisting she not buy a coupe.

A film of cold sweat broke out on her skin as the car gave
a screeching yaw. Whatever thread was holding it in place
wasn't going to last much longer. Why in God's name, she
wondered, stifling a desperate sob, had she gotten out of bed
this morning?

"Go," Tory ordered from directly behind her.

"I can't." She rattled the handle to no avail. "It won'
open."

"Yes it will."

Before she could react, Tory was hauling her against hi
chest. With his booted foot, he kicked the jammed door

striking it three times, each blow more forceful than the one before.

Beneath the pitching chassis, something snapped. Possibly the rear axle, but right then Kristian wasn't interested in specifics. The instant the stubborn latch yielded, she tumbled from the car, landing in an undignified heap on the gravel shoulder, not caring that Tory fell half on top of her. At least they were both out.

Even so, it hurt to accept what was happening around her. She didn't need to look to know that her shiny red car was no longer teetering on the brink of disaster. It was long gone, slipping and sliding, plunging over the rocky ledge, leaving nothing except a sickening crunch of metal and stone in its wake.

It cost Kristian an enormous amount of energy to lift her head, more than she could reasonably spare just then. Her hands and knees were scraped, her mouth tasted like dirt, every single muscle in her body ached.

Groaning, she twisted herself around, wriggling out from under Tory's lean body. "Is it over?" she asked in a thin whisper.

His shrewd eyes swept the now-silent cliff, coming to rest on her face. "For a while." He ran his thumb lightly over her dirt-smudged lower lip. "Can you move?"

She stared up at him, fighting the absurd desire to pull his head down and press her mouth against his. "I don't think so."

Concern darkened his face. "Why? Are you hurt?"

"Stuck."

"Come again?"

"You're lying on top of me," she explained, getting desperate. This wasn't a position her fragile emotions could deal with.

She held her breath as Tory rolled smoothly to his feet, catching her around the waist and bringing her with him. "Is that better?" he inquired. If the situation hadn't been so horrific she might have searched for a glimmer of mocking humor in his eyes.

"Much." Disconsolately, she peered into the gorge. Dozens of shapeless black blobs dotted the canyon floor, one of them being her once-perfect car. This hadn't been her day at all. "How are we going to get back to the park?" she asked as he took an assessing look around.

"We'll have to walk. Or hitchhike."

Kristian regarded her tattered, dirt-streaked dress and scraped knees. Who in their right mind would offer her a ride? She limped over to where Tory stood surveying a road he couldn't possibly see. "What are you doing?"

"Trying to figure out where that truck came from."

Shoving back the sleeves of his black bomber jacket, Kristian turned toward the space park. "Who cares? All I know is that it didn't stop, probably didn't even get a scratch. And if I ever find out who was at the wheel, I'm going to rip that person's useless eyes out of their sockets."

"I'd pay to see that show," Tory said, his lips twitching ever so slightly.

He draped an arm over her shoulders and, after a moment's hesitation, Kristian slid hers around his waist, letting him pull her against his warm, muscled body. She wanted badly to feel secure right now. While her intellect told her that this had been a freak accident, her instincts warned her of something altogether different. Something she didn't like one little bit. What were the odds of two cars leaving a road at the exact same place on separate occasions? Too low to risk a wager on, she decided.

A shiver ran through her. "This wasn't any coincidence, was it, Tory? We were just plain lucky."

His jaw was set in an unpromising line. "The truth?" He met her questioning green eyes. "No, I don't think it was a coincidence."

Kristian swallowed a renewed surge of terror. "In that case," she said, "we're in a lot of trouble."

THE WOMAN SAT cross-legged atop a craggy bluff, looking down at the shadowy twosome far below, angry but not entirely surprised that her latest plan had been thwarted.

"It didn't work, did it?" Her partner came up behind her, sounding so matter-of-fact, that she was tempted to toss him onto the road below.

"No, it didn't," she snapped. "You were right about Tory. He's a good driver."

"He's the best."

"He's lucky. So's Kristian. I promise you, though, their luck isn't going to last. And you better wipe that I-told-you-so look from your face. Your little computer warning didn't exactly send Kristian packing. She was chockful of questions earlier tonight."

"Questions can't hurt us," the man reminded her, blinking up at the familiar outline of Ursa Major. "I still think we should let them find the information for us."

"Well, I don't. It's too risky." She stood, facing him with a cold glare that had him stepping unobtrusively away from her. "Since we failed here, our only alternative is to move on to a new and better plan."

"Which is?"

There was no warmth in the smile she bestowed upon him. "I'll let you know. For the moment all you need to do is keep an eye on Tory and Kristian. Keep them away from the space park for a few hours."

"But how?"

"I don't know how," she snarled. "Figure something out. Be inventive for a change. Start a landslide; rope a cougar and sic it on them. I really don't care what you come up with, just keep them out of the park. I have work to do. I don't want them nosing around, getting in my way."

"Whatever you say," he capitulated, swatting at an invisible insect on his arm. "I hope you know what you're doing. I know I'll be glad when this is over."

"So will I," she agreed, laughing as she started toward the innocuous-looking van parked next to his car. "So, my dear partner, will I."

CHICKEN FEATHERS.

Kristian batted at the downey bits of fluff that clung to her ruined silk dress, sneezing as she followed Tory into a small wayside store five miles from the space park. She was allergic to feathers, which made it inevitable that they should be rescued by a pair of young farmers hauling a truckload of molting hens.

Tossing her unruly hair over one shoulder, she stifled another sneeze and sent Tory a smoldering glare. "I hope you know how much I hate you at this moment."

"I do." Grinning abstractly, he pulled a scraggly white feather from the collar of the too-large jacket she still wore. "You've been stabbing me in the back with those gorgeous green eyes of yours for close to an hour now."

"You're lucky that's all I've done." Exasperation won out over resentment. "A chicken truck, Tory? Honest to God, I think you will things like this to happen. What kind of farmers would be lugging hens through the hills at eleven o'clock at night?"

"Very amiable ones who mistakenly thought they were helping a damsel in distress."

Kristian passed him on the porch, pulling the squeaky store door open and smiling sweetly as she preceded him inside. "Don't worry. They're still under that false impression. Unless you saw fit to set them straight."

"Set who straight?" The question came from behind a stack of Count Chocula boxes. Seconds later, Evan strolled into sight, a pack of beer in one hand, a box of saltines in the other. A huge grin spread across his handsome face when he spied Kristian. "Hey, great getup. Maybe a little heavy on the dirt, but the feathers are a nice touch. Interesting new look for you."

If she hadn't been busy fighting off another sneeze, Kristian would have thrown a bag of marshmallows at him. But she couldn't do three things at once, and she had no choice but to deal with Tory whose unbearably sexy body was pressed against hers from behind. His arms might be resting with seeming indolence on her shoulders, but they were also doing a very effective job of holding her in place. Not that she really minded.

"I'd have thought you'd be long gone, Evan," Tory noted, his bland tone deceiving. "Was there a problem at the park?"

His partner shrugged. "A glitch in the Asteroid Adventure. Nothing compared to the problems you seem to have had." His dark eyes took in Kristian's disheveled appearance. "What did you do, get mugged by a chicken from the Black Lagoon?"

Tory shifted his weight, his stance still deceptively relaxed. "Close. We were run off the road by a truck. Probably a semi."

Kristian felt the tension that simmered just below the surface and couldn't help shuddering at the thought of how ugly things might get if it turned out that Evan was involved in anything that had happened. She knew she didn't want to be around if Tory ever truly lost his temper.

Fortunately, Evan's expression was one of complete bewilderment. "A semi?" he repeated, starting for the counter. "Where, on the highway?"

"In the hills," Kristian told him. "It should have come past this store." She transferred her gaze to the toothless old man who was playing checkers with his dog beside an outmoded cash register. "Have you seen any big trucks go by in the last hour, Mr. Ebenezer?"

The man lifted his head. "How's that?"

Belatedly she remembered he was hard of hearing, and adamant in his refusal to wear a hearing aid. She repeated the question and at the same time tried to duck gracefully out from under Tory's arms. Being this close to him was incredibly distracting. However, moving was a big mistake. With an imperceptible tightening of his wiry muscles, he obliterated the last discreet vestiges of space between them.

"Stand still," he murmured, his mouth next to her ear, his warm breath sending hot little tremors along her spine, causing a cramp of desire to strike low in her stomach.

Smothering a groan, she shoved a warning elbow into his ribs and watched the store owner purse his lips.

"A truck? Past here?" He shook his head. "Can't rightly say it did, 'cause it didn't. Course my eyesight ain't a patch on what it used to be."

Tory glanced at Evan, who shrugged and tossed a couple of bills on the counter. "Don't look at me; I just got here. Best I can do is offer you and Kristian a lift to your ranch."

"To the space park," Kristian said firmly.

"Whatever." He picked up his purchases. "Give me a couple of minutes on my car phone. I have a date with a hot canasta dealer that's going to be slightly delayed."

The door banged shut behind him, setting off a loud cowbell, which in turn set off the old proprietor. "No, sir, ain't been hardly a single rig since they rerouted the freeway." He chortled merrily. "Course, people have been known to get themselves lost."

"But not tonight." Tory plucked another feather from Kristian's hair. "You sure you didn't see or hear anything, Eb?"

"Sure as I can be. Just cain't say how sure that is." Still cackling, the store owner scooped up the money in front of him and turned back to his checkerboard. "Flip the Closed sign round on your way out, and have a nice night."

This time Kristian did groan. Have a nice night? Unintentional or not, it was a cruel blow.

Determinedly, she shook off the hand that circled her upper arm and reached for the door. "Leave me alone, Tory," she ordered wearily. "I can't think straight when I'm with you." God, now why had she said that?

One dark brow lifted, acknowledging the accidental admission. "Is that why you want to go to the space park?"

"Partly." She lifted her chin. "I also know you'll come up with a thousand reasons why I shouldn't go home, and I certainly don't want to go to your ranch."

"No?" His slow smile challenged the veracity of the statement, but he let it pass and settled for a disconcerting "Maybe I can persuade you to change your mind."

"You could try," she replied guilelessly, then gave the door a defiant tug, opening it to a cranking car engine that managed to sound worse than the screeching hinges behind her.

"This is ridiculous," Evan grumbled, climbing from the driver's seat. "It was working fine ten minutes ago."

His rare display of temper diverted Kristian's thoughts from the man so close behind her. With a glance over her shoulder, she went to stand beside the front fender as Evan raised the hood.

"You ever worked on a BMW before?" he asked Tory who was already leaning over, studying the snarl of hoses, wires and cylinders.

One long finger tested the battery connections. "No. Do you have a flashlight?"

"In the trunk."

While Evan banged around in search of a light, Kristian watched Tory fiddle with a foreign-looking gadget that was probably the carburetor. A neon Coke sign in the store window illuminated his arresting features with a soft white glow that made her heart give a painful lurch.

For all her sarcasm, she knew it would take very little persuasion to change her mind about accompanying him to his ranch. But if she relented, what then, she wondered in desperation. It would be Germany all over again. Wouldn't it?

Confused and very tired, she pushed away from the car with her sore palms, noticing with disgust that instead of dirt, she now had oil on her hands. And on her dress. If she was going to look like a hobo, she might as well go for the full effect.

She paused suddenly, staring at her palms, then at the BMW's smeared fender, then at the front of her dress. How could there be oil on the car? Evan had only now popped the hood, hadn't he?

Of course he had, she answered the question, shaking herself soundly. She was being paranoid. There was no reason on earth for Evan to cripple his own car. Still, this unexpected breakdown did seem awfully convenient. To what possible end, though, she hated to think.

Rubbing her hands on her ruined dress, she watched Evan return and hand Tory a powerful flashlight. And wished she could ignore the icy chill that crawled down her spine.

TORY, YOU'RE NOT LISTENING TO ME. That oil didn't spontaneously jump out from under the hood and land on the fender.'' Ignoring the fact that she was in the one place she knew she shouldn't be, Kristian limped into the large central bathroom of Tory's ranch house. ''And don't tell me those ignition wires came loose all on their own, because I won't believe you.''

''You never do.'' Crouching, he turned on the taps in the Mexican-tile bathtub, then sat her down on the edge and gently pulled off her dusty Italian pumps. ''Evan told you he stopped for gas this morning. The attendant could have gotten oil on the fender. Besides, what would anyone, Evan included, stand to gain by disabling his car?''

She studied the hands that were inspecting her scraped knees. Tory had beautiful hands, fingers that were long rather than wide and a touch that had the most wonderfully anesthetic quality about it.

She pulled up short, giving herself a firm mental slap. ''I don't know,'' she answered him truthfully. ''That's the problem. There's too much going on that we don't know about.''

Tory eased the jacket from her shoulders. "Anything computer related is bound to be complicated. Particularly when someone of Annette Barrows's considerable talents is involved."

He set about unfastening the belt of her dress, but it was his words, not his actions, that captured Kristian's attention. "Annette couldn't have stolen anything from NOR-Star's computers, could she?"

"I doubt it. More likely she used the NORStar computers to hack into some classified corporate file."

"Which could explain why my computer was on the night Simon was shot." She stopped speaking to stare at the hands that were in the process of unwrapping the remnants of her black silk dress. "What do you thing you're doing?"

The grin that curved Tory's lips was completely unrepentant. "I think I'm being nice."

"By undressing me?" She tried to stand, but he pulled her back down with no effort at all. "I knew I should have made Evan take me to the space park," she murmured as a wave of utter exhaustion and numerous other emotions assailed her.

In all fairness, she'd tried to remain firm on that point. But it had taken the better part of an hour to find and fix the problem with Evan's car, and while the breakdown might have been suspect, Kristian couldn't bring herself to delay his much-anticipated date any longer than necessary. Nor could she hope to hold out against the feelings that were currently leaping around inside her.

Smiling, Tory sat back on his heels. "Would it help if I promised not to jump on you?"

Only if he also promised not to let her jump on him. Or run her hands through the thick, dark hair that was so close it actually brushed her shoulder when he moved.

She shifted her gaze to his mouth, for one brief moment letting her guard down. No one could arouse her with the immediacy that Tory could. All he had to do was kiss her with that incredibly sexy mouth of his.

A blush stained her cheeks, and she lowered her lashes quickly, praying he wouldn't notice her involuntary reaction, or if he did, that he would attribute it to the steam rising from the tub.

"You can bandage my knees," she said, relieved that her voice sounded more or less steady. "But I'll take my own bath."

His blue-green eyes revealed nothing. For the longest time he didn't move, just stared at her from such close range that she was tempted to forget all about common sense and slide her arms around his neck and pull him with her into the water.

She held herself very still, waiting, fighting a desire so strong that it was a tangible ache. Fortunately, she didn't have long to wait. Through her lashes, she saw Tory reach onto a shelf behind the door and remove a thick white towel. His smile was obscure and completely unfathomable. If he was anywhere near as discomposed as she was, he certainly didn't show it.

"I'll get the peroxide," he said finally, and she breathed a sigh that was as much relief as regret. With that enigmatic smile still hovering on his lips, he stood, holding the towel out to her, distantly polite, yet not to be trusted, her suspicious mind cautioned. "There's a clean robe in the cupboard when you're finished."

If he could be civil, so could she. She rose smoothly to her feet. "Thank you."

"Don't mention it." A wicked spark of humor and something else glinted deep in his eyes. Then one hand slid around the back of her neck. And before she realized what he was doing, his mouth came down to cover hers.

SHE WAS A FIGHTER, and not a fair one by any means. The instant Tory's lips caught hers, she bit him. Not hard, but enough to let him know that she didn't appreciate being taken off guard.

Ignoring the negligible pain, he pulled her against him, fitting her to his taut length, feeling the warmth of her body, the tension and that fast-rising surge of excitement that had always fascinated him. Slowly, yet with a determinedly persuasive insistence, he rubbed his mouth across hers, teasing her, testing her response with an equal amount of curiosity and urgency.

The balance shifted rapidly as the tension in her gave way to something bordering on passion, as her tongue met his and her nails dug into his shoulders. Damn, but he wanted her, needed her. It was the first time in his life he'd ever admitted that, even to himself, and while this was no time for a long-overdue bout of self-analysis, he couldn't shed the sense of surprise that realization evoked.

Shoving it aside, he ran a hand along Kristian's slender spine, savored the heat of her, tasted the sweet defiance that lingered on her kiss and knew in the back of his mind that he couldn't take much more of this. Not without scooping her up in his arms and carrying her straight to his bed.

It was a tempting thought, damned near irresistible in fact, but of course he wouldn't do it. It was too soon, and he was too tired, to say nothing of how she must feel.

Reluctantly, he raised his head, aware that she wasn't pulling away from him. He knew her response had been real enough. He also recognized the wary light that entered her eyes as she stared up at him.

"Go ahead and yell," Tory invited, his voice low, one finger tracing the outline of her slightly swollen lips. "Just don't expect me to apologize."

Amazingly, she did neither. She didn't even look as if she wanted to shove him into the bathtub. Was it possible her attitude toward him had softened? Or was it simply that they were two different people now? More than friends, but not lovers. Not yet....

Looking down, he saw that she was studying him circumspectly. "You're worried, aren't you?" She tipped her head back. "Is that why you kissed me?"

With a reticent smile, he bent to flip off the taps. "Yes. And no." He turned her toward a well-stocked cabinet. "You'll find everything you want in here. When you're through, I'll bandage your knees and put you to bed." Put, not take, he reminded himself dryly. Much as he wanted to make love to her, he also wanted that feeling to be reciprocated. "Relax, Kristian," he murmured gently. "I'm not up to anything more strenuous."

She sent him a grudging smile. "That would be a first, but I'm going to give you the benefit of the doubt for once. And in case you're interested, your phone's ringing."

At midnight? "Must be Lydia." He shrugged, indifferent to anything his avaricious stepmother might have to say. "Her particular brand of mourning requires a constant cash flow."

"That sounds awfully cynical, Tory."

"It wouldn't if you knew her." He pulled the door open, calmly meeting her puzzled eyes. "Take your bath, Kristian. I'll be back in half an hour."

Such a dispassionate stance, he thought as he made his way to the kitchen. He'd gotten good at hiding his feelings over the years. Maybe he'd hidden them too well, locked them away for too long from the one person who could have made his life complete.

He glanced idly at the flashing light on the wall phone near the fridge. Messages on his answering machine didn't interest him in the slightest, though he would have to remember to call Jon Hayes first thing in the morning. It was just a little too convenient that Kristian's car should be run off the road tonight. Someone wanted them dead.

Fingering the bruise on his temple, Tory reached into the refrigerator for a cold beer. There were too many thoughts blasting around inside his head, too many emotional bullets he couldn't hope to dodge. Overlapping pictures of Kristian and Simon, the past and the present, his partners, and even the space park itself. And then of course there was Simon's message about Ibo and the Southern Cross. About a betrayal as well, he wondered tiredly. Maybe, but he couldn't believe he'd screwed up so badly that he'd let himself become partners with a murderer.

From the bathroom, he heard music and felt himself relax a little. Kristian must be feeling better. She loved stargazing with the old masters, dancing till dawn to classic rock and making love in the moonlight to whatever song nature saw fit to play. Making love, taking chances, breaking rules—and now as then, getting under his skin.

"Damn you," he murmured, pressing the icy beer bottle against his burning forehead. If circumstances had been anything other than what they were, he would have given in to temptation long ago and—what? Made love to her? It wouldn't stop there, and he knew it. There was something going on between them. Something that had nothing to do with the past and everything to do with the people they'd become in the present.

Smiling to himself, Tory wandered into the living room, leaving the lights off and flipping his answering machine on. Not surprisingly, Lydia's was the first voice he heard. The second was a hang-up, the third his lawyer, the fourth June calling with a message from Morton and the fifth Morton himself.

Morton Nash making a personal call? Now, that was unusual. Tory tossed himself onto the sofa and swallowed a mouthful of beer as his partner's raspy voice filled the air.

"Good evening, Tory. Yes, believe it or not, it's me. I know, I sound as though I'm calling from deep inside the Carlsbad Caverns. In a sense, I am. To be precise, I'm in my limousine en route to Paradise, perhaps literally as well as geographically. I'm told there's a young man who lives near there who might be able to cure my particular affliction. He's a psychic healer by trade, a shaman, for lack of a better term."

"More likely a sham," Tory retorted as the tape played on. "You're wasting your time, old friend."

"You'll have an opinion on this, I'm sure," Morton continued, his voice threadier now than before. "No matter, I didn't call to ask for your approval. I only want you to know where I'll be, and to say I hope all goes well with the grand opening tomorrow. Perhaps one day, I'll be able to see it for myself." His tone saddened. "Miracles, I'm told, still occur from time to time. Second chances are rare. Take my advice, Tory, count your blessings. As my grandfather once said: life is seldom as we would like it to be, but live it we must. Until the day life is no more. That day when death creeps through our door...."

Chapter Ten

Life, death, dreams. Morton's message to Tory, an anonymous computer message to her. There had to be a connection somewhere in all that, Kristian decided as she staggered into her office early Friday evening. It was just unfortunate that she hadn't had a spare moment to think about anything except her work since the opening of NORStar's two new exhibits Wednesday morning. She still didn't, though that might prove to be a blessing in disguise. No time to think meant no chance to dwell on Tory or any of the myriad feelings she was no longer able to fend off.

"Thank heaven for small favors," she breathed, dropping into her chair and pushing back the sleeves of her navy blue jumpsuit.

"And thank me for putting in more overtime." Priscilla marched through the door, dishevelled and dirt-streaked. "I am not a magician, Kristian. Nor am I a robot. Unless you want Earth to continue orbiting the moon in the Blue Star Voyage, you'd better put out an APB on either Crux or Crater. Pronto."

Kristian stared up from the depths of her comfortable chair. "Aren't they here?"

"In a word, no. Lilith's been hoarding Crater for two days now, and I have no idea where Crux has disappeared to." She frowned. "Unless Morton has him. He was asking about the robot the last time we spoke."

"Was that before or after he went to Paradise?"

A sparkle pushed the annoyance from Priscilla's eyes. "Word certainly does travel at light speed around this place. It was after. He got back late last night."

"Any luck in his quest?"

"His wild-goose chase, you mean." Priscilla snorted. "This so-called shaman lives in the side of a hill. Kind of like a groundhog, if that tells you anything."

"Did Morton say that?"

"No, I got a psychic transmission from the fraud in the hill. Of course he did. Or rather June did." She sauntered over to the adjoining office. "Speaking of June, where is she?"

Kristian's smile was unshakably genial. "Good question. When you find out, let me know. I've been trying to track her down all day."

Priscilla grinned. "Poor Kristian. I'd take pity on you if I weren't so tired myself. Did you call Morton's suite?"

"Five times. He isn't answering his phone."

"Smart man. I'm going to try that sometime." Her expression droll, she strolled back to the door. "For your sake, I'm going to be a nice person and wrestle with the Blue Star Voyage moon sans robot or magic wand. But I want you to know I'm getting tired of pandering to Lilith's weird craving for a soul mate." She tapped the miniature communication device attached to her tool belt. "Give me a ring if any more disasters crop up. I'm sure I'll be stuck in the control room for two or three hours."

Kristian rose, pouring herself a cup of the Brazilian coffee she couldn't live without. "Why don't you get the Colonel to help you?"

"No can do," Priscilla announced over her shoulder. "He's busy. George is nowhere to be found, and one of the holographic projectors in the Planet of Dreams is acting like a prima donna. I swear, people around here pick the worst possible time to disappear."

"Tell me about it." Kristian looked morosely at the floor where Simon had fallen.

"No offence intended," Priscilla said. "And not including that alleged computer thief the FBI was so keen on grilling everyone about. I was speaking of those individuals whose identity and whereabouts should be relatively determinate. June, George, Lilith; I'm not even sure where Evan's gotten to. It's been like *Invasion of the Body Snatchers* lately, only in a more literal sense than the movie. I wonder what Kevin McCarthy would do in these circumstances?"

"Demand to see our fearless leader?" Kristian suggested, draining her coffee.

"In that case, good luck to him. Unless you want to do the honors, our fearless leaders presently number among the vanished."

Kristian's heart skipped a beat. "All of them?"

Priscilla seemed not to notice her sharp tone. "No, just the two. We always know where Morton is, and I saw Tory a while ago, heading for the Cosmic Theater."

The relief that swept over her was perfectly natural, Kristian told herself firmly. Not true, a voice in her head whispered, but right then she didn't have the mental energy to sort through the confusion. Actually, she might do well to think about something completely different—like acting on a piece of her own advice and bearding one of her fearless leaders in his darkened den.

Wisdom dictated that she keep her plans to herself. She looked out the window at the bustling NORStar thoroughfares. "Maybe I should take a walk through a few exhibits myself," she said to Priscilla, who was already halfway out the door. "How is everything at the Omni Sphere Theater?"

"Ten times larger than life and rolling along smoothly—knock wood." With a wave and a sweep of her red-brown mane, Priscilla headed toward the main ramp while a more sedate Kristian struck out for the service stairs.

Sedate because she was dead tired after spending the past three nights tossing and turning in Tory's not uncomfortable double bed.

Despite her efforts, she couldn't seem to stop herself from thinking about him. Why on earth had she let him talk her into staying on at his ranch? Certainly not for safety's sake, though that consideration had unquestionably played a minor role in her decision.

Be honest for once, her brain practically screamed at her. *You stayed because you wanted to, because it isn't over between you.*

Did she love him? Had she fallen *in* love with him? Was she being a fool?

Yes, yes, and possibly yes **ag**ain. Terrific. With a sigh, Kristian exited the central complex, joining the crowd of space park enthusiasts who were awaiting the spectacular fireworks display and laser light show held every evening at 10:00 p.m. What a wonderful conclusion to come to now, in the middle of a debacle the size of Jupiter's Great Red Spot.

She'd fallen in love with Tory for the second time in her life. If she had an ounce of good sense, she'd go to Jon Hayes and his FBI shadows, tell them everything she knew, including the shooting she'd witnessed, then board a nonstop plane for Casablanca. No one would accuse her of cowardice, least of all Tory. He'd probably be grateful.

She'd be gone, the police would take over the investigation and everything would be back to normal. No one except Tory believed her story about Simon, anyway. And despite a more than respectable amount of government interest, no one seemed particularly upset at the thought of having had a computer thief's daughter on staff.

Of course, to be fair, the name Willard Barrows meant nothing to the vast majority of NORStar's employees. Nor did the code name Telstar. And if the park manager's car had tumbled over a cliff three nights ago, well, that was unfortunate, but these things happened. Even the police agreed on that point.

Unable to thread her way through the swarm of people who'd stopped to watch one of the park's traveling alien side shows, Kristian fell in behind a gaggle of visiting Trekkies decked out in Vulcan ears and Star Fleet uniforms. She made a detour through the Planet of Dreams, pausing only briefly to look in on the Colonel, who was obviously hard at work deep in the glass-encased, upper-level control room.

"It's been a busy night," one of the security guards observed as she turned to view the holographic fairyland below her.

"It's been a busy week," Kristian countered, leaning on the balustrade that ran around the top half of the building. "By the way, have you seen Crux or Crater anywhere?"

"Haven't seen Crux. Saw Evan with Crater a while back, though."

"With Evan, not Lilith?"

"No, but I saw Lilith with George, if that's any help."

"It isn't." She pushed herself from the rail. "Keep an eye on Norres down there in the Iolian Rain Forest. His wings look a little pale."

She left the way she'd come, ducking out the rear exit and picking a slow path through the maze of rides and exhibits to the elegant Pallas Hotel. As usual the casino was jampacked. So was the dance floor in the Plutonian lounge. Kristian bypassed both with scarcely a glance.

Propriety decreed that she phone Morton from the lobby. But what if he was the partner Simon had alluded to in his final message? Who was to say whether his photosensitivity was the real thing? Even if it was, that didn't necessarily preclude his leaving the hotel. He'd gone to Paradise, hadn't he? No, she couldn't risk warning him of her visit.

She took the sleek guest elevator to the twentieth floor, then switched to the private car that could only be operated with the use of a pass key. Thank God it was only one flight, Kristian thought, suppressing a shudder. She might have been standing in a sarcophagus for all the light she could detect. The walls were draped with thick ebony curtains that felt like crimped satin and smelled faintly of sandalwood. The black carpet was no less than two inches thick, and the eerie strains pouring from a hidden speaker system sounded closer to the wail of some prehistoric animal than any music she'd ever heard.

The door slid open with an unnerving whoosh, and she stepped gratefully into the hall. For a second, her determination faltered. With the exception of a few pinpoints of silvery light, the corridor was as dark and forbidding as the elevator behind her. Perhaps more so.

"Who's there?"

The harsh voice seemed to spring from the woodwork, and Kristian immediately jumped back against the wall. "June?" Heart racing, she probed the heavy shadows with her eyes, finally sensing a slight movement. "Is that you?"

"Kristian?" The harshness vanished, supplanted by a shaky laugh. "Yes, it's me. You scared me half to death, popping out of the elevator like that."

"Touché." Limp with relief, Kristian nevertheless forced herself to straighten. "Where have you been all day?"

"Right here," June said a trifle too quickly. "Didn't you get my message? I asked Evan to give it to you."

"I haven't seen Evan since last night." Kristian's dubious gaze flicked to what she assumed was a door at the far end of the hall. "Isn't Morton's phone working? I called several times today."

"So did a lot of other people, kiddo. We unplugged midmorning. Was it anything urgent?"

"I was looking for you."

"And now you've found me. Shall we go?"

Kristian frowned, mistrust blotting out a portion of her trepidation. "Not yet. I want to have a word with Morton."

"No!"

June's commanding tone stopped Kristian in her tracks. "I beg your pardon?" she demanded, a taut edge creeping into her own voice.

"I'm sorry." June hastened to apologize. "That didn't come out right. I meant, now? Tonight?"

"Yes, tonight."

"But—"

"Don't push it, June. I've had a truly lousy week. What's wrong? Is Morton in bed already?"

"No, but—"

"Fine, then he can give me a few minutes of his time." Ignoring her assistant's spluttering protestations, Kristian brushed firmly past and began making her way down the gloomy hall, almost banging into the double doors at the end. "It's like a tomb up here," she declared, her misgivings temporarily forgotten. "Why aren't the corridors lit?"

"Morton doesn't have many visitors," June informed her from directly behind. "I really don't think this is a good idea, Kristian. He's not in the best of health."

"I want to talk to him, not put him through an inquisition." As she spoke, she knocked softly on one of the thick walnut panels. "Why are you so protective of him?"

June's response, if she intended to make one, was forestalled by a burst of static from a speaker to Kristian's right and a mechanical-sounding "Yes? Who is it?"

"It's Kristian." She hesitated, then shook herself. Uneasy or not, she wouldn't back out now. "I'd like to speak to you."

"Certainly, my dear. Come right in."

A muffled click signalled that the door had been unlocked. Conscious of June on her heels, Kristian stepped across the threshold. Out of one black hole and into another, she reflected, feeling for the nearest wall. Why hadn't she thought to bring Tory with her?

"Turn left," June instructed, not sounding pleased. "Where are you, Morton?"

"Over here." The raspy voice came from a distant corner of the suite, from a huge, high-backed chair that sat in front of a wall, which wasn't really a wall but a screen, or in a more fanciful mode, a holographic portal to deep space.

Stars and planets, meteors and moons appeared to zoom past at a fast and furious pace. Even knowing it wasn't real, Kristian had a hard time getting her space legs. "What is this?" she asked June at her elbow.

A low chuckle emanated from the depths of the chair. "It's Morton's Cosmic Wonderland, my dear. A Night Flight to Venus. Tory's idea, George's handiwork and my salvation in more ways than you can possibly imagine."

"I told you this wasn't a good idea," June whispered, tugging on Kristian's sleeve. "We should leave."

"By all means, June, leave," Morton invited, still nothing more than a disembodied voice to Kristian's searching eyes. "You can talk to Kristian any time you wish. This is a pleasure I'm seldom afforded."

"Yes, I realize that, but don't you think—"

The outline of a pallid hand became visible as it passed in front of the three-dimensional projection. "I choose not to think tonight," he interrupted rather impatiently. "Now please, go."

Releasing a disgruntled breath, June nodded, thin-lipped. "If you insist." To Kristian she added a barely audible, "Try not to upset him." Then wheeling around, she moved with her usual sprightly speed toward the door.

Despite the star groups that seemed to be whizzing past a suite that had all the earmarks of a space ship, there was still very little light in the room. At least there wasn't until a series of intersecting blue beams began to emit a soft glow overhead, and even that didn't amount to much.

"I'm afraid this is the best I can offer," Morton told her, and in the gloom Kristian caught a flash of long, pointed teeth.

Space vampires would have teeth like that, she thought, shivering as she recalled a long-ago conversation with June.

Certainly it was an absurd notion, but then so were the surroundings. Battlestar Galactica had a homier atmosphere than this place. "It's fine," she lied, hunting blindly for someplace to sit.

"The sofa is two feet to your right." Again the pale hand made a waving motion. Pale, bony and very frail looking, Kristian noted, her unease mounting. "Can I offer you a drink? White wine, perhaps?"

Whiskey; two fingers, straight up was on the tip of her tongue, but she bit it back and would have negated the offer completely if she hadn't suddenly realized that the shadows beside the chair were moving. And talking.

"Maybe you'd prefer a glass of cognac. It's French, of course. Very old. Very smooth."

Very strange, Kristian added silently. Somewhere along the line she'd made the false assumption that Morton was incapacitated beyond his obvious aversion to light. Not paralyzed but definitely not as fluid as the silhouette before her seemed to be. The robed silhouette whose loose, flowing garment fluttered and danced like a cape of black silk.

Vampires wore capes, didn't they? They also lived in the dark. And it went without saying that they were pale. She clenched her fists in exasperation. She was being ridiculous. This man was Tory's partner. "Cognac will be fine, Morton," she said. "Thank you."

"You're quite welcome." One bony white hand held out a crystal glass, but its owner's face remained invisible, hidden in the folds of a voluminous black hood. With a rustling swish of his robe, Morton returned to his chair. "Now tell me, my dear. What can I do for you?"

It was a fair enough question. Kristian only wished she had an answer. Taking a deep breath, she fixed her gaze on the enveloping black chair in front of her. "I wanted to talk to you about Simon," she said more bravely than she felt. "About his disappearance."

"And the shooting that preceded it." Morton's glass sparkled in the faint blue light. "June told me your story earlier this week."

"It isn't a story."

"You seem quite certain of that."

"I am."

"You're sure it couldn't have been . . . a dream?"

Kristian knew she hadn't imagined the discriminating pause or the subtle shrewdness of Morton's tone. The incident in the hotel came back to her in a rush as she remembered Dracona's blue-skinned minion and the way it had hovered over her. No, that hadn't been any dream. Someone had attacked her, and unless her instincts were dead wrong, the man across from her was well aware of that fact.

"Who told you?" she asked softly and was rewarded with a parchment-dry chuckle.

"I have my sources, Kristian." A delicate cough preceded a slightly throaty "This is my park, too, perhaps more than you and many others are aware. Whatever happens here, no matter how large or small, invariably comes to my attention. I feel very strongly about NORStar, about what it represents. The past is nothing more than a collection of memories; the present is a stepping stone and need only be endured. The future—the space park—is my focus, my purpose, my life's blood, if you will."

"I don't understand."

"Yes, you do." The smile that invaded his voice took on an occult quality that made Kristian's skin crawl. "For one so young, you see the future with remarkable clarity. You understand what will happen to this planet if those who inherit it continue to abuse it, if those with the power to change the course of their slow destruction aren't somehow convinced that they must learn to act for the greater good rather than for their own selfish ends."

Those who inhabit this planet? Kristian shifted uncomfortably in her seat. "Morton, I—"

"Holes in the ozone layer, destruction of the South American rain forests, chemical emissions, carcinogenic dioxins, CFCs, PCBs—it must stop! You humans must learn that you are not the sole form of intelligence in this universe, that this thing you call life is a fragile thing indeed." One waxen fist hit the arm of the chair. His voice was strained, raspy and frighteningly impassioned. But only for a moment. Then his teeth flashed in the blue murk and he settled back in his chair. "So tell me, my dear," he said calmly, "how is your cognac?"

She stared at the white hand, the gleaming teeth, envisioned a pair of burning red eyes and felt herself nod. "Delicious." Good Lord, had she actually spoken? She must be braver than she realized. Either that or on the verge of getting panicky. Setting her drink aside, she ventured a discreet "Uh, Morton, I think I should leave."

"Nonsense," he said, clucking his disapproval. "You haven't finished telling me about Simon yet."

With difficulty, she banked down the worst of her fears. This couldn't be what it seemed. She was not having a close encounter of any kind. "There's really nothing more to tell," she managed weakly. "He's supposed to be on vacation."

"In Brazil." Morton spread his narrow fingers and for a split second Kristian expected to see gossamer webs strung between them. "Has anyone tried to locate him?"

"He didn't board his scheduled flight out of Las Vegas, and his reservation at the Paissandu Hotel in Rio was canceled."

"Most interesting." Morton continued to flex his thin fingers. "How do you suppose a dead man could cancel his hotel reservations?"

"A dead man couldn't. A murderer could." Why was she saying these things, she wondered in desperation? Why was she still here? Summoning a determined smile, she stood. "Morton, I really do have to leave. I just wanted to make sure you were aware of what's been happening at the park."

The fingers curled into claws. "And out of it, as well?"

She hesitated. "What do you mean?"

"Anita Brace, also known as Annette Barrows, the loss of your car..." His robe rustled. "As I said, I have my sources."

Might those sources stem from personal involvement? Kristian's instincts came up dry in that area, though her palms were anything but. Rubbing her damp hands along the legs of her jumpsuit, she inched away from the sofa. Away from the three-dimensional asteroid belt on Morton's theater-size screen and away from the man himself.

"I'm here for you any time, Kristian." His hoarse voice floated out from deep in the chair. "You'll remember that, I trust."

"I'll remember," she promised rashly. "Good night."

This time he made no attempt to forestall her. For that small blessing Kristian uttered a prayer of thanks to the heavens. Unfortunately, in doing so she came perilously close to slamming into a coat rack she almost mistook for a person.

At first glance, it appeared to have a head. A closer inspection, however, revealed a shiny, black helmet of Harley Davidson vintage perched atop a jumble of outerwear. Still, if she hadn't known better, she would have thought she'd just avoided a collision with...

She halted abruptly, the name hitting her like a physical blow.

Darth Vader! The quintessential *Star Wars* villain; evil in its most diabolical form. And the selfsame character Colonel Nathan Brenda claimed to have seen in the Cosmic Theater the night Simon had been shot.

Knees shaking, Kristian stepped back from the apparition. Certainly she could be wrong in her line of thinking. Lots of people owned motorcycle helmets. Of course, those people usually owned motorcycles as well. Unless she'd missed something, Morton wasn't likely to number among them.

It took every ounce of her courage, but she managed to turn around, actually forced herself to advance on the imposing black chair. "Morton," she began, then frowned and stopped, slowly reaching out a hand to touch the smooth leather upholstery.

It felt cool beneath her fingers. Cool and luxurious. And empty. Or rather, almost empty. The silk robe was still there, lying in an expensive heap on the padded seat. But there was no one in it.

Chapter Eleven

"Evening, Kristian."

George came up behind her at the precise instant the fire-works display began, placing a hand on her shoulder as a fiery pink and gold starburst exploded in the desert sky. In her discomposed state, Kristian thought she'd been speared by a stray rocket. She hadn't, but it was all the same to her splintered nerves.

"Evening, George." She plastered a smile on her face. "Have you seen Tory anywhere?"

"Four o'clock and closing." While she twisted her head around to watch Tory, who was strolling toward them with Crux at his side, George arched a dark brow at her. "You feeling okay? You look a little pale."

"There's a lot of that going around," she murmured, then, at his quizzical expression, gave her head a shake. "I was in the Planet of Dreams earlier. Norres's wings seemed a bit anemic."

George grinned. "Well, you know what they say about being green. According to the venerable Kermit, it ain't easy."

"That would wash if Norres were a frog instead of a dragon." Tory joined them, and it took all of Kristian's self-control not to throw herself into his arms. For a change he was wearing a standard NORStar uniform, open at the throat, with the sleeves rolled up past his wrists. He looked incredibly good, unbearably sexy and blessedly real. "Sounds as though our computerized projectors need a major overhaul," he noted, running a hand through his long hair.

"Just the ones in the Planet of Dreams." George slid a slender cigar between his lips and lit it. "Relatively speaking, they're the dinosaurs."

Kristian glanced up. "By whose standards? The space park's only been in operation for a little over a year."

"Things change fast in the world of computers." Gently, Tory brushed a lock of hair from her cheek, replacing it with the back of his fingers. "Are you feeling all right? You look—"

"Pale," she supplied wearily. "I know. I've already been through this with George."

"And gotten nowhere." Blowing out a stream of blue-grey smoke, George squinted at the colorful laser beams that were shooting across the night sky. "This looks good, but I'd better go check on the dinos. The Colonel can only do so much." He gave Kristian's cheek an affectionate tap. "Take care, huh? Running yourself into the ground isn't likely to help Simon at this point."

Would anything, Kristian wondered, smiling distractedly as George moved off. She waited until he was out of ear-shot then looked sideways at Tory whose hooded eyes, as usual, revealed nothing. "I went to see Morton tonight," she told him without preamble.

His lips twitched. "Should that surprise me?"

"It surprised me. Are you aware that he's living in another world, or to put it in simpler terms, that you have a crazy person for a partner?"

"Not crazy, just a little eccentric."

Hands on her hips, Kristian faced him. "Tory, I have an eighty-seven-year-old great aunt who sleeps on a cot in the attic of her Copenhagen home in the hope that the ghost of her sister, who fell out the window at the age of eighty-two, will come back to visit her. Don't talk to me about eccentric. No way is my sweet cookie-baking Aunt Elsa in the same league as your disappearing Jedi knight partner who, by the way, refers to the human race in the second and third person rather than the first."

Tory's eyes glinted. "You're trying to tell me something, right?"

"Good guess." Tossing her hair, she began walking away, confident that both Tory and Crux would follow. "To put it delicately, it sounds to me as though your partner thinks he's a little green man. Even setting that small detail aside, you might want to consider making a thorough search of his intergalactic suite."

Tory caught her easily, dropping a casual arm across her shoulders. "Okay, that detail aside, why would I want to search his suite?"

Briefly she explained about Morton's frenzied outburst, his silent vanishing act and finally the black helmet she'd discovered on the coat rack. "There's no way you can rationalize that one," she charged. "Green or not the man can't possibly own a motorcycle."

"He doesn't."

She allowed herself a smug smile. "I knew it. He's crazy."

"He's eccentric. And he owns three."

Kristian ground her back teeth, pushing Tory's arm from her shoulders in a spurt of irritation that stemmed more from a feeling of utter futility than from any true sense of anger. "Three motorcycles?" she repeated evenly.

"Two Harleys and a Honda. He keeps them at his house in Boulder City." Undaunted, Tory replaced his arm, urging her forward with very little effort. "Of course, he only rides them at night and only then in the desert."

"Of course." Kristian wondered idly whether anything anyone said or did from this moment on would surprise her. "Tell me, does he also wander around the park after hours wearing the aforementioned helmet?"

Tory shrugged. "I doubt it, but he might."

"If he does, then it's possible, too, that he might have strolled through the Cosmic Theater the night Simon was shot."

"And been the person the Colonel mistook for Darth Vader," Tory finished for her. "The answer is yes."

She sent him a sweetly sarcastic look. "In that case, you can defend him all you like, but the man's nuts."

"On the other hand," Tory continued his previous line of reasoning, "someone else could have been wearing that helmet as a disguise."

"To make Morton appear guilty?" She contemplated the idea for a long moment. "I see your point, but it's awfully thin."

"This whole conversation is thin—unless the person who shot Simon was wearing a motorcycle helmet."

"He wasn't. He also didn't intend to have an audience. Of that I'm certain. Therefore, he probably wouldn't have foreseen the need to frame anyone." The massive Space Walk pavilion rose up before her and she knit her brow in confusion. "Wait a minute. Why are we going in here?"

With a nod at two departing security guards, Tory drew Crux's remote control from his pocket, directing the dutiful little robot toward a large domed area that was all stars, interstellar dust clouds and deep space darkness. "He's been acting up lately. I don't want him running around the central complex bumping into computer panels or falling off ramps."

Kristian watched as Crux appeared to float through the Milky Way. "That reminds me, Priscilla was looking for Crater earlier tonight. Have you seen him anywhere?"

Tory returned the control to his pocket. "He was with George the last time I saw him."

Lilith, Evan, George—how could one small robot be in such great demand? Leaning against an electronic hatch, one of several that opened into a panoply of Space Walk air locks and shuttle pods, she motioned at the slightly less-versatile Crux. "Between the two of them, he's the dinosaur, isn't he?"

Tory grinned. "Yes, but you don't have to look so sad about it. Crux is the prototype. We're not planning to dismantle him."

"But isn't the Colonel working on a newer model?"

"Three of them, actually."

"That number's beginning to bother me," she muttered under her breath. "What will happen to Crux and Crater when the new robots are finished?"

Tory came up in front of her, his aquamarine eyes catching her shimmering green ones, his beautiful hands catching her waist, drawing her forward into the circle of his arms. "They're valuable. I imagine Evan'll want to sell them. Morton won't care, and George will undoubtedly go along with what I want."

She held her breath, willing the sudden rush of heat that suffused her body to abate. "And what's that?"

"To let you decide." His thumbs traced the line of her rib cage. "Why are you shivering?"

"I'm cold," she lied, not quite sure why. "The air conditioning must be turned up too high."

His smile was a trifle too knowing. "It's eighty degrees and climbing. The maintenance crew is coming in at midnight to give the system its weekly inspection."

So much for lame excuses. Eyes sparkling defiantly, she lifted her head. "Well, in that case, maybe you should—"

The teasing challenge she'd been about to issue died suddenly in her throat as her eyes caught a flash of something at the far end of the tubular hall. Fingers tightening on his wrists, she pushed herself upright with a jerk. "Tory, there's someone in there."

"In where?" He didn't seem the least bit concerned, but then he hadn't seen the face behind the shuttle pod door. For that matter, Kristian wasn't altogether certain she'd seen it herself, wasn't sure she dared believe it.

"I'm not—no, wait. There it is again."

"There what is again?"

"Who," she corrected, pulling out of his restraining grasp and starting down the long corridor at a run. "It's Simon."

"What?"

She heard the disbelief in his voice; it trailed her along the passageway, past safety-locked hatches, space suits and portholes that showed a panorama of shifting, swirling galactic nebulae. "Down here," she called over her shoulder. "I know I saw him."

She'd reached the end of the corridor now. The metallic hatch in front of her stood half-open, permitting only a partial view of the pod's interior. With one mighty tug, she dragged the heavy door back all the way and slipped inside.

"Simon?"

Something, perhaps a premonition that all was not as it should be, had her inching forward tentatively. The lights in the pod had been dimmed for effect to a low amber glow. It was difficult to distinguish the motionless figure in the NORStar uniform from the chair it sat in.

"Simon?" She whispered his name again, then jumped as a strong hand ensnared her wrist.

"It isn't Simon," Tory said flatly, reaching past her to grab the figure's limp arm. "It's a dummy. Someone's idea of a sick joke."

Only a joke? Kristian stared at the rubber mannequin that bore a striking resemblance to Simon Juniper and wished she could believe there wasn't a more sinister explanation.

"I saw him," she insisted stubbornly, averting her gaze from the bland, painted features. "He was moving."

Tory tossed the mannequin aside in a motion of disgust. "You don't have to convince me, Kristian. I believe you."

Although she couldn't imagine why he should, Kristian kept her mouth shut, rubbing her hands on her arms and wandering around the compact pod, which, oddly enough, hadn't been shut down. The sensation of tumbling languorously through space was strong, as was the feeling of apprehension that tugged at her. Was it possible that they'd been lured into this chamber?

While Tory squatted to inspect something on the mannequin's uniform, Kristian made a hasty but cautious inspection of the outer corridor. Nothing, she noted, expelling a relieved breath. Not a soul in sight. Just Crater who somehow managed to look forlorn as he wheeled down the long hallway alone.

A tiny smile crossed her lips, fading slightly as something clicked in her brain. "Tory, what's Crater doing here?"

An unintelligible response drifted back to her, but she was too busy peering around the passageway to try to decipher it. "Where did you come from?" she asked the robot instead. "More important, who did you come with?"

In a whir of circuits and joints, Crater glided to a smooth halt directly in front of her, as though he'd been programmed to do so. But that was absurd. Who would want to tamper with such a sophisticated piece of machinery? Then again, who would put a rubber dummy in a shuttle pod? Certainly Tory was half-right in his earlier assessment. Whoever was behind all this had to be sick. Or crazy.

"Come on, Crater," she said, giving him a preoccupied nudge. "Let's see if we can find a security guard. Tory, I'm going to take Crater into the star dome. If I can get him to move," she added in a puzzled undertone. "What's the matter with you?" she asked the obstinate robot. "Crux is the one who needs a remote control. You're supposed to respond to the touch of a hand."

From deep inside Crater's barrel chest a small hiss emerged. A minor malfunction, Kristian assumed, disregarding it. Then she did a double take. Rattlesnakes hissed, robots didn't. Neither did they glower. But that's precisely what Crater appeared to be doing.

Before her startled eyes, two metal arms slowly rotated upward to point at her. "You will listen to me," a horrible, nether-dimensional voice ordered.

Kristian's blood froze in her veins. It was Crater who'd spoken! But that was impossible. The robots could beep up a storm, but they couldn't talk.

"Listen!" Crater's alien-sounding command shot holes in that theory, and at the same time destroyed the last traces of her faith in anything mechanical.

"Tory..." His name came out in a disbelieving whisper. Eyes riveted to the now-advancing robot, she edged backward. "Tory, this thing is talking to me."

"You have interfered in matters that are none of your concern," Crater warned, crawling forward, forcing Kristian to back into the pod. "You will not interfere again."

"Tory..."

"I hear it." She felt him move up behind her. Fingers curling around her upper arm, he eased her to one side. "Where did he come from?"

"I have no idea. He was just—there." She swallowed unsteadily. "Why is that red light flashing on his head?"

"Someone's tampered with his programming, probably introduced a foreign object into his workings."

The picture of a gun or some equally nasty weapon raced through Kristian's mind, but, even discomfited, she recognized the absurdity of that thought. Intelligent though he was, Crater wouldn't be capable of using a gun. "Maybe he's possessed," she murmured as the robot rolled to a halt in the middle of the pod.

Tory treated her to a humorously mocking look before crouching to inspect Crater's outer casing. "You need a vacation, Kristian. The only thing possessing this little guy is a miniature compact disk." He flipped the chest panel open, pausing as he scanned the wires inside. "And a bomb. Damn!"

Kristian's head shot up. "Bomb? Did you say bomb?" The terrifying question had scarcely fallen from her lips when the pod's outer hatch suddenly began to swing shut.

Swearing volubly, Tory launched himself at the door—and very nearly caught it in time, she realized in a distant part of her mind. Far, far in the distance. At the moment only one thing registered with any real clarity.

Bomb! The word was a shriek in her head. Acting purely on instinct, she forced her trembling legs to function and stumbled across to the computerized panel that should have overridden any and all external commands. "Don't do this," she begged the unobliging master switch. "Don't go down now. At least give us an emergency line to the central complex."

Nothing. Only a series of dead clicks that succeeded in making the situation seem that much more dire.

The red light on Crater's head flashed. "Five minutes to detonation," the mechanized creature-voice intoned.

How could a machine sound as if it was laughing, she wondered frantically.

Still swearing, Tory flipped her his black communication box. "Try to contact George," he said. "If he's in the Plane of Dreams, he might be in range."

He might also be a murderer, Kristian wanted to point out, but didn't. Tory would never, not even for a moment, suspect his best friend of any involvement in this. Biting her lip hard, she punched George's code number, then Evan' and as a last resort, her own. June might have returned to the complex, and Kristian knew her communication box was sitting atop the cost reports beside her computer.

Head bent over the unresponsive device, she raised her eyes, regarding Tory, who was studying the array of circuits and wires inside Crater's chest. His calmness was deceptive but it helped. Bomb notwithstanding, she'd never be able to live with herself if she fell apart in front of him.

"Four minutes to detonation," the increasingly malicious voice announced. "Time to say your final prayers."

Kristian smacked the communication box against the lifeless control panel. "The signal must be blocked. I can't get through to anyone."

"Three minutes, thirty seconds to detonation." The mechanical voice warbled another warning. "Soon you'll be dead."

"So will you, Crater," she countered, using anger to fight her mushrooming terror. "One way or the other."

"Preferably the other," Tory dragged the robot into an area of marginally stronger light. "This isn't a complicated mechanism. I might be able to defuse it."

A burst of hope and adrenaline tore through her, and she dropped to her knees beside him. "Can you do it in three and a half minutes?"

"Three minutes to detonation," the robot contradicted.

He seemed to be taunting them now, but Kristian refused to listen. No little bucket of bolts was going to make her panic. She took a deep, calming breath. "Is there anything I can do to help?"

Carefully, Tory tapped a small metal plate with his finger. "You can tell me you have a tiny screwdriver in your pocket."

She could, but she'd be lying. Hastily, Kristian hunted through her pockets. Two quarters, a set of keys, an unmatched earring—and a bent bobby pin. Prying the plastic tip off with her thumbnail, she thrust it at him. "Will this work?"

"Two minutes, thirty seconds to detonation."

Tory grabbed Kristian's hand, placing it inside Crater's chest and pressing her fingers down on a collection of loose wires. "Try and keep them out of the way, and whatever you do, don't let him move."

"I won't."

"Some things never change," Tory murmured, deftly working at a tiny screw with the flat end of the bobby pin. "You always did have a 'won't' of iron. I seem to remember you saying the same thing the night you left me in Heidelberg."

Kristian tightened her grip both on the robot and on her rising fear. "You volunteered for a test flight, knowing we already had plans for the weekend," she reminded him. "You didn't care how I felt. All you ever cared about was your career."

His expression remained impassive. "All I *wanted* to care about was my career. It didn't work out that way."

"One minute, thirty seconds to detonation."

Kristian blocked out the mocking declaration. "Why are you telling me this?" she asked, not quite able to prevent herself from starting a mental countdown.

"I'm not sure." One screw clattered to the floor. "Maybe I just wanted you to know that it wasn't your life I was trying to control. It was mine."

"Maybe we were both just too young," Kristian murmured. Her fingers were slick with perspiration now. The air in the pod was becoming increasingly hot and stuffy. Unfortunately, even Tory's startling admission wasn't sufficient to obliterate the horror of the situation. "What are you staring at?" she asked.

He'd removed the metal plate from Crater's chest cavity and was currently probing the area behind it. "There are two wires attached to the detonator," he told her. "One red, one blue."

"One right, one wrong," she interpreted as an icy shiver crept along her spine. "What would happen if you disconnected both of them at once?"

"Thirty seconds to detonation," Crater disclosed evilly. "Time to die."

"He'll explode."

He'd do that in a moment, anyway. So would her heart if it didn't slow down. "Pull the red one," she croaked.

"Fifteen seconds to detonation," Crater warbled. "Fourteen, thirteen, twelve..."

Tory's fingers closed around the red wire.

"Pull it!"

"Ten, nine, eight..."

"Tory..."

"Five, four, three..."

He glanced at her, smiled recklessly, then dropped a quick kiss on her terrified lips.

And pulled the blue wire....

"BANG, THEY'RE DEAD," the man whispered. "I wonder how it feels."

His partner's lips curled in disgust, but she said nothing. Let him wonder. He'd have his answer soon enough.

She turned to Hubie Bittman, who stood just inside the solar corridor of the Constellation exhibit. Clouds of orange and magenta, gold and black billowed up around him. He looked uneasy, frightened in fact. Good. His fear would keep him in line, and for the moment that was all she needed.

"It's time," she told him and smiled when she realized he was staring uneasily at her partner who was staring dreamily at the North Star. "Now, Hubie," she added with just an edge of impatience. "I want you to make sure they're dead."

"But he just said—"

"I don't care what he said. If you value your life, you'll do as I say."

Hubie swallowed shakily. "You're that person, aren't you? The one everybody's talking about."

She maintained her even expression. "I wouldn't ask too many questions if I were you," she advised coldly, but it was hard to keep the smugness from her voice. "It doesn't matter who I am. Just do as you're told, and I'll let you live."

He seemed to relax a little and she had to swallow her rising laughter. These men were such fools. Didn't they know that they were nothing more than loose ends that had yet to be tied up? A smile touched her lips. Perhaps they didn't, at that.

But they would.

Chapter Twelve

"Two, one... It's over!" Crater warbled with apocalyptic certainty.

Was it? Dead silence reigned in the pod. Beyond the porthole, the asteroid Eros somersaulted past. The light on Crater's head continued to flash. Tory stared at the blue wire in his hand, at the robot in front of him, at Kristian, then released a slow breath that could have been a little steadier. Her nails were embedded in his forearm, a not unusual occurrence when she was frightened and loath to let it show.

Eyes fixed on the wire he held, she dug in deeper. "You didn't pull the red one."

The accusation in her voice brought an end to the silence in the pod and a flicker of amusement to Tory's lips. "I know."

"We could have been killed!"

"But we weren't." Giving her no chance to object, he hauled her into his arms and pulled her head onto his shoulder. She was trembling, a perfectly natural reaction under the circumstances, and while his own reaction had a slightly more needful edge to it, he made no attempt to push her. It was enough simply to hold her, to know that she was alive and willing for the moment to let him comfort her.

He ran his hand along her spine, turned his face into her hair and felt her slowly begin to relax against him. He loved her too much, he realized with a dry smile. Even more to-

ay than in the past, and that had been difficult enough to
ccept. Of course he was older now, less inclined to avoid
hose feelings he couldn't change—and perceptive enough
o know that for all her voluble protests to the contrary, she
vas, if not in love, still strongly attracted to him.

He felt the terrified beating of her heart, and the sweet
liant curves of her body as she stirred in his arms. A surge
f tenderness rose inside him when he thought of how things
ould have turned out. It was a protective response, tinged
vith a slow burning anger that had him hungering for ven-
eance.

Against whom, though? Not Crater, and certainly not a
ubber dummy. One of his partners, then? If Simon's mes-
age was to be believed the answer had to be yes. God only
new the signs of guilt were beginning to point more and
nore strongly in Morton's direction. Why then, Tory won-
lered, couldn't he make himself believe that Morton Nash
night be mixed up in any of this?

"Eccentric," he murmured and could have cheerfully
itten his tongue out when Kristian lifted her head from his
houlder.

"You think Morton's behind this?" She sounded shaken
out alert, as though her thoughts had been running along
hose lines.

Tory didn't fight her withdrawal, at least not physically,
lthough his mind and body both resented the imprudent
nuttering that now literally had her regarding him at arm's
ength. "Morton's behavior tends to be a bit more deviant
han Evan's," he conceded, torn between a desire to haul
ler back into his arms and a more sapient urge to get them
ooth the hell out of here.

A tiny creak from Crater made the decision for him. They
vere sitting on a powder keg that still had the potential to
olow them into the next dimension. No murderer with half
a brain would assume that Crater had exploded on sched-
ile and go on about his business. Someone, possibly a sac-

rificial lackey, was bound to show up sooner or later, and Tory preferred not to be caught in a defensive posture.

"Maybe Morton's working with an accomplice," Kristian theorized, warming to her subject with the enthusiasm of a modern-day Sherlock Holmes. "June's awfully protective of him. Then again, maybe he's formed a secondary partnership with Evan. And there's always the chance that he's talked Priscilla into helping him do whatever it is he might be doing. After all, she is his goddaughter."

"She was also in the Cosmic Theater the night Simon was shot." Tory released her with tremendous reluctance, letting his arms fall to his sides. "I can vouch for that one personally. Besides, I didn't say I thought Morton was guilty; I simply said he was less predictable than Evan."

Kristian pushed the hair from her no longer pale cheeks. "The word you used was deviant, and it happens to be an apt description."

"In your opinion and after a single offhand encounter. Give the guy a break, Kristian. He lives in the dark. He's bound to be a little odd."

"Odd, yes, but not extraterrestrial." She crossed to the control panel, giving Crater a wide, mistrustful berth, and started poking at the dead buttons, leaving Tory to ponder the limited alternatives. "Are you sure Morton's photosensitive?" she asked thoughtfully.

"I've never dragged him into the direct sunlight to find out, if that's what you mean."

"I was thinking more along the lines of a medical report. Have you ever seen any of them?"

"No, but I've talked to his doctor a few times."

"And?"

Shrugging, Tory resumed his crouch, drawing the remote control unit from the pocket of his uniform. "And nothing. The man's a respected physician."

"Respected by whom?"

"Probably not by the criminal underworld. You're wasting your energy, Kristian. First, let's concentrate on getting out of here, then you can jump to all the conclusions you'd like.'' She could also jump back into his arms, he added on a more libidinous note; however, he wasn't going to count on that simply happening. It would take patience and a great deal of persuasion to overcome her not inconsiderable resistance. Fortunately, he had both those qualities in abundance.

He felt rather than saw her kneel down beside him. "What are you doing with that?'' she asked in a skeptical voice.

Using the tip of her bobby pin, he unfastened the screws that held the remote together. "I'm going to try and adjust the control.''

"To Crater's frequency?'' A shudder ran through her. "Don't you think that's a bit risky?''

"It's very risky. And next to impossible. Crux is well within range. If we can get a signal through to him, he might be able to help us escape.''

Amazingly enough, she smiled at him, a smile of genuine amusement that caused the bobby pin to slip and gouge a hole in his palm. "I just knew those mendacious tendencies of yours would come in handy some day. I've always believed that you and George would one day wind up hot wiring the gates of hell as easily as you did every security gate **on** every air force base you were assigned to in your eight-year careers.''

That was a double entendre if ever he'd heard one. Grinning slightly, Tory dropped another kiss on her unsuspecting lips and shoved the revamped control at her. "When the chance to test that belief rolls around, I'll make sure you have a front row seat. In the meantime, pretend you're putting the screws to me and see if you can coax Crux out of the star dome while I disconnect his evil stepbrother.''

With a final glare at Crater and a more guarded look at him, she carried the control over to the hatch. "What is it you have in mind, anyway? Crux can't open this door. For one thing, he's not tall enough to reach the outer panel.''

"He doesn't have to be." Unwilling to fiddle with the individual wires in Crater's exposed chest, Tory ripped them all free of their connections. "What time is it?"

She stared at him in aggravation. "Who cares?"

"I do."

"You would. It's 10:29."

"Is he out of the star dome yet?"

"Tory, if I could see through these walls, chances are I'd be able to walk through them, as well. For all I know, Crux could be whizzing out the main entrance even as we speak."

"Somehow I doubt that." He propelled Crater into the far corner of the pod. "Push the ALT button, and bring him toward the air locks."

"I'll do my best," she said, then looked around as a high-pitched scream suddenly penetrated the heavy door. "What's that? It sounds like an animal in pain."

"Try a robot on alert."

Kristian stared at the box in her hand. "You managed that with a bent bobby pin?"

"You said it yourself, I have a way with wires." Tory came up behind her in time to see Crux wheeling full tilt along the empty corridor. "Slow him down a bit," he suggested. "You're not on the open road, and contrary to popular belief, robots aren't indestructible. Crux would make a decidedly ineffective battering ram."

"Maybe," she retorted with false geniality. "But I'll bet you'd make a fine one. Why don't you take a shot at it?"

A smile pulled at the corners of Tory's mouth. "Nice try, but it won't be necessary." He hooked an arm about her waist, bringing her back against him just as the pod's door swung open on its electronically controlled hinges. Reaching down, he plucked the remote from Kristian's hand and depressed the alert button that had sent Crux into a screeching frenzy. The mechanical screams subsided instantly, leaving only a bewildered security guard in front of them to be dealt with.

"I thought Crux might be trying to tell me something," the man hastened to explain. He flapped a hand at the dutiful little robot. "I was doing my thirty minute walk-through when he came shooting out of the star dome and started spinning around in circles and screaming like a stuck pig. I thought he'd gone crazy for a minute there."

Tory nudged Kristian out of the pod ahead of him. "Crux is fine," he said mildly. "It's Crater who's not working properly."

The guard peered past his arm. "Looks kinda dead to me. Maybe he needs a recharge."

"He needs more than that," Tory muttered under his breath. "Thanks for getting us out."

"Out? You mean you were—?"

"Locked in," Kristian stated plainly. Her smile was completely guileless. "No doubt someone's idea of a joke."

Tory shook his head as the guard opened his mouth to question them further. "Don't ask," he advised, his tone affable but firm. "Just seal the hatch and post one of your men in the hall for the night. I don't want anybody going in or out of this pod, and I especially don't want anyone touching Crater unless Kristian or I authorize it. When you're finished, take Crux over to the Colonel's workshop and leave him there."

"Yes, sir." The man nodded, then twisted his head around to follow Tory's suddenly intent gaze down the corridor. "Is . . . something wrong?" he asked hesitantly.

"Nothing important."

The bland denial was good enough to convince the security guard, but Tory could tell by the gleam deep in Kristian's green eyes that she wasn't as easily fooled. With an obligatory nod, he slid his hand to the base of her spine and gave her a little push.

"What is it?" she demanded the second the guard could no longer hear them. "Did you see someone? Was it Simon?"

"Not even close," Tory murmured, making a covert sweep of the air locks. "Whoever it was, he had blue skin and pointed ears."

Her eyes widened in surprise. "Dracona's minion?"

"More likely a murderer's minion."

She concealed a tremor of fear as she glanced into the thankfully deserted star dome. "We're not out of this yet, are we?"

"Not quite," he said softly, taking her hand in his. "We still have to make it out of the park."

SIMON'S KILLER WAS WATCHING. Kristian could feel a pair of beady snake eyes staring at her from every black shadow, every misshapen patch of darkness they passed. And there was an inordinate amount of darkness, especially in the Martian Terrace Restaurant, through which Tory insisted they take a shortcut.

"I suppose it would be asking too much to hope that Scotty might have our coordinates," she said after banging her knee on a chair that someone had conveniently left in the middle of what she assumed was an aisle.

"You can probably rule it out." Tory's voice came back to her in a wryly humorous drawl that didn't for one second diminish the insistent pull he was exerting on her arm, or the purposefulness of his long stride. "Let me know if you see anything out of the ordinary."

"I'll let you know when I see anything at all." Kristian groped blindly for the counter in the massive kitchen, smacked her elbow on a chopping block and wailed a softly whispered, "Tory, for God's sake, what's going on at this park? We've got aliens following us, robots threatening us, dead people haunting us and a crazy person who thinks he's E.T. living in the penthouse suite of the Pallas Hotel. And that's just tonight's update." She let him drag her through the rear door. "You don't think Simon could be alive and mixed up in all of this, do you? No, of course not," she answered her own question. "That would be stupid. If that were the case, why would he leave you a message? Even if the shooting was some kind of weird setup, he couldn't possibly have known that I'd be coming back to my office at eleven o'clock at night. Still, he always needed money. Maybe he finally found a way to get some."

"And maybe the person you thought was Simon was actually someone dressed up to look like him."

"Maybe." Kristian wished she could convince herself of that. Tilting her head back she stared at the building in their path. "Why are we going into the Planet of Dreams?"

Tory tightened his grip on her hand. "Because the lights are on and George might still be around."

Around and lurking like a hungry jackal in the shadows, Kristian added silently, keeping her mouth clamped firmly shut. She really didn't want to believe that George could be involved in any of this. And luckily she didn't have to. Right now Morton seemed like a much more viable suspect than either George or Evan.

"Cimmeron, Cressida, Abbadan, Shantar.... Well now, I know that's not right."

Kristian heard the Colonel muttering to himself as they entered the Planet of Dreams' spectacular Electric Swamp. Tongues of white lightning forked across a black-and-crimson sky, illuminating the malformed trees and all the thick, twisted vines that hung from the heavy boughs. Like boa constrictors, she thought, her fear dissipating somewhat despite the eerie setting.

Interspersed among the mossy red trunks and thick brown creepers, a small group of pandits, droopy-eared bunnies with gossamer, jewel-colored wings, played an airborne game of tag, while below them, lounging against the base of a shimmering sparkle tree, a crafty-featured dragon used the streaking lightning bolts to sharpen his already razor-sharp claws. His bored yawn ended with a crackle of orange flames and a world-weary flick of his tongue, which just happened to nab him a passing swamp gnat.

"I see Peverell's his usual haughty self," Kristian observed, almost able to forget the horror of the past hour. Peverell, with his superior attitude and lethargic dragon mannerisms, was one of her favorite holograms.

Tory released her hand, only to drop his arm securely across her shoulders. "Figures you'd like a snotty dragon," he remarked, then raised his voice. "Evening, Colonel. Is George here?"

One elegant, faintly ironic white brow arched. "Hello, Tory, Kristian. If you're referring to your partner, I haven't seen him all night."

"He must have gotten sidetracked." Tory glanced around and at the same time managed to tug Kristian closer to his maddeningly warm body. "What about Evan?"

"I'm afraid not."

"Morton?" Kristian tried, disregarding the pressure Tory's arm immediately exerted on her neck and the feel of his hip bone where it dug into her backside.

The Colonel merely chuckled. "Not him, either. George and Evan might have slipped past me, but I'm certain I would have noticed if Morton had put in an appearance." A slender hand rose to adjust his glasses. "If I might ask, what are you two doing here? It must be close to eleven now."

"We've had a few problems tonight," Tory told him, his hand poised to cover Kristian's mouth at the first sign of an unrequested color commentary. "One of them with Crater. How hard would it be to rewire the robot for speech?"

Lips pursed, the Colonel stroked his chin. "Oh, I shouldn't think such a thing would be too terribly difficult." He blinked, then looked from Tory to Kristian and back again, as though realizing belatedly what he'd been asked. "Are you telling me that Crater has been reprogrammed for speech without my approval?"

"Without anyone's approval," Tory confirmed. "And it gets worse. Someone also rigged him to explode."

"My little Crater exploded?"

Kristian honestly thought the Colonel might have a heart attack on the spot. Ducking out from under Tory's arm, she hastened to the older man's side. "He's fine," she promised, patting his thin hand. "Tory defused him."

"And locked him away for the night." Tory imprisoned Kristian once again, this time by sliding an arm around her waist. With his head, he motioned the Colonel out of the Electric Swamp, into the purple-and-gray mists of Beldam Dracona's underworld realm. "I'll see that he's brought to your workshop first thing tomorrow morning. For the moment, I want you to go home. The holograms can wait for George to fix them."

The Colonel sighed heavily. "Perhaps you're right. This isn't a job for a toy maker. I seem to be missing a pandit, Dracona's looking rather grainy, her minions are more green than blue, and to top it all off, now you tell me that someone's been tampering with Crater. This has simply not been my day."

"Mine either," Kristian echoed in a fervent undertone.

She did a double take as they passed Dracona's saber-toothed cave entrance. As usual, all the beldam's minions, trolls and toadies were gathered in a slothful cluster, milling about, antennae bobbing, pointy ears rotating, spouting nonsense from their slimy mouths. One of the older toadies, Brutus, looked particularly crabby. He sat on a boulder outside Dracona's cave, banging a magic glitter staff on the purple ground. While one three-fingered hand plied the staff, the other stroked his pet parvine, a vicious cross between an aardvark and a porcupine. But it wasn't any of those things that caught Kristian's eye and made her swing her head around for a second look. It was the sight of Brutus's third hand that caused her blood to run cold.

She stopped dead, shock and a horrible sense of doom slashing through her. Toadies only had two hands! And neither of those hands carried guns.

"Tory, look out!"

Her warning cry came a split second too late. From behind Brutus's stumpy, holographic back, one of Dracona's minions surged upward. Taking careless aim, he pulled the trigger, then vaulted over the boulder, a growl emanating from deep in his blue-skinned throat.

"Get out of here!" In a single lithe move, Tory shoved Kristian and the Colonel through a hologram of the evil beldam herself.

He must have literally dodged the bullet, Kristian realized gratefully, clawing for something to support her as she stumbled over a pile of purple rocks. What she found was the Colonel who'd banged into the side of Dracona's cave and was struggling to regain his balance.

Her fear for Tory's life was too great to permit any other thoughts. "Go," she hissed, righting herself and snatching up a gnarled pepper-stick. "Find security. And turn off the holograms."

For an older man, the Colonel's reaction time was amazingly swift, though his hearing seemed to have deserted him. Kristian knew he was directly behind her when she wheeled around and crawled back through the folds of Dracona's ragged shroud. However, it was hardly a point to be quibbled over with the uniformed minion making a snarling lunge for Tory.

"No!" The scream burst hotly from her throat, and for a blessedly long moment the minion faltered.

Grunting, she drew back and swung the pepper-stick with all her might. It struck the creature across his beefy shoulder blades with a whack solid enough to knock the breath from his lungs. Not surprisingly to Kristian, Tory managed to shoot her a thin-lipped look of anger as he grabbed the minion's gloved wrists and forced them upward.

A second bullet blasted from the gun's barrel, lodging itself in the metal rafters. Using the pepper-stick, Kristian took another swing at the leathery-skinned head. Whoever this creature was, he had a good seventy pounds on Tory—

and biceps that threatened to burst the seams of his navy blue sleeves.

"Here." She thrust her speckled stick at the Colonel who'd picked up and launched a handful of purple stones at the wide back in front of him. "Keep hitting him."

A whisper-fine rain began to fall as Kristian scrambled onto Brutus's boulder. The holograms responded by huddling closer together and raising their studded fists to the angry heavens. Unfortunately, they were venting their rage in a haphazard circle that encompassed both Tory and the now-sweating minion.

"Get the gun," Tory growled, obviously resigned to her participation in the struggle.

After several futile attempts to grab the correct set of upraised arms, Kristian's fumbling fingers closed around a pair of glove-encased wrists. Above them loomed the gun; below them lurked the blue-skinned mask. Feelings of anger and resentment and plain old spite erupted inside her. Damn this hideous creature, whoever he was. He didn't deserve another second of anonymity.

Snarling, she brought her hand down and snatched the mask from his head. Then felt her breath hiss out at the beet-red face she encountered.

"Bittman," Tory grated, wrenching hard on the security guard's visibly tortured arms. "You slimy bastard."

A somewhat more obscene description flitted through Kristian's head, but she said nothing. With her nails, she raked at the cloth gloves. Beside her, the Colonel slammed the pepper-stick into Hubie's back, while Tory, an icy smile curving his lips, gave the wrists he held a final painful twist. Eyes cold, expression unrelenting, he brought his booted foot up, catching the stocky guard in the most sensitive part of his body and causing him to drop like a rock to his knees.

Hubie's mouth lolled open. He knelt on the purple ground for a long moment, swaying back and forth, making no sound at all. Suddenly, his eyes popped in their sockets. "It's a hologram," he gurgled, then let out a single

strangled cry and slithered into an ignominious heap a
Brutus's wart-covered feet.

By some stroke of luck he'd released the gun before h
fell. It landed in Kristian's hands, startling her, but not s
much that she let it slip from her grasp. Holding tight to th
snub barrel, she slid from the boulder and staggered int
Tory's waiting arms.

Cheek resting against her hair, he took the gun an
shoved it into his uniform belt. Kristian stole a quick side
ways look. Although Hubie seemed disinclined to move, sh
still didn't trust him. Evidently, neither did the Colonel. H
kept the pepper-stick pressed to the base of the fallen man'
spine while he straightened his vest and tie and smoothed th
waves of his thick white hair.

"It would appear that you immobilized him, Tory," h
noted with characteristic diplomacy. "A good shot, I mus
say. Not in the RAF handbook, but a highly efficaciou
tactic nonetheless. Shall I call security?"

"Call the night-duty officer at the central complex,"
Kristian interceded, the words muffled against Tory's broa
shoulder. "Tell him to find George and Evan if he can."

"What about this one?" The Colonel prodded Hubie'
inert form. "Shouldn't we bind and gag him?"

"We should hang him upside down from the rafters,"
Tory put in mildly. "Go on, Colonel. Get us some help
We'll take care of Hubie Bittman."

Through a veil of holographic rain, Kristian stared dow
at the massive security guard. For someone who should hav
been writhing in agony, he was remarkably still. "Wimp,"
she accused in disgust. "Who faints from a little kick?"

"Only a woman would ask that question," Tory said, hi
voice rich in meaning. Pressing a kiss to her temple, he re
leased her and squatted next to where Hubie lay. "Colonel
you'd better call Jon Hayes, too. And shut off the holo
grams."

For the first time in what felt like days, Kristian drew
semisteady breath. Sinking down, she rested her bac

against Brutus's boulder and let her gaze stray to the Electric Swamp where Peverell was idly picking his teeth with one newly sharpened claw.

"What did Hubie mean when he said, 'It's a hologram?'" she wondered out loud, then shook her head. "You know, Tory, the moment this is all over, I've decided I'm going to take a nice long vacation in some wonderfully remote spot where there are no holograms, where people still believe the moon is made of green cheese and where murder is considered a four-letter word." When no response was forthcoming, she switched her attention to Hubie, who still hadn't moved a muscle. "Don't you think you should tie him up or something? He's bound to come around sooner or later."

"I don't think so," Tory said slowly, withdrawing his fingers from Hubie's thick bull neck. "This man isn't unconscious. He's been shot."

"Shot!" Kristian scrambled unsteadily to her knees. "What are you talking about? Hubie was the only person with a gun."

"Not the only person. Someone shot him in the chest."

Her heart pounded against her ribs. "Is he—" she swallowed the lump in her throat "—dead?"

Nodding grimly, Tory reached out and grabbed her into his arms. "Whoever did this is a marksman. Hubie Bittman was dead before he hit the floor."

Chapter Thirteen

"I can't take this," Kristian moaned to June who'd just strolled into her office. It was three o'clock Saturday afternoon on what should have been her weekend off. After an all-night session with the police, Kristian was sprawled facedown on the sofa, unable to move, much less work. "There's a dead man in the county morgue, a million plainclothes cops wandering around the space park and a turncoat robot with a bomb in his chest sitting in the Colonel's workshop."

June pushed a cup of coffee between her limp fingers. "Crater's in the workshop," she agreed. "But the bomb's gone." She settled into a buttery leather armchair and propped her feet up on the low coffee table. "So where's your heavenly male shadow?"

Kristian buried a groan in the sofa cushions. In one part of her mind or another, she'd been thinking about Tory all the previous night and most of today. She didn't want to do it anymore. Didn't want to recall how safe he made her feel, how cosseted and protected in spite of the gruesome nightmare that continued to unravel around them both. It was just too confusing.

"If you mean Tory, I have no idea," she lied.

"I do. He's locked in the conference room with George and Evan." Lilith's wooden monotone drifted inward from the open doorway. "Can I have a word with you, Kristian? Alone?"

Without raising her head, Kristian murmured a blunt "Certainly. Go away, June."

"Go where? I'm not even supposed to be here today."

"Fine. Go home, then. Better yet, go tell Morton everything that's happened since last we spoke."

"He already knows."

Of course he did, Kristian acknowledged, forcing her eyes open. The question was, how did he know? Through report or involvement? "In that case, take the rest of the afternoon off."

"Well, I suppose I could rent 'Krull' and—"

"Excuse me," Lilith interrupted stiffly. "But if you don't mind, I have a great deal of work to do."

"Trust me, we don't mind at all." It was Priscilla who made the blithe comment as she stuck her head into the office. "We're wanted upstairs, Kristian."

"We, who?" June inquired.

"All of us who are working this weekend when by rights we should be stretched out under a palm tree, sipping a banana daiquiri."

Somehow Kristian found the energy to drag herself from the sofa. "Okay, you and June go ahead. Lilith and I will be right up."

Priscilla shrugged. "Better make it snappy. I saw a tray of hot cinnamon Danish fly past a few minutes ago. You know how long they'll last with George and Tory in the room."

Kristian waved her off. "I know, five minutes." She carried the still-steaming coffee to her desk and fell into her padded chair. Lilith's expression was stern, her posture rigid, her lips compressed to an almost nonexistent line. Not good signs, but then with Lilith, positive body language was hardly commonplace. "You wanted to talk to me?" she prompted, eyeing the woman's large lab-coat pockets warily. She'd already decided that she didn't trust anyone at the park, and guns could reside all too easily in pockets like that.

"Yes." Lilith squared her thin shoulders. "About Anita Brace."

Kristian came perilously close to choking on a mouthful of coffee. She swallowed instead, summoned a congenial smile and asked, "You mean you know something about her death?"

"No, I mean her death is bothering me."

Kristian kept her expression blank but eased her chair surreptitiously closer to the telephone. "Bothering you in what way?"

Fists clenched, Lilith paced the floor. "Isn't it obvious? She's no longer here at NORStar. She's dead."

"You're upset over her death?" Kristian hated to think where this conversation was leading. She tugged on the telephone cord. "Was Annette Barrows a friend of yours?"

"Certainly not." Lilith sounded affronted. "She was a computer programmer. A very good computer programmer."

"She might also have been a computer thief. What's your point?"

"I just told you." Jerkily, Lilith jammed her fists into her pockets. "She's dead. Gone. Not coming back."

"So's Hubie Bittman," Kristian said evenly. And Simon, she added to herself. Eyes on the large patch pockets of Lilith's lab coat, she asked again, "What's your point?"

"I need a replacement."

"I beg your pardon?"

Lilith's face was a complete deadpan. "I need another programmer."

"That's it?" Kristian stared at her, incredulous. "That's what you wanted to talk about?"

"Is it a problem?"

"Yes—no." Maybe she'd accidentally stepped into the Twilight Zone, Kristian reflected, too dazed to try and understand Lilith's dispassionate thought processes. "I'll speak with Marie in personnel first thing Monday morning."

"I'd appreciate that. Oh, and with regard to Crater..."

"Yes?"

"I heard he was...indisposed?"

Kristian wondered if she detected a note of smugness in the woman's otherwise stilted tone. "That's one way of putting it. He had a bomb in his chest."

"Yes, I heard that, too. How fortunate that it didn't explode."

"I thought so."

"It would appear there's something unwholesome going on in the park."

"You're just realizing that now?"

Lilith's eyes hardened perceptibly behind her glasses. "Don't underestimate me, Kristian. I might prefer not to associate with humans, but that doesn't mean I'm blind to what they do." And setting her lips in a dour smile, she turned on her heel and marched from the office.

"IT'S VERY SIMPLE when you stop to think about it, Tory. We've been invaded by beings from another star system."

Grinning slightly, Tory sat Kristian down on the edge of his double bed and tugged off her ankle boots. She was exhausted and making absolutely no sense, but he was enjoying listening to her babble. "Invaded, huh?" He moved to sit beside her. "You mean the planet, or just the space park?"

Eyes half closed, she swayed against him as he began unbuttoning her uniform. "They infiltrated NORStar first," she said, stifling a yawn, "but they're spreading. Morton's one of them. Lilith's another. God knows how many more will follow."

"What about me?"

"No, you're too arrogant to be an extraterrestrial." She offered no resistance as Tory slid the uniform from her shoulders. In one smooth move, he lifted her hips and pulled the material down over her long legs, leaving nothing but a lacy cotton bra and a pair of matching high-cut briefs to cover her. "Cops and aliens and maybe a homicidal secret seller." Her head fell onto his shoulder. "People have no idea what they are really getting into when they pass through NORStar's main gates." She pushed the hair from her face. "Are the FBI agents still looking for Telstar?"

"Not wholeheartedly. They're sticking with the current theory that Telstar is in fact dead and that Annette Barrows was mixed up in an unrelated computer theft."

"What do you think?"

His grin widened a bit. What he was thinking at that moment had nothing to do with any code-named seller of high-tech secrets. However, if he answered her truthfully, tired or not, she might very well knock him off the bed and halfway to Pluto for good measure.

Keeping a supporting arm around her waist, he drew down the bedspread and navy blue top sheet. "I think we're dealing with Telstar," he said calmly.

"And a computer theft," she murmured sleepily, curling up on her side and wrapping her arms around the feather pillows as he tucked the covers around her.

"That too," he agreed softly. An indulgent smile played at the corners of his mouth at her innocent expression. "Close those gorgeous green eyes, Cinderella. The ball's over for now. It's after midnight."

In actual fact, it was only a little after 6:00 p.m., but as neither of them had had any sleep for close to thirty-six hours, it might as well have been the dead of night. Dead being the operative word, he reflected, letting his fingers trail a dangerously tempting path along her collar bone and lower to the firm swell of her breast visible above the top of her soft-pink bra.

He resisted at the last second and settled for kissing her cheek. She was sound asleep already and likely to remain in that state for several hours—which was just as well, since awake she was bound to go looking for trouble. Not consciously, but that's how it would turn out.

There was a murderer at NORStar Center, an as yet unknown commodity who apparently had no qualms about killing people. And Tory knew Kristian was a very definite target. For that matter, so was he. They'd bought a little time by defusing Crater last night, but nobody's luck lasted forever, especially when that luck was completely blind.

Telstar. Gut instinct told Tory they were dealing with the code named middle man—or woman as the case may be. What his instincts couldn't tell him was why Hubie Bittman had been the only person shot last night. Why not kill him and Kristian, as well? Had the Colonel's presence in the Planet of Dreams been significant in some as yet undetermined way? Could he have shot Hubie?

Not unless he had the power to be in two places at once, Tory thought, recalling the relative positions of everyone involved. The trajectory of the shot indicated that it had been fired from the direction of the Ionian Rain Forest, Norres's densely foliated home. No, the Colonel hadn't killed Hubie, and he'd been on the far side of the park the night Simon was shot. Someone else had pulled the trigger in both instances. Someone—but not one of his partners.

"It's a hologram...."

Hubie's dying words came back to him. Had the killer been hiding behind Peverell or one of the other holographic images? Had Hubie seen the fatal shot coming? Possibly, but if so, the knowledge had died with him.

Running a tired hand over his face, Tory stood, shaking the unpleasant thoughts away and looking down at the woman sleeping so soundly in his bed. Damn, but he loved her. Loved her temper and her stubbornly defiant attitude and the genuine feelings she had for those people she considered true friends.

Did she think of him as a friend? Probably not, he decided, stripping off his uniform and kicking it aside as he closed the heavy curtains. She probably wouldn't like what he was about to do, either, but he'd deal with her cries of outrage later. Right now, he was exhausted, mentally, physically and emotionally. An earthquake might wake him once he fell asleep, but little else would get through. And that wasn't a risk he was willing to take. If someone broke in and tried to hurt her, he wanted to be within strangling distance, not off dreaming lustful thoughts in another room.

She made a tiny sound that might have been protest or approval as he stretched out beside her on the too-narrow mattress. Head resting on one bent arm, he stared up at the ceiling and let his mind wander where it chose. Naturally it chose Kristian, and for a few tantalizing minutes he drifted into a past he could still recall as if it had happened only yesterday.

He was in a misty version of Baden-Baden with Kristian and in the process of exploring her beautiful body with his mouth and hands when something slammed down hard across his throat, momentarily cutting off his air supply. He came awake in an instant, ripping away the arm that had landed on his neck.

At first he thought Simon's murderer had tried to bludgeon him and missed. Then he realized who the arm belonged to, and he smiled a little as another part of the past came back to him, a lesson he'd learned very quickly after waking up one morning with a black eye.

Kristian was a restless sleeper with a brutal right cross and a kick that would have been more than enough to deter most men. Unfortunately, most men would never know what they were missing.

Careful not to disturb her, Tory curled his fingers around her wrists and turned onto his side, wrapping his arms and body around her and fitting her securely against him. "Time out, slugger," he murmured against her hair. "Save your punches for Simon's killer."

She mumbled something but offered no objection, and he forced himself to relax a bit as she snuggled closer. It wasn't as difficult as he might have anticipated. His mind was a jumble of half-formed thoughts and images, some provocative, some provoking, others almost too gruesome to contemplate. But he had to consider them, had to accept the fact that Telstar wanted them dead.

And that wasn't the worst of it. There was an even more bitter acknowledgement to be made, one that had him groaning deep in his throat when it finally fought its way into his mind.

If Simon's message had any merit at all, one of Tory's partners might very well be in league with Telstar. Hell, for all he knew one of them might even be Telstar. And Telstar was notorious for betraying partners.

THE WOMAN snapped her fingers impatiently as she paced the stuffy storeroom floor. What was holding him up now? It was after 1:00 a.m. and they had an inordinate amount of work to do in a ridiculously short space of time.

She whirled around at the sound of the door being stealthily opened. "It's about time," she complained when her partner emerged from the shadows of a dozen slatted wooden crates. "Is everything ready?"

He nodded. "There shouldn't be any problem. Tory's gone home, and the police are mostly watching the Planet of Dreams and the Central Complex."

With her teeth, she pulled on a pair of leather gloves. "Let's go, then. This is getting too messy. I don't like it."

"Neither do I."

"But not for the same reason, my friend. I only want everything to be tied up neatly. You're squeamish, afraid of getting blood on those lily-white hands of yours."

"Unlike you," he said quietly. "I know you shot Hubie."

She stared at him. "Now there's a real news flash."

"That's not what I mean. I know you killed him. What I don't understand is why you didn't shoot everyone in the exhibit when you had the chance."

"Believe me, it would've been my pleasure," she said, her upper lip curling at the memory. "Unfortunately, my gun jammed. I could only get off the one shot. Hubie had to go first. We'll simply have to think of something more inventive."

His brows rose. "More inventive than an exploding robot?"

"Yes, well, something more terminal, then. Besides, the robot didn't explode, did he? And that musclebound ape I hired to help us only succeeded in making matters worse. No, we need a new plan. Luckily I have the beginnings of a brilliant one."

"Will it get us the information we want?"

"In due time," she said, shoving a bundle of clothing at him. "First we're going to muddy things up, make them squirm a bit. Then we'll finish it off."

"How?"

"I'll let you know when I've decided," she lied, but it was hard to bite back the laughter that swelled inside her.

He didn't know it yet, but his usefulness to her had just about reached an end. One day more, maybe two, and their partnership would be dissolved. Permanently.

TELSTAR WAS CHASING HER! Kristian could hear the sounds of pursuit as she raced down an endless cosmic corridor. Only it wasn't a human crooning her name over and over again; it was the real Telstar, or at least a personified version of it.

Why was a satellite chasing her? Why couldn't she outrun it? In her panicked mind's eye, she looked down and saw the reason. There was a mechanical arm snaked about her waist, a skinny little green thing that got tighter the harder she struggled.

Where was Tory? How could he have left her alone to battle this wretched mechanical monster? What did Telstar want with her anyway?

She pounded on the metallic arm with her fists, but stopped abruptly when the satellite gave a high-pitched yelp, yanked its wiry, green tentacle away and whizzed past her on an erratic course similar to that of a deflating balloon.

"Stop hitting me."

A man's familiar voice overrode Telstar's angry howls, and glancing down, Kristian realized the arm she was pounding on belonged to Tory. "How did you do that?" she demanded, relieved and inexplicably excited by his touch.

"I haven't done anything, Kristian." She felt herself being pulled backward until she was pressed against his tautly muscled body. "Not yet, anyway."

The words were a silky promise in her ear, surreal in some ways, all-too-real in others. Where was she, she wondered in confusion. Not running through the Milky Way—that much was certain. The darkness lingered, but someone had stolen the stars. Either that or she'd fallen into a black hole.

"Just like Alice," she said dreamily. Smiling to herself, she twisted around in Tory's arms and was simultaneously disconcerted and fascinated when her hands encountered nothing but a wall of smooth bare skin.

Something was definitely wrong. Or wonderfully right. She couldn't decide which. Someone's lips were also nuzzling her neck, making her skin tingle and creating a delicious warm spot that started in the region of her chest then spread like wildfire to a much more needful part of her body.

"Come on, Kristian." Again Tory's voice came to her, a gentle persuasion that seemed to spring from the twilight shadows of her own mind. "Time to wake up."

"No." Her protest was a fractious grumble. She didn't want to wake up, didn't want to fight with Tory or with herself anymore. This was the fantasy she'd been longing for, that blissfully erotic moment when her memories took control, blotting out everything except the warm German nights she'd spent wrapped in his strong arms.

"Yes." His tone was more insistent now, though not quite forceful enough to slice through the fiery sensations that had begun to dance around inside her.

She'd reached a delightfully somnolent state, a heavenly place that existed somewhere between sleep and wakefulness. Every one of her senses seemed to have been magnified a hundredfold. The lightest brush of his lips across her skin sent waves of desire pulsing through her. She felt his breath on her face, the heat of his body, the touch of his hands through the lacy fabric of her bra.

The shadows around her began to shift. In the darkness, her fingers found the nape of his neck and pulled. She neither expected nor received any resistance from him. He let his head be drawn down, let her seek out and explore his mouth until she was kissing him with an eager abandon that had the power to rip away the last vestiges of her slumber.

Shocked, she tore her mouth from his. Her breath was coming in jerky spasms, her lips were damp and slightly swollen, her mind a roil of tangled thoughts and images. The transition came with remarkable swiftness, making real the dream she'd both feared and coveted most. She was in bed with Tory, and for the life of her she couldn't remember how she'd gotten there.

He was smart enough to have hooked a restraining leg over her knees before propping himself up on his elbow to stare lazily down at her. "It's about time," he noted, his voice rich with amusement and a host of other emotions she was too jolted and bemused to identify. "For a while there, I thought you were going to seduce me in your sleep."

"What are you doing in my bed?" She whispered the question in a raw voice, forcing her traitorous body to stiffen.

His expression remained aggravatingly unperturbed. "My bed," he corrected, his impassiveness belied by the glint of desire that lurked deep in his blue-green eyes. "But I don't mind sharing."

"Well, I do."

"You didn't a few minutes ago."

She managed to glare at him. "A few minutes ago, I thought Telstar was chasing me."

"Telstar probably is chasing you. What does that have to do with us sharing a bed?"

"Your bed," Kristian reminded him, pushing weakly at the beautifully toned chest that hovered so temptingly above her. "I'm going home."

"Like hell you are," he murmured. And lowering his head, he caught her mouth with his.

Chapter Fourteen

Kristian's muscles tensed. Don't let this happen, her brain cautioned as his lips moved with deliberate, arousing slowness over hers. But then his tongue began a delicious invasion that brought a hot, shuddery feeling to her stomach and sent a cramp of desire shooting through her limbs, and she forgot all about caution. Almost.

She broke away just enough to give him a smoldering look that had not a shred of conviction behind it. "I won't live in the past, Tory. And I won't let you hurt me again."

There was a certain wry wistfulness in the smile that curved his lips. "I didn't hurt you the first time around," he said softly, running a finger along the side of her neck.

She refused to react to the spiky little tremors that assailed her. "Someone did."

"Uh-huh." He slid his mouth across her warm brow. "You."

"All right, that's it." Planting her palms on his shoulders and exerting the last remnants of her self-control, she gave him a mighty shove. "I'm going home."

"Running away, you mean." Tory shifted his weight so that he was hovering above her in a distinctly menacing if not physically obstructive fashion. "We're not as different as you'd like to believe."

"We're different," she said firmly. "I never ran away from you, or any man, for that matter."

He held her in place with nothing stronger than a hand on her jaw—and a look that was just a little too incisive for Kristian's comfort. "Maybe not," he agreed. One dark brow arched. "Tell me something. Why did you marry Donald?"

"Daniel."

"Whatever. Did you love him?"

"Of course I loved him. You're being impertinent."

"I'm being reasonable, and believe me I've done easier things in my life."

"Like marrying Susan?" she inquired sweetly.

"Suzanne. And no, that was just plain stupid."

"Something like this conversation."

A wicked smile that never failed to make her heart pound lit his shadowy features. "Something like that," he agreed, and suddenly, unexpectedly, she didn't want to fight the fiery urges that bolted through her.

Removing her hands from his shoulders, she ran her fingers across the satin-smooth skin of his back, over the tiny scar that was a souvenir of all those reckless days and nights he'd spent in the Air Force Academy, until they were tangled in the long hair covering his neck. "In that case," she said, "we're wasting our time talking." And digging her fingers in, she pulled his mouth down onto hers.

His hands slid along her sensitized body, moving with a practiced ease that was so familiar that it made the ache inside her tighten to a painful knot. It had been so very long, an eternity since any man had kindled more than a passing spark of desire in her. With a single slow caress, Tory brought it all back, every kiss they'd shared, every touch, every wonder-filled minute of their first-time lovemaking.

"No kicking," he drawled against her mouth, and for an answer, Kristian sank her teeth into his lower lip. Not hard enough to draw blood, but enough that he immediately deepened the kiss. "No biting either," he told her, although she had trouble hearing him above the sudden rush of blood in her ears.

His breath was hot on her face, his tongue wet and seek
ing in its thorough exploration of her soft mouth. She wa
trembling as she responded to him, but it had nothing to d
with fear or uncertainty. She wanted this, wanted him, no
just physically but emotionally, as well. Her nipples wer
hard and exquisitely painful beneath the crushing weight o
his chest; her breasts were swollen, her skin burning wher
his fully aroused body pressed into hers. For all she knew o
cared, time itself could have ground to a halt, leaving noth
ing except the two of them and a starless shroud of dark
ness behind.

No trace of light crept in around the edge of the curtains
only a faint glow from the general direction of the hallwa
allowed her to see him, and then only when his mout
wasn't devouring hers with kisses that made her feel posi
tively drugged.

Love drugged, she thought, kissing him back. No chemi
cal narcotic could send her head into the stratosphere whil
her body remained behind to enjoy all the earthly pleasure
known to woman. Only Tory could do that.

A soft moan rose in her throat as he slid his mouth to he
ear and along the side of her neck to her shoulder. She fe
his hands on her spine, and a second later saw her bra sa
to the end of the bed. Her lacy briefs followed, althoug
how he managed to dispose of them so easily was a ques
tion she didn't care to examine. He shed his own unde
wear with equal ease, and then he was raising himself abov
her, cupping her breasts in his hands, bringing a tiny cry o
pleasure to her throat.

A smile grazed his lips as he lowered his head to her ere
nipples. "You're holding out on me, Kristian," he mu
mured, setting his mouth on one darkened peak and ci
cling it luxuriously with his tongue. "That isn't like you."

A thousand fiery splinters shot through her, and she ha
to swallow another low moan. "Maybe I've changed," sh
managed to choke.

"And maybe you're afraid of what might happen if you let your heart rule your head. This isn't the past, Kristian. This is you and me. Now."

She opened her mouth to say something, but heard her own sharp intake of breath instead as Tory continued teasing the aching bud of her breast with his lips. He never had fought fair, damn him. "You want too much," she whispered in desperation.

He lifted his mouth from her glistening breast. In the darkness, his expression was strained and more than readable. "I want you," he agreed. "All of you. Not just your body."

"But—"

"No compromises, Kristian. All or nothing. It's your decision."

"But . . ." This time the objection died of its own volition. His gorgeous tanned body was poised mere inches above hers. His eyes were unusually dark and somber, his features taut with desire, the same desire that now sent a series of shivers sweeping across her heated skin. Taking a deep breath, she met his impassioned gaze and smiled at him. "In that case," she said simply, "the answer is, all."

If she'd surprised him, he didn't show it. Nor did he waste a second of reaction time. Threading one knee between her legs, he ran his thumbs over her cheekbones and dropped his mouth back on hers.

He was right; she knew it. She'd been holding out on him and on herself. But that time was gone. For tonight at least she would cast aside all her doubts and fears and let herself be swept away to a place where even the past couldn't reach her.

With her hands, Kristian sought out the hard, heavy length of him. His reaction was instantaneous, a tightly hissed breath followed by a groan deep in his throat as he once again took her nipple between his teeth. Somehow he twisted them both around so that her body covered his. He made no attempt to hold her there but continued to run his mouth over her silken flesh.

For a terrified second, the directives of her rational mind broke through, and she almost bolted in panic. Loving Tory was so very easy. Making love with him would be easier still. Easier and frighteningly, enticingly dangerous, like testing some exotic forbidden fruit.

Did she want that forbidden fruit, or did she want him? Surprisingly, the question that should have been so difficult to answer posed no problem at all. Tory was no longer forbidden to her. This was her choice. And his. She'd been a self-denying coward long enough. It was time to take her courage in both hands, time to take a chance.

Alternating feelings of dizziness and longing tore through her as Tory once again reversed their positions. She felt his hands slide across her ribs, felt his lips follow their lead, trailing a tantalizing path over her stomach and along her inner thighs, teasing her until there was nothing whatsoever left of her self-control. She knew his name burst from her throat, heard his approving response, felt the ripples of shock and amazement and delight that ricocheted through her. Wave after glorious wave crashed over her, receding slowly as Tory brought her back down and some more primitive need within her began to assert itself.

She wasn't submissive by nature. Not quiet, not docile, not content to let him dictate the pace or conditions of their lovemaking. If he truly wanted all of her, then he knew that. As her heart at last began to resume its normal rate, her fingers twined in his hair. However, before he could begin another intimately erotic invasion, she pulled away, breathing hard, but determined not to let him have everything his way.

"Running again, Kristian?" he asked, trapping her ankle before she could elude him.

Grinning, she pushed at his wrist with her free foot. "If I were, I'd be long gone."

"Maybe."

He advanced on her cautiously, unsure what to expect, his desire for her not dampened in the slightest. He might have sounded faintly skeptical, but he wasn't. Unless being here in this bed with him was what she wanted, she would have been out the door and halfway to Las Vegas by now.

She watched his approach with feline intent. Her blond hair hung in thick waves over her shoulders and breasts; her slender body shone in the meager light from the hall; her wide, attentive eyes sparkled with humor. He knew her so well, yet she never ceased to fascinate him, never failed to enchant and amaze him.

"Now who's holding out on whom?" she queried, and there was a challenging light in her green eyes. Was she playing a lover's game? Some wary inner instinct told him no, and he stopped his forward progress, ignoring the edicts of his demanding body.

To his surprise, it was Kristian who moved toward him. Kristian who pushed him down onto the mattress, who ran her hands and mouth over his shoulders, his ribs, his hips, his thighs, until his body was covered with a fine film of sweat and his heart pounded like a steel drum in his chest.

A sense of wonder filled him. He hadn't expected this from her, couldn't quite believe what she was doing to him. Considering the constant stream of surprises she'd thrown at him in the past, he probably shouldn't have been so startled. But he was. Startled, dazed and utterly, completely mesmerized by the incredible power she had over him.

Her mouth was like liquid fire on his skin. He felt his own instinctive reaction to her bold touch, felt her lips on him and knew she was pushing him dangerously close to the edge of his endurance. An incredulous smile touched his mouth. She was either going to be the death of him or gift him with a lust for life such as he'd never known.

Tapping the splintered fragments of his self-control, he reached for her, bringing her back into his arms and flipping her onto her back. "You," he croaked against her beautifully damp lips, "are making me crazy."

"All's fair, Tory," she retorted, then wound her arms around his neck and pulled his mouth onto hers.

He thrust his tongue past her lips, delving deeply, testing her, absorbing the sweetness of her kisses while his hands slid beneath her hips. She was ready for him, hungry for him, wanting him inside her, wanting all the things she'd been denying herself for so long.

She stopped thinking as the fire in her blood turned into an inferno, clinging to him tightly, letting the waves rock her, shocked and excited by the feel of him inside her. With his mouth, his hands, his body he drew her up and up. Higher than they'd ever flown before.

Wherever they were, it wasn't on Earth. There was something exquisite in the darkness around them, something fragile and beautiful and fleeting. Kristian caught back a strangled breath as the moment and the darkness and all the mysteries of the universe culminated inside her. Tory's name was a strangled cry on her lips, his sweat-slick body hot, hard and straining beneath her hands as the world and everything in it exploded in a burst of white light that seemed to sweep down and envelop them both.

She wasn't sure how long they stayed there on that supernatural plane, but gradually Kristian became aware of more than their lovemaking. Had she fainted? She didn't think so, but anything was possible. The darkness hung heavy around them, brushed by a soft ray of light that skimmed across the sleek, golden flesh of Tory's back and shoulders. With a start she realized that he'd collapsed on top of her. She knew, too, that if she moved a muscle, he'd roll away, and that was something she definitely didn't want. Not yet. Not until she figured out how it was humanly possible to love someone as deeply as she loved him.

Immersed in thought, she didn't see him lift his head to stare at her. It wasn't until he caught her lower lip between his teeth that she even realized he was awake.

"That bad, huh?" he said, though the gleam in his eyes dared her to agree with him.

She didn't. "That good," she admitted, wrapping her arms around his neck and stretching beneath him. "But don't let it go to your head. I seem to recall better."

He grinned and brushed her hair from her face, deliberately misunderstanding. "With Donald? Sorry, Kristian, I find that hard to swallow."

"You would. And it's Daniel."

"If you insist." His grin widened. "Why did you marry him?"

"None of your business."

"Did you really love him?"

"Yes."

"As much as you loved me?"

Past tense? Maybe he wasn't quite so arrogant after all. Smiling, she slid her fingers through his sweat-damp hair. "No," she said softly. "Not that much." And reaching up he set out to prove just how true that statement was.

BACON SIZZLING, orange juice chilling, toast toasting, coffee brewing. Not her usual Brazilian brand, but close enough. Satisfied, Kristian shoved back the sleeves of the blue-and-black flannel shirt she'd swiped from Tory's closet and wandered over to the kitchen window. With a shake of her shower-damp hair she looked out over the bristly desert terrain and tried to pretend it was seven in the morning instead of four in the afternoon.

Had she really slept through the day? Well, no, in fairness, she hadn't actually slept for more than six or seven hours all told, but that wasn't entirely her fault. All things considered, she'd been lucky to manage even that much.

"What are you doing?"

Tory's amused voice floated across the kitchen. Turning, Kristian hoisted herself onto the counter—and had to bite back a sigh when she spied his bare chest. No man had a right to look so devastating. She managed a placid smile. "I don't know about you, but when I get out of bed, I eat breakfast."

"Even when you get out of bed at 4:00 p.m.?" He strolled toward her, his feet bare, a pair of well worn jeans hugging his long legs, a wine-red shirt hanging open over the unbelted waistband. Amusement still gleamed in his eyes, but it wasn't the only visible emotion.

She held up a forestalling hand as he drew closer. "Back off, Tory. I'm hungry."

"So am I."

"You're relentless."

He grinned, catching her. "That's a polite way of putting it."

"I'm trying to keep this conversation on a polite level."

He brought her fingers to his lips and kissed them. "Then you must really be hungry."

She shouldn't have let him get within twenty feet of her, should never have let him touch her. Wasn't there some old proverb about abstinence being good for the soul? Of course, a lot of people also believed that fasting was good for one's body, though Kristian's own experience in that area had merely left her feeling weak and irritable.

Lashes lowered, she savored the feel of Tory's lips on her shoulder, her neck, her jaw. She probably would have forgotten all about food once he claimed her mouth; unfortunately, a shrill summons from the telephone stopped him before he reached that point.

"Saved by the bell," he murmured in her ear. "It must be George calling to find out what happened to us."

Kristian hesitated, torn between disappointment and interest. "Why? Did we miss a meeting or something?"

"Nothing that exciting. Just Griselda Payne's literary guild."

"I thought they were coming next week."

Tory reached for the phone. "They were—until Griselda heard about Hubie Bittman's death. Morbid curiosity's a powerful magnet."

"Only for vultures." Hopping from the counter, she crossed to the refrigerator and pulled out a carton of eggs. Her monthly cholesterol fix, she thought, pausing long enough to pour two mugs of coffee. She pushed one toward Tory who'd taken over her makeshift seat on the counter, then continued on to the stove.

It occurred to her that food was the last thing she should be thinking about right now. On top of the nightmarish chain of events transpiring in and around the space park, she had yet to deal with her feelings for Tory. Even isolated, the latter would most certainly be a monumental undertaking. She did love him, there was no doubt in her mind about that. But she'd also loved him eleven years ago. Maybe she'd never stopped loving him. In any event, that wasn't the crux of the problem.

Crux... The moment the Latin word passed through her head, her mind took a quantum leap into a far less pleasant arena of thought. Telstar, Ibo, the Southern Cross, Simon...

How were all those things connected? It was pretty much a foregone conclusion that Annette Barrows had used the NORStar computers to steal classified information. But what had she done with it? For whom had she been working? And where did Simon fit into the picture? Had he interfered with the murderer's plans, caused them to backfire in some way? That made sense, but it didn't really clarify the situation. Regardless, the exact sequence of events probably wasn't as important as determining the identity of the murderer. To that end, Simon's message almost certainly had to be the key.

In the back of her mind, she heard the click of the telephone receiver. Seconds later, Tory's hands were sliding around her waist, tugging her back against his lean body while he leaned over her shoulder.

"Was it George?" she asked, deliberately pressing herself into him.

"Uh-huh. He can't find Evan."

"It's Sunday, Tory. Evan's allowed to take a day off."

He smiled, "No one's denying that. George just wants to talk to him." Before she could stop him, he'd snatched a crisp slice of bacon from the draining rack. "It's good," he said, chewing. "Hot, but good."

She couldn't resist a small laugh. "You know, this scene seems awfully familiar to me. Wasn't the heroine in *War of the Worlds* cooking breakfast about the time the Martians landed on the roof?"

"Are you back on that kick?" he teased, his tone humorous.

She frowned. "What kick?"

He lowered his mouth to her shoulder, pushing the flannel shirt away rather impatiently with his fingers. "Last night you kept insisting we'd been invaded."

"By Martians?" In the back of her mind, she vaguely recalled some reference to extraterrestrials, but the specifics of the conversation eluded her.

Tory's teeth closed lightly about her earlobe. "No, by Morton and Lilith. I'm not sure, but I got the impression you thought they were breeding a race of interplanetary conquistadors."

"Maybe they are," she replied, jabbing him with a playful elbow. "They're probably growing their offspring even as we speak, planting them seed by little green seed in the desert."

"Just like in *The Thing*."

"That's right. Before you know it, super carrots will control the planet."

"I have news for you, they're already controlling your brain."

His breath was warm in her ear, the scent of him clean and vital and uniquely Tory. Removing the skillet from the burner, she tipped her head back onto his shoulder. She was about to suggest they forget breakfast and concentrate on satisfying a more urgent hunger when the phone began to ring again.

"The machine's on," Tory said against the corner of her mouth.

"It might be Evan."

"It also might be Lydia."

"Or the police," Kristian added, lifting her head as Jon Hayes's voice reached her ear.

"I know you're there, Tory." The sergeant's gravelly tone had an irritated edge to it. "Pick up the damned phone."

"This better be important," Tory muttered. He grabbed the receiver. "What is it, Jon? I'm busy."

With a sigh and a toss of her nearly dry hair, Kristian started to scoop up the eggs. By the time they got around to eating any of this, it truly would be morning.

"Where?" she heard Tory demand. There was a pause, then a wary "Are you sure?"

"Sure about what?" she asked, leaving the stove. "Did the police find something at the park?"

His hand came up from behind to cover her mouth. "Okay, we'll be right there."

Kristian tugged on his wrist until he released her. "Be right where? Tory, what's going on?"

"Get dressed," he said by way of a reply. "We're going to the city."

"The city!" Ignoring the nudge he gave her, she stared at him. "What for?"

"Because," he told her softly, "that's where the Martians have landed." At her puzzled expression, he gave her another firmer push. "There's been a body found in an alley, Kristian. Jon thinks he recognizes the corpse."

"I—" Her eyes grew suspicious. "Who does he think it is?" Somehow, instinctively, she knew what the answer would be, but she wanted to hear it anyway.

Tory slid a hand around the back of her head, looking down at her. "He thinks it's Simon."

"WE FOUND HIM RIGHT HERE," Jon Hayes revealed. With the toe of his boot, he scuffed a chalk outline in the reeking alley that separated two of Las Vegas's more disreputable hotels. "The medical examiner can probably give you the time of death, but we reckon it likely happened sometime late this morning."

"This morning!" Kristian exclaimed, then promptly masked her disbelief. Unless she wanted to spend the next full week describing to the police the crime she'd witnessed in her office, she'd better make an effort to keep a tight rein on her tongue. "Isn't that, uh, rather unusual?"

Jon knit his brows. "What, a shooting?"

"Is that how he died?" Tory inquired with the perfect balance of curiosity and grimness in his voice.

"Yup, but I wouldn't call it an unusual occurrence. Leastways not in a neighborhood like this one."

Kristian looked around at the chipped and discolored bricks, the overflowing dumpsters and badly rusted fire escapes. No one should have to live in such squalor, she thought, concealing a shudder of disgust. "I was referring to the crime itself, Jon," she said. "Isn't late morning an odd time for someone to be killed in such a public place?"

"Maybe a little," the sergeant conceded. "But I've seen stranger things."

So had she, Kristian thought forlornly. "You're sure you're not mistaken about the time of death?" she asked.

"Don't take my word for it. I'm just telling you what we think from looking. The coroner will know more than I do. At this point, the only thing I'm sure of is that the prints match the ones in Simon's military file and that he was killed with a single .45 caliber bullet."

Tory's eyes narrowed consideringly. "Point of entry?" he questioned, and Kristian felt the warning squeeze he gave her hand.

Again, Jon shrugged. ''About what you'd expect in such a low-life area. Neat, but not quite up to professional standards. Whoever killed him put the bullet right through his chest.''

Chapter Fifteen

"Whoever killed him put the bullet right through his neck," Kristian maintained, her jaw set in a stubborn line. "I know what I saw."

Tory wasn't about to argue with her. They were sitting in a noisy casino lounge on the famed Las Vegas strip, waiting for the deputy coroner, a long-time acquaintance of his, to put in an appearance. "Drink your drink," he suggested, flicking a hand at the beer she'd ordered but not touched. "Rob should be here in a few minutes."

With a sigh, she picked up her glass. "Is there anyone in this state you don't know?"

"Telstar," he replied, swallowing a mouthful of his own beer and watching a man in a cowboy hat who was watching Kristian with more than a passing amount of interest.

"I wouldn't count on that. If Telstar's at the space park, chances are we both know him." She followed the line of Tory's gaze. "What are you looking at?"

"There's a guy in a tan Stetson staring at you."

She grinned. "So? There's a guy in a black Stetson staring at you."

Tory munched on a salted pretzel. "Jealous?" he asked, arching a guileless brow.

"Of a slicker in a rhinestone suit? Not likely."

From the end of a busy slot machine row, a lanky man with thinning brown hair and glasses hastened toward their table. "Sorry I'm late," he apologized, tossing his gray sportcoat onto the seat of an empty chair and smiling at Kristian. "We've got a backlog like you wouldn't believe."

"That paints a pleasant picture," Tory noted dryly. "Rob, this is Kristian Ellis. She manages the park. Kristian, Rob Pfeifer, deputy coroner."

"Overworked deputy coroner," Rob supplemented. "By the way, Tory, did you know there's a guy in a black Stetson staring at you?"

"So I've been told," he murmured, not missing Kristian's swiftly hidden smile. He waited until Rob had ordered a beer, then asked, "What do you have on Simon's death?"

"Officially, a big fat zero. Unofficially, one hell of a weird discrepancy."

"Weird in what sense?" Kristian queried carefully.

"Well, for starters, we're having trouble establishing the precise time of death. By precise, I mean accurate within certain medically established parameters."

Tory leaned back in his chair. "What's the problem?"

"Body temperature."

Kristian glanced up, but Tory merely moved an uncomprehending shoulder. "You'll have to explain that one, Rob."

The other man sipped his beer. "I shouldn't really be explaining any of this," he said, giving his tie a tug. "But since you're almost family, I guess I'll risk it."

"Family?" Kristian echoed, and Tory made a dismissing motion with his hand.

"Rob's father was married to Lydia eighteen years ago."

"For twenty-three of the darkest months of my life," Rob put in, his distaste evident. "Getting back to Simon Juniper, the problem we're having stems from the very simple fact that the temperature of the corpse was several degrees lower than it should reasonably have been, which in turn leads us to believe that your friend was shot in one location, then moved to another."

To a certain twisted extent, Tory knew that made sense. Aloud, he asked, "Where was he shot?"

"Where in his body?" Rob jabbed a thumb at his ribs. "In the chest. Right through the heart, in fact."

Kristian's eyes narrowed slightly, but she said nothing.

"What was he wearing?" Tory pressed.

"Street clothes. You know, jeans, T-shirt, sneakers."

"Any visible marks or bruises?"

"None that we've been able to detect, but you have to remember that this is only a preliminary report. We still have to account for the temperature differential. Best theory we have so far is that he was killed in one of those warehouses that are used for cold storage, left there for a few hours then dumped in the alley where he was ultimately found." Rob glanced at his watch, frowned and looked again. "This thing better be wrong," he said and shook his wrist. "It can't be seven-thirty. I told Sadie I'd be home by seven. Sadie's my wife," he added for Kristian's benefit. "She'll be royally ticked if I've left her alone with my sanctimonious Aunt Martha for half an hour."

"An hour and a half," Tory corrected mildly. "It's eight-thirty."

"Oh, damn." Gulping his beer, Rob jumped from his chair. "I'm in the doghouse."

"Bring Sadie to the space park next weekend," Kristian suggested. "I'll have a complete set of passes sent to the Pallas Hotel. Maybe that'll help."

"It will. Sadie loves science fiction." He grabbed his jacket. "Have we covered everything, I hope?"

Tory ran a thoughtful hand across his mouth. "As well as possible. Thanks, Rob."

"No problem. Catch you both later."

Kristian waited until he was gone, then pounced on Tory. "He said cold storage. That would account for the discrepancy in Simon's body temperature and partially explain how he could have been murdered at NORStar a week ago but not have turned up until today. The only thing that doesn't make sense is the way he died. I know he was shot in the neck." She hesitated. "Unless..."

"What?"

She bit her lip and tried to remember exactly what she'd seen. "I told you the gun looked a little strange. And there wasn't any blood on the carpet. Maybe Simon wasn't shot with a bullet. Maybe he was only doped."

"Sounds reasonable," Tory agreed, eyeing the man in the tan cowboy hat who was still staring lewdly at Kristian. "He could have been shot with a pellet, hauled to a meat locker, murdered and literally put on ice."

She grimaced. "Lovely concept. And you thought Rob painted a pleasant picture. So what do we do now? Start checking out meat lockers?"

"Freezers," he said, his expression hardening.

"You don't sound very happy," she noted softly. "Do you have something specific in mind?"

"Someone," he countered and reached for her hand. "Morton has a house in Boulder City. And that house has a full-size freezer."

BENEATH THE BLACK-AND-PURPLE shadows of an uncharacteristically somber twilight, Morton's Boulder City home looked to be a huge, Victorian affair, more of a mansion than a house. A little on the melancholy side, Kristian decided, but she supposed that was to be expected given the man's bent for darkness. On closer inspection, she found no trace of the Spanish architecture so prevalent in the area. Although that surprised her a little, perhaps it shouldn't have. Color, style and form weren't likely to be of much concern to someone with Morton's ocular affliction.

A rumble of thunder rolled ominously through the blackened heavens. Just what they needed, Kristian thought as Tory stopped his car outside the high wooden gate that encircled the grounds. An electrical storm to supplement their hunt for a freezer that might very well have been used to store a human body. Even Freddy's nightmares weren't this lurid.

Leaning from the car, Tory punched a long series of numbers into a computerized panel on a post near the gate, waited a few seconds, inserted his NORStar pass into a hidden slot and hit a few more buttons. When nothing happened, he gave the panel a resounding whack with the heel of his hand. As if by magic, the gate slid slowly back.

"So much for modern technology," he said, but it was an abstracted comment. Clearly his mind was on something else, and it didn't take a genius to figure out what that something was.

No matter how she looked at it she couldn't get past the horrible realization that they were about to search a freezer in hopes of determining whether or not Simon's body might have been stored inside. Maybe they should reconsider this particular plan. After all, what could they reasonably expect to find?

Kristian eyed the mansion before them with more than a few misgivings. "Tory, are you sure you want to do this?"

"No, but I'm going to."

"*We're* going to," she told him firmly, pushing her doubts aside. "Where is this freezer anyway?" If he said it was in the basement, she was going to scream.

"In the utility room."

"Where's that?"

"Behind the engineering section."

She snatched her head around in time to see the faint smile that quirked his lips. "Very funny," she muttered, and he moved an unrepentant shoulder.

"Just trying to lighten things up a bit. Besides, that's what you're expecting, isn't it?"

"No," she replied quickly, then released a pent-up breath. "Well, maybe." She slid him a calculating sideways glance. "I am going to be disappointed, aren't I?"

"Let's say you'll probably be surprised."

"That's not a very reassuring answer."

"I know." He looked around the neatly manicured estate, letting his gaze come to rest on the unlit front porch as a second clap of thunder, this one closer, grumbled menacingly overhead. "I wonder where Hugo's gotten to."

Now why did a vision of Igor immediately pop into her head? Kristian huddled deeper into her seat, unable to ignore the crooked fork of lightning that streaked through the soot-black sky. "Maybe he's dusting the dilithium crystals," she said, but the sarcasm in her voice sounded hollow even to her own ears.

The corners of Tory's eyes crinkled. Reaching over, he pulled her across the gearbox and out his side of the car, his fingers retaining their strong grip on hers as they mounted the wide stoop. "Hugo's perfectly harmless," he promised, repeating the ritual he'd performed at the outer gate. "And perfectly ordinary. Quiet, diminutive, efficient. He's been Morton's groundskeeper for years."

Kristian wasn't convinced. "If he's so efficient, why isn't he waiting at the door with a candle?"

"Be consistent and say a light saber. And I don't know. He could be out on an errand." The door swung open with a twist of the ornate brass knob, and Tory drew her into an entrance hall that was darker than a solar eclipse. A sharp click preceded his vaguely disconcerting "The power must be out."

No surprise there, Kristian reflected. "Doesn't Morton have an emergency generator?" she asked.

"Somewhere." He kicked the door closed with his heel. "Hugo, it's Tory. Are you home?"

Nothing. Not even the evil cackle Kristian's overtaxed imagination had been half anticipating. "I guess he's not here," she said, pulling insistently on Tory's hand. "Let's find the freezer and get out."

"We will, but first let's find a flashlight."

"Why? As I recall, you used to have exceptional night vision."

"Depends what I'm doing." The note of amusement in his voice was unmistakable, and Kristian was tempted to hit him. Or launch herself at him and see what transpired from there. She refrained, out of deference to Simon and a situation that seemed to be growing more complicated with each passing hour.

"All right," she agreed, resigned. "We'll find a flashlight. Which way?"

"How should I know? I'm not a bat."

As if to justify the statement, he bumped into a statue that in silhouette looked suspiciously like Sagittarius. "Yes, I see that," she remarked. "You also don't appear to know the house very well. But you must have been here before."

"It's not the house, it's the furniture. Morton likes to move things around."

By telekinesis, no doubt, Kristian wanted to add, but she bit her tongue and stayed glued to Tory's side as he forged an amazingly surefooted path to a room he said was the study. However, she wasn't certain she would have called it that, particularly after he dug a flashlight out of a cupboard by the door and ran the powerful beam around the walls.

The mosaic figures adorning them looked positively cabalistic. Was Morton dabbling in the occult, she wondered with a shiver. A dot inside a circle, a crescent moon, something with horns and the head of a pitchfork. She opened her mouth to make a comment, then snapped it shut again when the beam landed on two symbols that were more familiar to her.

"Male, female," she breathed, more relieved than she cared to admit. "Mars and Venus. They're planetary signs." She hesitated. "All two hundred of them? That's not right. What is this place?"

Tory shrugged. "Whatever it is, it's new. A lot of these symbols probably came straight from Morton's imagination. He enjoys envisioning other solar systems."

"Why wouldn't he? He undoubtedly comes from one. You know, I don't like to keep harping on this point, but the man isn't working on all boosters—" she brightened perceptibly "—which, if you think about it, isn't necessarily a bad thing. At least it lessens the chance of his being Telstar."

"True, but he could still be in league with Telstar."

She glared at him, exasperated. "I hate it when you get logical."

"So do I. Let's find the freezer and get out of here."

To reach the utility room, they first had to pass through a kitchen that was almost as large as the one in the Martian Terrace Restaurant. Between the myriad roots and herbs that hung in thick bunches from the ceiling beams, the cobalt blue marble floors and counters, the thunder crashing around the roof and the lightning bolts that continued to snake to the ground beyond the windows, the overall effect could only be deemed unearthly. And then there were the creaky little noises that kept filtering down from the rafters, sounds not quite obstructed by the thunder.

A fine film of perspiration broke out on Kristian's skin. Wiping her free hand on the leg of her jeans, she whispered a tentative "Does this Hugo person like to wander around on the second floor?"

Tory's teeth flashed in the shadowy light. "Hugo has his own suite of rooms in the east wing. Don't worry about the noises, Kristian. This is an old house. It has the right to a few creaks and groans."

"Under normal circumstances, yes, but not during an electrical storm." Her sharp eyes caught a long white object visible through a partially open window. "Is that the freezer?"

He nodded. "Do you want to wait here?"

"Are you crazy?"

"That's what I figured. Come on."

His fingers tightened briefly around hers, but only until they'd reached their destination. It was a fickle attitude, but now that they were here, staring at the offending appliance, Kristian was no longer sure she wanted to look inside. Why? What did she expect to find, she wondered uneasily. A stack of frozen bodies? Blood-smeared ice-cream boxes? Telstar waiting in frosty ambush?

She held her breath as Tory raised the heavy lid—and released it when the flashlight beam revealed nothing more sinister than a freezer filled to the brim with fish sticks, TV dinners, numerous flavors of frozen yogurt and box after box of vegetables. She would have turned away, satisfied, if some pesky little voice in her brain hadn't cautioned her to take a second look.

Chewing on her lip, she stared at a packet of brussel sprouts, aware that Tory was examining a similar box of string beans. "Something's not right, is it?" she ventured, poking one of the TV dinners. "There's no frost on a lot of this stuff."

Tory hunted through the various packets. "At least half of it," he confirmed after a lengthy search, which wasn't made any less nerve-racking by the thunderbolts beyond the mansion's aging walls.

The implication was clear. Yet for some reason, Kristian had an utterly absurd impulse to defend Morton, or barring that to give him the benefit of the doubt. "Is it possible that Hugo stocked up on supplies recently?" she asked.

"I don't think so." Tory picked up two of the TV dinners, one coated with frost, the other completely ice free. "The expiry date's the same on both of these boxes."

She refused to follow his line of reasoning. "So?"

"They came from the same shipment. They were purchased at the same time."

"It could be a fluke," she maintained stubbornly and with absolutely no idea why she was being so hardheaded about this. Since her visit to his penthouse suite, hadn't it been her contention that Morton was the traitorous partner Simon had alluded to in his final message? "Maybe they were bought one or two days apart. It happens, you know."

Tory's eyes glinted grimly. "Not likely, Kristian. Take a look at the date. More specifically, the year."

"September seventeenth, nineteen..." She broke off midword, nails biting into her palms. "That's last year!"

"Over ten months ago." He tossed the boxes back into the freezer. "Half this stuff's been thawed and refrozen again."

That did it. Kristian's feeble attempts to rationalize the situation vanished with the speed of the lightning bolts that crackled through the night sky. So, too, did her burning indignation when the truth of what had taken place in this room suddenly hit her. She backed away from the offensive appliance that now bore a frightening resemblance to a coffin.

"My God," she whispered in revulsion. "Simon's been here all this time. Frozen. Like a human Popsicle." She drew a deep, shuddering breath. "Who would do something so sick?"

"Telstar," Tory stated with no discernible inflection.

"It's depraved."

"It's murder." He slammed the lid, curled his fingers around her wrist and pulled her against him. "Don't think about it," he said, his voice a low, soothing sound in her ear. "You can't alter the past no matter how much you might want to."

She pressed her forehead into his shoulder. "I know that. But to freeze him. It seems so...so sacrilegious somehow."

"Murderers like Telstar are notoriously lacking in compassion," Tory reminded her. "You can't expect them to care."

"I don't." Lifting her head she shot the freezer a vengeful look. "But I can want this particular murderer to pay for his crimes." Her gaze shifted to Tory's face, implacable in the streaking lightning. "What do we do now? Call Jon Hayes?"

"No."

She sighed. "I knew you were going to say that. You want to talk to Morton yourself, don't you?"

"There's a chance he wasn't involved," Tory pointed out, taking her former stand on the issue. "He only spends about two months a year in this house. He's certainly not the only person with access to it."

"That's true," Kristian conceded. "If you could get in, so could Evan and, uh—" she choked back George's name "—well, lots of people."

"Like George," Tory supplied, slanting her a shrewd look as he drew her back into the kitchen. "I know how your mind works, Kristian. But you're wasting your suspicions. You of all people should realize that."

She felt a twinge of guilt. "I know. It was George who talked you into hiring me."

"That's right." Tory's smile was wry. "Evan wanted to run the park himself, Morton wanted June, and I was undecided."

She stared at him in genuine surprise. "You mean you were the swing vote?"

"Something like that."

"And you voted for me?"

"I had my reasons," he disclosed, his murmur barely audible above the crack of thunder that shook the house.

Something about that violent sound shattered Kristian's momentary distraction and brought all the horror of their discovery crashing back into her head. What were they doing in this tomb? They should be halfway back to the space park by now. Actually they should be talking to Jon Hayes about now, but she could get around that uncomfortable thought easily enough. After all, they couldn't really prove a single one of their suspicions.

She stayed plastered to Tory's side as they headed back to the entrance hall. This time he bypassed the study and cut through the living room, a relatively normal-looking area of the house if one didn't count the glass-fronted cabinet on the wall opposite the old stone fireplace. Wreathed in shadows broken only by the dying flashlight beam and an occasional fork of blue-tinted lightning, the figures contained inside seemed to be staring at her. Glowering at her, in fact. A preposterous notion, but Kristian had trouble shaking the creepy sensation.

Why couldn't Morton have a weird fascination with Alf? Why did he have to collect Dracona's minions? Why did those minions all of a sudden look so vicious?

"How do we get out of here?" she wailed in a whisper to Tory.

"Shhh."

He's stopped moving and snapped off the flashlight. His body was rigid, his muscles taut, his eyes combing the corridor visible at the far end of the room. Kristian listened between thunderclaps, but heard nothing. "What is it?" she hissed.

"Quiet," he warned, his voice a mere thread of sound in the blackened room. "There's someone upstairs."

She heard it then, the distinct groan of a floorboard responding to the pressure of a stealthy footstep. Her skin went clammy. They weren't alone in the mansion, and she wasn't fool enough to hope that they might be standing in the east wing. But if not Hugo, then who was up there? Surely it couldn't be Morton.

She swallowed the lump in her throat and ordered her slamming heart to slow its breakneck pace. Tiny marble eyes glared at her from inside the cabinet, followed her as she and Tory moved soundlessly along the opposing wall. It was so very dark, like being in a crater on the far side of the moon. No, not a crater, her terrified mind retracted. She wouldn't think that word, that name. Wouldn't remember the bomb that had come within an inch of blowing them to microscopic bits.

The footfall overhead came again. And again and again. Kristian glanced at Tory. "Maybe whoever's up there doesn't realize we're here."

Tory nodded, his expression enigmatic in the brief flicker of lightning that shot through the room. "Maybe. At any rate, he doesn't seem to be coming down."

"Does that mean we're going up?"

"No, it means I'm going up." His tone was inflexible, but Kristian was having none of it.

"Forget that," she retorted fervently, grabbing the flashlight before he could stop her. "I'm coming with you."

His only response was a knowing look and a muttered comeback she couldn't decipher above the thunder. She let him take the flashlight from her, watching as he flicked the switch, and grimacing when the once-strong beam stuttered and faded and finally settled down to a mere trickle of light scarcely powerful enough to illuminate the mantel...

... Or the heavy iron poker that was poised like a deadly blackjack above their heads.

Chapter Sixteen

Kristian wasn't sure how long it took for the malignant image to register in her stunned brain. Half a second, perhaps less. Whatever it was, Tory's reaction was that much faster. With one arm, he shoved her out of harm's way while the other went up to block the mighty downward blow. She heard a grunt that could have been her own as she sprawled backward into the fireplace screen and past it into a pile of ashes. Through a wall of soot, she saw the poker come down again and someone who looked like an angry Pan hopping around the carpeted floor, keeping just out of Tory's range.

She grabbed the first thing that came to hand—a heavy brass bellows—and scrambled to her feet. And almost jumped out of her skin when a strong arm came from nowhere to clamp itself down on her shoulder.

A strangled cry stuck in her throat. Whirling, she swung the bellows, catching the person behind her squarely in the biceps. Another grunt reached her ears. Female, unlike the owner of the hand that was now twisting painfully on her arm.

A round of obscenities underscored the crashing thunder. The windows rattled angrily in their panes. Razor-thin slashes of lightning momentarily turned the room an eerie shade of blue. Kristian felt the pressure on her arm increase and in her peripheral vision saw Tory intercept the poker in midswing. He snatched it away cleanly, then without pausing set his sights on the man from whose grasp Kristian couldn't manage to escape.

More obscenities filled the sooty air. The woman, minus her poker, launched a vase at Kristian's head. It missed crashing harmlessly in the fireplace. Free now, thanks to Tory, Kristian rounded on the smaller female, snatched up a large throw pillow and gave her a solid thump that sent her over a low footstool and into an ornate floor lamp beside the figures of Dracona's minions.

"Damn you!" Kristian snapped, advancing furiously. "You killed Simon, I know you did."

The woman's head shot up. "Kristian?" Her voice was little more than a disbelieving croak. "Is—is that you?"

Bellows long since lost, pillow poised to slam down on the fallen woman, Kristian forced herself to check the motion. "June?" She frowned into the darkness, waited until her assistant had crawled to her knees, then exploded. "For God's sake, what are you doing here?"

A choked growl prevented an immediate response. "Oh, no! Stop!" June flapped an agitated hand at the men in front of her. "It's Evan!"

Tory let loose a curse that would have lit the room if the lightning hadn't chosen that moment to do it for him. He was straddling Evan's legs, pinning him, spluttering and indignant, to the carpet. "You've proved your point, Tory," the other man rasped, his face pressed into the thick fibres. "My arm doesn't bend that way."

"I should break it," Tory snarled, releasing his partner in disgust. "What the hell are you doing here?"

It was the question Kristian had asked, and this time June hastened to answer. Picking herself up off the floor, she rubbed a sore spot and winced. "Morton wanted a few things brought over to his suite. Papers and books and such. It took us a while to collect everything. By the time we finished, it was dark. I didn't think we should drive during an electrical storm, so we decided to spend the night here."

Evan rolled onto his back, panting. "The plan, however, was to sleep, not get into a wrestling match. Where did you two come from?"

"Kristian has a cousin in Boulder City," Tory lied without batting an eyelash. "We planned to have dinner with her, but she got tied up in Las Vegas. Then the storm started, and we came to the same conclusion you did. As soon as we got here, I called George and told him where we'd be in case there was a problem at the park."

"Terrific." Giving his arm a shake, Evan sat up and squinted at the fireplace. "Well, now that we've cleared that mess up, what say we figure out how we're going to explain this other one to Morton. I could be wrong, June, but I think that vase you threw at Kristian was Ming."

June lit a candle on the piano. "It was handy," she said with a shrug. "Morton will understand."

"That's a cavalier attitude," Kristian remarked, brushing the soot and ash from her hair.

Tory, who'd been watching June closely, sat down on the arm of the sofa. "Where's Hugo?" he inquired with seeming disinterest.

June lit more candles, then calmly blew out the match. "Out," she said simply.

"Visiting his mother, I think," Evan put in quickly.

Tory obviously wasn't buying it. "He has a mother?"

"We all do, Tory," June teased. "Or didn't yours tell you about the birds and the bees?"

His impassive expression didn't alter. "She told me lots of interesting things," he said, but from the edge in his voice Kristian could sense the confrontation that was coming.

"Well, as long as we're all straight on the facts of life," she inserted smoothly. "Why don't we go into the kitchen and see about finding something to eat?"

June's eyes sparkled. "Good idea. I have a craving for strawberry ice cream. I think Morton has a carton in the freezer."

Kristian forced herself not to gag. "On second thought, maybe Tory and I should just go—" she recalled their excuse for being in the house a split second too late and had to add a hasty "—to bed."

One of June's penciled brows rose. "Oh, really?" Her smile broadened. "Is there something you're not telling us?"

Evan snorted. "That's a subtle question." Ignoring the acerbic look she sent him, he turned to Tory. "Listen, as long as we're all here, we might as well put our time to good use. I have a few ideas that just might up our profits considerably."

"Enough to replace a Ming Dynasty vase?" Kristian asked from her kneeling position by the hearth. "Why didn't either of you say something before you attacked us?"

Evan held up his hands. "Hey, don't bring me into this. June attacked. I only came on the scene because I heard a lot of scuffling under my floor."

That explained the footsteps they'd heard. As for the rest of their story, Kristian wasn't sure what to think. She frowned at her assistant, mistrust crowding in, but said nothing. For all her elfin smiles and seeming lightheartedness, June could be a real scrapper when she chose to be. Certainly, there were few people who could intimidate her, fewer still who could truly understand the way her mind worked.

Was that significant to Simon's death? June was here with Evan. She was also closely linked to Morton. Both men were Tory's partners, and Ibo Quan's partner had betrayed him.

"Damn." She sighed softly, then looked up and forced a tranquil smile to her lips when she realized that everyone was staring at her. "I broke a nail."

"Better a nail than a priceless vase." Evan surveyed the mess with a shake of his head. "Oh, well, what's done is done. So what do you say? Shall we sit down and discuss my ideas?"

Kristian stood and batted at the ashes on her jeans. "The rest of you go ahead. I'm going to take a hot shower."

"And I'm going to eat strawberry ice cream while I watch *Land of the Giants* on Morton's battery-powered TV," June piped up.

Evan regarded Tory without a great deal of hope. "Well?"

Tory shrugged and picked up a candle. "Let me find Kristian a room first. I'll meet you in the kitchen in ten minutes."

Stifling a glimmer of disappointment that he wasn't going to join her in the shower, Kristian let him draw her out of the living room and up a winding staircase to a guest bedroom pleasantly decorated in varying shades of apricot and green.

"Are you going to tell Evan about Simon?" she queried as he closed and locked the door.

"Do you think I should?"

One of the few times he'd ever asked her opinion, and it had to be under circumstances like these. "It might be a good idea, but I'd do it from a safe distance."

He grinned, rubbing his thumb across her smudged chin. "Such faith, Kristian." One dark brow rose. "Or could it be that you're worried about me?"

"You're not Superman, Tory," she informed him, neatly evading the question. "I doubt if cornered killers fight fair."

"You sound like a newspaper headline."

Maybe, but that wasn't the way she felt. Mindless of the soot on her clothes and skin, she threw her arms around his neck and pressed herself into him. "Don't get hurt," she said in a husky whisper.

If she'd caught him unawares, he recovered swiftly, sliding his hands over her hips and setting her firmly against his fully aroused body. "I don't intend to," he promised and brushed his lips lightly across hers.

A tight knot of longing formed in Kristian's stomach. She couldn't believe how much she wanted him, and at the most inappropriate time, too. But then again who could really say which times were right and which were wrong? Love had little or nothing to do with logic, and God knew, she did love him. Body, heart and soul.

His tongue delved deeply into her mouth, touching her in places that made her moan and pull his head down even more in response. Evan was waiting for him, she knew. But did she care? Not when Tory's mouth and hands were on her.

Thunder rumbled in the distance, and for a moment her conscience got the better of her. For Simon's sake, she told herself, pulling back but not away from Tory's persuasive lips. "You said ten minutes," she managed to murmur, though it sounded more like a groan.

"I know." Apparently unconcerned, he continued to kiss her and at the same time propelled her back toward the four-poster bed behind her. "Ten Venusian minutes."

IT HAD BEEN A LONG NIGHT. Tedious and fraught with moments of anger that could easily have been transformed into years of regret.

Careful now, the woman cautioned herself as she eased her car into its usual spot in the NORStar parking lot. Don't overreact.

There was a saying for situations like this. Kill in haste, repent at leisure, or words to that effect. To kill Kristian and Tory last night would have been a huge tactical blunder. She'd done well to remember that in time. There were better ways to handle the matter. Ways that would rid her of three problems instead of two.

Her partner looked at her from the passenger seat. He wasn't saying much this fine morning. Was he getting worried, she wondered, sending him a deceptively bland smile. "Tired?" she inquired with an innocent widening of her eyes.

"It was a long night," he affirmed, then regarded her apparent confusion, his customary state of mind these days. "Why didn't you kill them when you had the chance?"

"Because the 'chance,' as you put it, was loaded with risks I wasn't willing to take."

"They know about Simon."

She shrugged. "A lucky guess on their part. They can't prove anything. Besides, after today their knowledge will be a moot point."

"Only their knowledge?"

So he was worried, after all? Well, that was to be expected. She was working up a clever rejoinder when she spied Tory's car pulling into the lot.

"Tell Tory—common ground," she said, echoing Simon's final message instead. "Tell him. Remember Ibo." Her face contorted, the anger she'd been forced to tamp down so often came rushing back full force. "Damn you, Simon!" she cursed. "Damn you! I should have frozen you alive for doing what you did."

"Do you want to keep looking through the computer programs?" Her partner's question was quiet, a borderline whisper.

She ignored him, her eyes blazing as she watched Kristian and Tory enter the park. "I should freeze you, too," she whispered, her voice a sibilant hiss. "Both of you. Before you cause me any more trouble."

The man stared at her. "I don't think—" he began, but she cut him off with a savage growl that had him lapsing into an uncomfortable silence.

"You don't think," she spat the words back at him. "That's your problem, partner. You really don't think. Well, I do. And I'm very good at it." Calmer now, she faced him with a smile rich in meaning. "Every bit as good as Telstar."

LILITH, PRISCILLA, JUNE; one by one they stomped, strode and breezed into Kristian's office. And one by one she dealt with them, along with umpteen million other problems designed specifically to irritate.

"I truly hate days like this, Crux," she said to the little robot who now roamed the center alone while his turncoat twin sat in a dismantled heap in the Colonel's workshop. Priscilla wasn't happy about the situation. Neither were Lilith or Evan. But that was tough. Let them get locked in a space pod with a walking, talking time bomb and see how eager they were to have the little tin rat come zooming into their offices every two hours.

Exhausted, Kristian tossed herself into the chair behind her desk. A bizarre night had turned into an even more bizarre day. The imprint of Tory's touch was still strong on her mind—and on her body, she recalled, blushing as an uncustomary stiffness in her muscles made its presence felt. But that was hardly a problem. At least she wouldn't put it on the same level as Simon's death.

Drugged, shot, frozen and dumped in a Las Vegas alley, that was Tory's assessment of the situation, and it made perfect sense to her. Unfortunately, it was still an unsubstantiated theory.

Logic told her they should go to the police. Discretion told her they should talk to Morton and Evan. To that end, Tory had taken the first step last night—and come up empty. If Evan knew anything, he wasn't talking. According to Tory, he'd been properly shocked and outraged to learn that Simon's body had been found. But beyond that he'd revealed nothing, except an idea for a super-high-speed adventure ride and a new line of Peverell T-shirts.

"It's not fair, Crux," Kristian brooded. "Simon's dead, Telstar probably isn't, Tory doesn't want to believe Simon's message, and when you get right down to it, neither do I. So where does that leave us?"

"In limbo." Tory appeared at her office door, his face a stoic mask as he lounged against the frame, wearing his park uniform in his own inimitably casual fashion. "Morton's not in his suite."

"What?" Kristian glanced sharply at the brilliant afternoon sunshine behind her. "How can that be? I thought he was a creature of the night."

"That's what he claims." Pushing himself from the jamb, Tory strolled across the carpet and rooted through the half-eaten lunch of burritos and diet pop she'd had sent up from the Io Cafeteria two hours ago. "My guess is he's off to Paradise again."

"To visit the hermetic healer in the hill?" She watched him polish off her cheese burrito. "I don't see why he'd bother. Priscilla says the guy's a quack."

"June says he's a miracle worker."

"June also attacked us with a fireplace poker last night," Kristian reminded him. "Fond as I am of my assistant, I'm not giving her or anyone else the benefit of the doubt from now on. Too many horrible things have been happening lately."

"Fair enough," he agreed, then looked at his watch. "Three o'clock already. We'd better get going."

"Going?"

He summoned a grin at her wary expression. "To find George."

"Why do we want to find George?"

"Because we trust him, and we want him to help us figure this mess out."

Simply said, and Kristian found herself agreeing with him. Deep down, she knew George Straker was no more a killer than she was. Which left Morton and Evan and heaven only knew who else to consider.

"Do you know where George is?" she asked as they left the cool central complex for the dry desert heat of midafternoon.

Before Tory could respond, a cheerful young voice behind them chirped, "I do. I saw him going into the Colonel's workshop about five minutes ago."

Kristian smiled at the floppy-eared pandit, one of the many extraterrestrials who wandered throughout the park. "Are you sure it was George, Michelle?"

"Oh, yes." The teenage girl bobbed her furry head. "He whizzed past me so fast that I almost got whiplash, but then he came back and apologized. I think he had something major on his mind."

"Don't we all," Kristian said so softly that the girl couldn't possibly have heard her. Tory did; however, his only reaction was a distant smile and a nudge on her spine that got her moving in the direction of the Colonel's workshop.

The building was quiet when they arrived. No holograms romped on the floor of George's playroom. There was no sign of Peverell or Norres or even Brutus and, disappointingly, no sign of George Straker.

"Either Michelle's having hallucinations or George whizzed through here as quickly as he passed her." Hoisting herself up on a long black table, Kristian inserted a computerized disk into one of the projectors and switched it on, noting in an aside that the mechanism felt warm. A bug-eyed Plutonian fire-monger appeared instantly, oblivious to everything around him as he injected crystalline glow-seeds into various-sized bubbles and piled them up like a mountain of snowballs behind him. "That's good," she said, sidetracked by the ultraclear image. "Is it one of George's experiments?"

"Probably." Tory rested his hip against her leg as casually as if they'd been lovers for years. Which in a confused and complicated way they had. "Where did you find the disk?"

"Sitting by the projector, but there are more in here." She handed him a slotted leather box and sighed. "Why do I get this horrible feeling that Telstar is watching everything we do? I mean when you get right down to it, we're not even sure Telstar's behind all of this."

"It's a good bet, Kristian. I told you before, Telstar's notorious for establishing partnerships, then turning around and stabbing those partners in the back."

"Remember Ibo," Kristian repeated Simon's words thoughtfully. "Tell Tory—common ground."

Tory moved one shoulder. "Ibo's partner wanted the Southern Cross. It's a simple enough message."

Absently he slid a handful of disks into the projector, the muscle that twitched in his jaw the only hint of emotion Kristian could detect. This had to be incredibly hard for him to accept, she reflected, running her fingers through the ends of his thick hair. Morton and Evan were only her employers, but they were Tory's partners, his friends, people he'd trusted and believed in.

She opened her mouth to offer what little consolation she could, then closed it again when she caught sight of George in her peripheral vision. Except that it wasn't really George, she realized, recognizing the image she'd seen before. A 3-D image so real that it brought a strange chill to her skin. Especially when George's dark eyes met hers.

She was being absurd, she told herself. Holograms couldn't see. If this one appeared to be staring at her, it was simply that she happened to be sitting across from it. The same way she was sitting across from all the other projections that had magically appeared in the room: a Mercurian pit-clam, eyes blinking inquisitively at the end of its long antennae, a scowling Venusian lava tree whose limbs were launching molten silicon balls at a flock of playful cloud-drifters overhead, a sled-bellied European eel, Simon, a Martian dust-rooter, an automated lunar scout...

...Simon!

Kristian's eyes widened in disbelief. Simon? Here? Something tightened painfully in her chest. She wasn't seeing things. She couldn't be. "I don't believe this," she whispered, too stunned to do anything more that stare at the man in front of her. The man, the image...the illusion. "My God, Tory!" she rasped, clutching at his arm. "That's what

I saw the night we got locked in the space pod. It was a hologram. Someone made a hologram of Simon!''

"Someone did a hell of a lot more than that."

His angry growl cut through Kristian's shock, though she still couldn't drag her eyes from the startlingly real projection. At least she couldn't until a brilliant stream of light passed through her line of vision, nearly blinding her.

If Tory hadn't been holding her in place with his arm, she would have jumped from the table as a matter of reflex. Where once there'd been a relatively empty room there was now a huge pair of headlights, and behind that the indisputable outline of an eighteen-wheel truck. An enormous rig, bearing silently down on them with such a grim single-mindedness that for a second it seemed like a creature possessed, a mad thing bent on crushing everyone in its path.

Kristian kept her body rigid, watching, waiting, her mind in a chaotic jumble as the truck's speed increased. That it was actually doing no such thing made not a speck of difference to her sweating palms and constricted lungs. This was NORStar, not planet Earth. Anything was possible here. Including death.

She held her breath, not moving. The headlights grew stronger, the truck in front of them more malevolent. Then, suddenly, the lights disappeared, the truck vanished, the image dissolved, leaving nothing in its wake except a wall of darkness and a scattering of holographic figures, each calmly going about his or her business.

Kristian's lungs threatened to explode from lack of oxygen, she saw black spots in front of her eyes and the room seemed to be spinning in strange circles. Slowly, shakily, she released her breath, staring into the darkness as a multitude of conflicting thoughts and feelings pressed in on her. "We were run off the road by a hologram," she managed at length. "Lured into a space pod by a hologram. Almost killed on two separate occasions because of a stupid hologram." Anything else she might have wanted to add got stuck in her throat. In the space of a few short seconds, she'd gone from numbed shock, to relief, to incredulity, to a bout of icy fury that defied description. "The next thing we're going to discover is that Simon was murdered by a hologram."

"Maybe he was," Tory said softly but with an edge to his voice that stopped her bitter tirade in its tracks. "Maybe that's what Hubie was trying to tell us the night he died."

A feeling of dread washed over her, leaving her cold inside. "What are you talking about?"

For an answer, he slid his fingers to the back of her neck, turning her head toward the remaining holograms. "Look beside the Venusian firebrand," he instructed in the same quietly controlled tone. "Look at the two people standing there. This has to be the hologram Hubie was referring to."

Kristian located the familiar pair, a man and a woman working in tandem, and would have shrugged the matter aside if she hadn't caught the dangerous glitter in Tory's suddenly dark blue eyes. She bit her lip instead and turned her gaze back to the twosome. "What is it?" she asked, not understanding, yet aware in some obscure part of her mind that she should. "Are they doing something wrong?"

His low chuckle contained no trace of humor, and no hint of reassurance, either. "It's not what they're doing that's important," he told her. "It's what they're not doing."

"You're talking in riddles," she charged through gritted teeth. "What aren't they doing?"

"Well, let's just say we aren't sitting around twiddling our thumbs." A recognizable female voice drifted out from the shadows. Seconds later, the woman to whom it belonged emerged through her own holographic image, a cheerfully vicious smile on her lips, a sleek-looking gun in her hand. Her brows arched at Kristian's somewhat jolted expression. "Surprise, surprise, Kristian? Did I shock you?" She waved the gun tauntingly at Tory. "I know I shocked him. And here I thought you were both so good at rolling with the punches."

Kristian stared at the woman, feeling curiously detached from everything around her. There was no cause for alarm. This person couldn't possibly be pointing a gun at her. She was a hologram with the capacity for speech, that's all. Another of George's experiments. Surely she could be turned off.

Beside her, Tory regarded the woman with a smile that was as serene as it was wintry. "Not as good as you are at throwing them," he said in response to her remark, and inwardly Kristian tensed. This was no illusion, this was reality. Cold, hard reality. "Where's your soon to be ex-partner?" she heard him ask.

The woman's smile grew wider and just a trifle sarcastic. "Carrying out my orders, of course. Where did you think he'd be? At the bottom of a cliff? In an empty office?"

"In a freezer?" Kristian's anger returned in a rush. However, she knew better than to unleash her temper when she was staring down the barrel of a gun. "You killed him, didn't you?"

"Who, Simon?"

"Yes, Simon." Tory partly shielded Kristian's body with his own, keeping his eyes on the gun as she slid from the table. "Although it's understandable that you'd be starting to lose track of your victims by now."

"My, but we do have a mean mouth, don't we?" She moved a step closer. "Maybe I should remedy that situation by removing your entire head."

"It's all taken care of," a man's voice interceded, and thankfully, the woman halted her stony advance. "I've secured all the doors and windows. Unless they're beamed in, we shouldn't be troubled by any unwanted company." Her partner appeared to glide through the lava tree, his features placid, his eyes strangely glassy in the dim light. "Ah, I see they're not pleased to learn the truth."

"Did you think we would be?" Tory countered, pushing Kristian behind him as far as possible.

"To a degree, yes. I would think you'd at least be relieved."

"Right, they're relieved that I've got a gun pointed at their heads," the woman snapped. "I'm sure I would be."

Her partner subsided with a servile "I expect you're right." He indicated a door ten feet to his right. "Shall I take them to the storage room?"

Kristian's heart missed several beats. "Storage room?" she said weakly.

The woman passed the gun through her holographic image, seeming inordinately pleased with herself. "Yes, well, it's the best we can do, given that we don't have a freezer at our disposal." Her smile, directed mainly at Tory, became a triumphant gloat. "You had no idea, did you? But then it wouldn't have occurred to you that you were looking at a hologram the night Simon died."

Eyes darting to the telling projection, Kristian frowned, then glanced up at Tory. "Is this the hologram you saw that night?"

He nodded. "In the Cosmic Theater."

"Through two walls of glass," the man inserted quietly. "No one could have known it wasn't us."

Kristian's fists clenched at her sides. "So while your holograms appeared to be working at the Cosmic Theater, you two were really inside the central complex."

"Drugging Simon, as I'm sure you've guessed by now," the woman disclosed. "The rest, as they say, is history."

Drugged, shot, frozen and dumped in an alley. One by one the hideous word pictures raced through Kristian's head. These people were monsters, cold-blooded killers—and in the woman's case possibly a great deal more.

Swallowing the lump of fear in her throat, Kristian squared her shoulders and ventured an admirably prosaic "You're Telstar, aren't you?"

"Am I?" The woman's composed smile gave nothing away. "Perhaps. Personally, though, I've always preferred a more straightforward approach. Code names are fine for the masses, but I hardly think they're necessary among—oh, how shall I put this—colleagues? No, I find the truth generally works best in situations like these."

Tory, who hadn't taken his eyes off her face since she'd stepped out of the shadows, sent her a veiled look of enquiry. "And just what would that truth be?"

She stepped back a pace, separating herself from the troika in front of her, her smile now the picture of blithe self-satisfaction. "The truth is that I'm Priscilla, he's the Colonel . . . and I'm very much afraid the three of you are going to die."

As she spoke, she pointed the gun at each of them in turn. And squeezed the trigger three times.

Chapter Seventeen

The pain in Tory's head was brutal. He'd had a headache from a hangover once that hurt almost as much, but this one definitely took the cake. If some lingering reflex hadn't set off a thousand screeching alarms in his mind, he would have succumbed quite willingly to the black fog that wanted to pull him back in.

Somehow he forced his eyes open to a few thin shafts of light that intensified the pain in his head tenfold. Pity poor Count Dracula, he thought, groaning as he rolled away from the dusky beams. And Morton. If this was what it felt like to be either undead or photosensitive, he'd pass on both experiences.

He rolled onto his stomach and rested his forehead on the black lacquer floor. Death had to be better than this, he decided, then promptly retracted the thought as snatches of what had happened slowly came back to him.

Priscilla had shot them, hadn't she? Obviously not in a fatal sense, but she'd certainly pumped some kind of knockout drug into them. All three of them, including her ex-partner, the Colonel and . . . Kristian!

Tory swore out loud, as much to rouse himself as anything else, although it helped to hurl choice invectives at Morton's renegade goddaughter. "Bitch," he muttered when he ran out of more colorful terms. "Kristian, where are you?"

"Behind you, and stop shouting." She was on her knees by the time he found her, swaying and not particularly alert, but conscious. "I feel like I've been run over by a fifty-foot bottle of bourbon."

"Close enough," Tory agreed, folding her into his arms and almost slithering to the floor in the process. Damn, but he felt awful. "Are you hurt anywhere?"

"I hurt everywhere," she mumbled against his shoulder, "But it's better than the alternative. Where's the Colonel."

"He's here. I crawled over him to get to you."

"Is he alive?"

"I didn't stop to check."

She lifted her head just enough to look over his shoulder. "Don't you think we should? If nothing else maybe he can tell us why Priscilla didn't kill us—and I don't believe I just said that," she moaned, collapsing against him. "My God, I knew Priscilla in Las Vegas. We worked at the same hotel. She used to deal blackjack."

"She dealt something, all right," Tory charged dryly. "But I'd be willing to bet her favorite form of blackjack had nothing to do with cards."

A shudder passed through Kristian's body. "We've got to get out of here. Do you think the Colonel will help us?"

"He'll help us," Tory promised. Setting her away from him, he reached down and none too gently turned the older man from his stomach onto his back, checking the pulse in his neck as he did so. Not as strong as it could be, but there. He was alive if still unconscious.

In his peripheral vision Tory saw Kristian staring at the Colonel's relaxed features. "I don't trust him. Are you sure he's really out?"

"Positive."

"Can you bring him around?"

"Sure," he said and promptly gave the Colonel a right to the jaw that had more sound than force behind it.

Kristian was unmoved. "Hit him again," she ordered, and Tory knew if he didn't she would. Murder and betrayal obviously didn't sit well with her.

He cuffed the man again, and this time received a low grunt for his efforts. "Wake up, Colonel," he said, giving him a shake for good measure. "You're going to provide us with a little information."

"Information?" The Colonel's eyelids fluttered, then snapped wide open. "Information!" he repeated shrilly. "Did you find it? Where was it? I looked, I really did, but Simon hid it so well."

Tory gave him another shake. "Snap out of it, Colonel. Priscilla shot you with a drug pellet, remember?"

The Colonel managed to look highly affronted. "Certainly, I remember." He batted feebly at the hands holding him. "And now, my good man, if you'd be so kind as to remember your place."

"His place?" Kristian inquired doubtfully.

"Subcreature," the Colonel declared, flicking a disdainful finger at Tory as if he were contaminated. "Please, get back before one of your terrestrial germs rubs off. We're not so hearty healthwise on Alpha Centauri. No disease, you know, ergo no immune system."

"Maybe Priscilla shot him with a hallucinogenic drug," Kristian theorized. She tapped his arm. "Colonel, do you have any idea what's happened?"

He raked her contemptuously with his glassy eyes. "I beg your pardon?" he demanded, his tone haughty, almost comically indignant. "Are you speaking to me, human?"

At her skeptical look, Tory shrugged. "Don't ask me to explain any of this. You're the human here; I'm just a lowly subcreature."

"This isn't funny, Tory," she accused.

"Do I look like I'm laughing?"

He released the Colonel, who immediately began blowing imaginary germs from his shirt and vest, and dragged himself to his feet. Although his mind would have preferred to shut down, Tory knew they had to think of a way out of this storeroom before Priscilla returned from wherever it was she'd gone. His bleary eyes sought and located the one and only escape route open to them: an air duct that should be large enough to crawl through. Of course, they could try using the Colonel as a battering ram to knock down the locked door, but Tory wouldn't put it past Priscilla to have wired the damned thing to explode on contact. Even if she hadn't, God knew what other surprises might be awaiting them on the other side.

"Scheming witch," he grumbled as he crossed to the covered duct. "She must have used the Colonel's knowledge of holograms to make the ones we found outside."

Kristian joined him at the wall. "Much as I despise her at this moment, you have to admit it was a perfect plan. And it gave them both an airtight alibi."

"I gave them the alibi."

"You and a dozen red-zone security guards." She helped him tug on the duct cover. "Did it look like they were working in the control booth?"

"They appeared to be fixing a dead panel," Tory confirmed, recalling the night vividly. "They had it figured out beautifully. The intercom was dead, and the entry hatches to the control booth were jammed and they had their backs to the rest of the room. Through two layers of Plexiglass no one could reach them."

"Bug! Bug!" With a wild flapping of his elegant arms, the Colonel leaped to his feet, wobbled slightly and began stomping his feet on the floor like a Spanish flamenco dancer gone berserk. "She promised to kill them all for me. She lied to me." His foot came down hard on one of the lacquered tiles. "Lied!" Standing back, he straightened his tie, surveying the floor in seeming satisfaction. "There we are. I've killed it myself. Crushed the little Earth germ before it could infect me. Still, she did lie."

Kristian's expression was less than sympathetic. "Does everyone at this park think they come from outer space?"

"Space," the Colonel echoed, his voice and posture suddenly softening. "That's where I belong, where I and my following will go just as soon as she gives me the design to that remarkable new computer."

Tory's head snapped up. Abandoning for the moment his attempt to open the air duct, he advanced on the disoriented man, grabbing him roughly by the shoulders and pulling him up to his full height. "What computer, Colonel?" he demanded. The finger began to flick again, but Tory ignored it. "What design?" he bit out impatiently.

"The one our helper stole, of course. Please let go of me before I catch something."

Tory gave him a firm shake. "Was your helper Annette Barrows?"

The Colonel waved a dismissing hand. "Yes, I believe that was her name. Priscilla met her at some grand resort in Las Vegas. In any event, she's dead."

"So is Simon," Kristian added, her expression mutinous. "And Hubie."

"Subcreatures all of them," the Colonel snorted. "Such a troublesome lot, especially Simon. Priscilla said she heard something while she was strangling Annette." His finger continued to poke ineffectually at Tory's wrist. "Naturally I thought she was hearing things. She has a funny mind, even for a bloodthirsty and quite suspicious human. Still, as it turned out, she was right. Simon had seen everything. Knew all about us and our plan to steal the specifications for a revolutionary computer, one that can actually think for itself. Sadly, he overheard Annette giving us the access code to the program where she'd buried the information, and—well, I'm sure even creatures such as yourselves can guess the rest."

"More than you, it seems," Tory muttered under his breath. "What's Priscilla's plan now, Colonel? Did she tell you?"

The Colonel gave his head a regal lift. "As her partner, I refuse to answer that question. Moreover, if you don't unhand me in the next five Earth seconds, I shall transmit a telepathic message to my followers and have them do it for you."

Tory sighed. "Go right ahead. But I suggest you make it snappy. I have a feeling Priscilla wants us out of the way as quickly as possible."

Outraged, the Colonel regarded the hands that still held him. Mouth clamped tightly shut, he closed his eyes and began to hum. Summoning his troops, no doubt. Well, let him, Tory thought, too caught up in more pressing problems to concern himself with this one. Taking Kristian by the arm, he drew her back to the air duct.

"Unless I'm mistaken, this shaft leads right into the Colonel's workshop. If we can make it that far, we should be able to get out."

"Mmm."

Her distracted response had him averting his head. "What? Did you think of something."

"Yes and no." A crease formed between her delicately arched brows. "It suddenly occurred to me that if Priscilla and the Colonel are responsible for Simon's death, then his message couldn't have meant what we thought it did."

"I know." Tory pulled the duct cover off with a single hard tug. "Which leaves only one other explanation."

"And that is?"

"He wasn't trying to tell us who killed him."

"Then what...?" She hesitated. "You mean he was trying to tell us where he hid the information Annette Barrows stole?" Her eyes lit up. "That makes sense, doesn't it? He heard Annette give Priscilla and the Colonel the access code to the file she'd created, somehow he made it over to the central complex and used the computer in my office to change the code word."

"Makes sense to me."

She raised her gaze to his. "Yes, but what did he change it to? Not anything as simple as 'Ibo' or 'common ground.'"

No, nothing that simple, Tory reflected, measuring the size of the duct with his eyes. Simon had to have known Priscilla was in the vicinity or he wouldn't have shoved Kristian out of her office. Therefore, whatever information he'd wanted to convey would scarcely have been shouted out for his murderer to hear.

"Tell Tory—common ground," Kristian murmured. "Tell him, Remember Ibo. Ibo Quan, Lee Dong—"

"And our common ground," Tory finished the sentence. Groaning, he squeezed his aching eyes closed. "Common ground. Dammit, it was right there all along. Ibo's bar was where Simon and I met. It was our common ground. He must have changed the access code to Southern Cross."

"Come! Come! Come!" the Colonel chanted from across the small room. His lashes flew up. "They can't hear me," he declared, sounding put out. "It's this building we're in. It simply isn't conducive to telepathic waves."

Tory studied the man's aggrieved expression, then gave his mind a clearing shake. Act or not, drug-induced reaction or not, he had a first priority to get out of here. When Priscilla was in custody, he'd deal with the Colonel's fixation, not before. In the meantime, it was enough of a struggle simply to deal with the Colonel's protests as he and Kristian half-coaxed, half-shoved him into the duct.

"Watch him," Tory instructed her once they'd reached the workshop at the end of the tunnel. "This almost feels too easy."

"In your opinion." Kristian steered the Colonel away from a table full of toys. "Maybe Priscilla got tied up in another part of the park. Much as she might want to, she can't shoot everyone in her path."

Tory crossed to the side entrance and punched in the computer release code. "She wouldn't have to. Priscilla's nothing if not blunt. She can get rid of just about anyone with a dirty look."

The door popped in front of him. Easing it open, he scanned the surrounding area, more than a little surprised to discover that night had fallen. Jaw set, he glanced at his watch: 9:15. Why hadn't he thought to check the time before? Because, dammit, his brain was now only beginning to function at a halfway normal level.

"Okay, it seems clear," he said, extending his hand to Kristian. "We'll take the main thoroughfare back to the central complex. There'll still be lots of people wandering around the park."

"People?" the Colonel piped up, appalled. "Human people?"

"No, cat people," Tory growled. "Move it."

Arms beating the air, the Colonel did as he was told, fussing all the way. "I can't associate with such germy creatures," he insisted. "You must let me return to my workshop."

They'd joined the lazy flow of pedestrian traffic now. Calmly, Tory clamped a hand about the Colonel's slender wrists and dragged them down. "Knock it off," he warned, his tone just short of a snarl.

An edginess he'd long since learned to appreciate crept over him. Something didn't feel right. Actually, nothing felt right. He knew it, and from the look on her face, so did Kristian.

"Where are we going?" It was the Colonel who posed the question in a confused fashion that made it seem as though he'd just awakened from a deep, deep sleep.

Kristian's eyes panned the crowds. "To the central complex," she told him absently.

"Oh, no, I don't want to go there."

Tory's fingers tightened around his wrists. "Tough," he said flatly.

"Isn't it, though?" The husky voice, rich with amusement, came from directly behind them, and Tory felt his muscles clench. "How nice of you to come and meet me." Smiling pleasantly, Priscilla strolled into sight, hands jammed into the pockets of her baggy uniform jacket. "I don't suppose I need mention that I've got a gun pointed at you. Hidden, of course. We don't want to alarm our paying guests, do we? That wouldn't be good for public relations. Oh, and by the way, Tory, I'd be grateful if you'd let go of the Colonel. I said I had a gun, but if the truth be known, I really have two. One for me and one for my not entirely sane but still relatively manageable partner."

Tory said nothing, and pulling free of his slackened grasp, the Colonel stepped back. "Germs," he sighed, rubbing his wrists. "I'm undoubtedly contaminated."

"Snap out of it," Priscilla chided scornfully. "You can take a sonic shower later." Unobtrusively she slipped him a snub-nosed hand gun. "Tuck it in your belt," she instructed. "Unless they're incredibly stupid, you won't need to use it."

Tory watched the Colonel's face, watched the glassy sheen vanish from his pale blue eyes, saw his deportment change swiftly, as though he'd been hit with a jolt of electricity. "I'm sure they'll behave," he said in his usual diplomatic way. Or was it closer to subservience?

With her head, Priscilla motioned Kristian and Tory forward. "Slow and easy," she advised, keeping her partner at her side, and her sights trained on the pair in front of her. "Did you follow my orders?" she queried, and the Colonel nodded.

"You know I always do." A vaguely enigmatic note entered his voice. "I told them about our helper, Annette, and about Simon. I told them everything you wanted me to, and then I listened."

The curse that erupted from Tory's mouth couldn't possibly have been heard by the twosome behind him. They'd been set up all the way, and he'd fallen for it. It was an old and often effective rule of thumb, one that had been drummed into his head time and time again in the military. If you can't figure something out and you think the enemy might be able to do it for you, leak a little information and see what develops. Damn, he should have seen this coming.

"Common ground," the Colonel was saying now. "Apparently, that was the key to Simon's message."

"And what is this common ground?" Priscilla inquired in a silvery tone.

"A bar," the Colonel returned, shifting his gaze to the evening's first stars. "Simon changed the access code to Southern Cross."

"IN HERE." The cold smile that seemed permanently etched on Priscilla's lips didn't waver as she closed the heavy door behind her. They were inside the fireworks storage building, an impenetrable fortress situated on the outer rim of the park, well apart from the other structures. "Back there," she said, nodding toward a rear storage chamber. "Now that I've finally gotten what I want, you're of absolutely no use to me."

Kristian could well imagine what was coming, but she refused to panic. She hung on by a thread, forcing herself to face the icy maintenance woman. "What if we're wrong about Southern Cross being the computer access code?"

Priscilla shrugged. "Then I guess I'm back to square one. But at least I won't have you two breathing down my neck." Her smile took on a penitent cast, and she turned to the Colonel beside her. "Oh, dear, I seem to have miscounted yet again. Sloppy of me. I meant to say I won't have you three breathing down my neck."

The Colonel's eyes clouded in puzzlement. "Three? But I don't—"

"Understand?" Priscilla gave him an impatient little push in Tory's direction. "Okay, I'll spell it out for you one last time. I needed your help. You gave it to me. Now you're nothing but deadweight, soon to be simply dead. Is that plain enough for you—partner?"

Obviously, it was. The Colonel made an odd strangled sound in his throat and quickly began fumbling for the gun he'd tucked under the bottom of his vest. As he did, Tory calmly reached out and snared Kristian's arm, pulling her off to one side.

"I have a feeling we're in for one hell of a show," he murmured, and if the situation hadn't been so desperate Kristian would have kicked him to wake him up.

"This woman's going to kill us, Tory," she hissed, anger and terror clashing within her. "How can you stand there and be so composed?"

"I'm not composed, I'm thinking."

Of a way out, she prayed but kept her mouth shut as Priscilla's laugh rang out, filling the dusty crate-jammed room. "You really are a fool, aren't you, Colonel? Did you honestly think I'd give you a loaded gun?"

"You said we were partners," the Colonel replied, still fumbling with his belt, but in a fretful fashion. "You told me I could use the stolen design for my own private purposes, that it wouldn't matter what I did since you were going to sell the plans to an overseas buyer. You said we'd both benefit in the end."

The corners of her mouth gave a perfunctory quirk. "I lied," she countered without a trace of remorse.

The Colonel's normally serene face flushed, but Priscilla merely chuckled and turned to Kristian and Tory. "Would you believe this space cadet wanted to use the stolen specifications to create his own artificially intelligent computers—as if that were even possible—so that he could then implant them in his toys and robots and such? He actually believes they're his followers, his interplanetary disciples, if you will."

Kristian banked down her fear long enough to ask, "You mean he really does think he's from another planet?"

"Sometimes." Priscilla gave her gun a desultory wave. "Most times, in fact. But even invading extraterrestrials know they have to try and blend in with us lowly Earthlings in order to avoid detection. I think it's a rule of some sort."

"It's something," Tory agreed mildly and not quite loud enough for Priscilla to pick up. He pushed Kristian a little farther to the right and arched an indolent brow. "I take it you've lined up a buyer for this design you stole."

"I've lined up several," she said, grinning at the Colonel who now looked as dazed as he did wounded. "Who wouldn't be interested in a computer that can think for itself? All I have to do now is choose which de—arghh!"

The cry of pain that broke from her lips effectively wiped away her smile. "What the...?" she snapped angrily, whirling around, and Kristian caught a fleeting glimpse of the two metallic arms that snaked out from behind a crate to close their viselike claws about the woman's ankles. "What is this?" Priscilla thundered, fighting ineffectively to back away. "Tory, you bastard!"

Tory! Kristian snatched her head up, but Priscilla's piercing shriek of outrage made her turn. "Let go of me!" she shouted and began swearing at a fast and furious rate.

Even though she was in shock, Kristian's first instinct was to bolt for the door. To her astonishment, however, Tory hooked a strong arm about her waist, holding her firmly in place, not looking at her when she endeavored to wrench herself free.

"Don't move," he said, his eyes locked not on Priscilla's flailing form, but on something else. On someone else, she realized with a start that stopped her struggles cold.

"Very good, Tory," the object of his attention congratulated. "Most impressive. You knew the truth even before we came in here, didn't you?"

"I had an idea."

"An idea!" Priscilla's furious screech rent the air. "What are you talking about? What's going on? You traitor! What's Crater doing here? Why is he cutting off the circulation in my legs?"

Lips compressed to hold back the scream that was burning in her throat, Kristian stared at the robot. The fully functional robot, whose arms gave a sudden jerk that sent

Priscilla crashing to the floor with an undignified splat, halting her bitter diatribe midstream.

"Thank you, Crater." Unruffled, in fact the complete antithesis of the man who moments before had been flicking imaginary germs from his clothing, the Colonel removed the robot's remote control from his belt and pushed a series of buttons. Crater immediately opened his mechanical claws and rolled away from his spluttering victim. "I'm terribly sorry, Priscilla," her ex-partner apologized. "But you do tend to go on. The drawback of a violent temper, I suspect—though, I confess, psychology isn't my forte."

Priscilla's face was purple with the force of her rage. "You treacherous old coot," she spat. "You can't do this to me! I won't let you!" Snarling, she grabbed the gun she'd dropped and squeezed the trigger.

The Colonel patted back an exaggerated yawn, then offered her a tranquil smile. "Blanks only," he revealed, once the resounding blasts had subsided. "Really, Priscilla, you could learn a thing or two from Tory and Kristian. You don't see them charging about in a panic. They realize that such a thing would be pointless. They know that Crater isn't—now how did you put it earlier—twiddling his thumbs here beside me. No, I've equipped him quite well. Quite well indeed."

A feral growl emanated from between Priscilla's bared teeth. "I don't care if he's equipped with enough explosive to blow this park sky-high. You won't get away with this."

Smiling wistfully, the Colonel appealed to Tory, whose arm was wrapped like a steel band around Kristian's waist. "She's not overly perceptive, is she?"

"Not overly," Tory agreed, his steady gaze never leaving the Colonel's face.

"Oh, really?" Priscilla's voice grew ominous. "And just who are you to make such a judgment?"

"How dreadfully rude of me." With appropriate thespian decorum, the Colonel executed a polite bow that encompassed all three people before him. "Please, forgive my shoddy manners and allow me to introduce myself. As you might imagine Nathan Brenda is only one of numerous aliases I use. Most of them you wouldn't know. But there is one you might recognize. In business circles both at home and abroad, I'm referred to simply as Telstar.''

Chapter Eighteen

Telstar.

Kristian squeezed her eyes tightly closed, unable to believe what she'd just heard. The Colonel, not Priscilla, was the code-named secret seller. It was the Colonel who'd been using Priscilla all along. Manipulating her by allowing her to think that she was manipulating him. God, but this was complicated. And terrifying, Kristian thought, swallowing shakily. The only thing that was crystal clear in all of this was that Telstar intended to kill them.

"Dreadful business, this," the Colonel stated sadly, ignoring Priscilla's abusive snaps and barks as he watched Tory bind her wrists and ankles at gunpoint. "So much death. I must admit it was a relief to let my partner do the killing this time. Annette, Simon, Hubie—yes, it was much easier to let her do the dirty work."

Morbid curiosity prompted Kristian to venture a tremulous "Weren't you taking an awful risk letting her kill Hubie in the Planet of Dreams? What if she'd decided to shoot you instead?"

The Colonel bent to plaster a piece of wide tape across Priscilla's scurrilous mouth. "It was a calculated risk," he agreed. "In my line of work, one is forced to take such gambles from time to time. In this case, and knowing Priscilla as I do, I felt certain she would dispatch Hubie first. He was, after all, a bigger threat to her at that point. Needless to say, I saw to it that her gun jammed after one shot."

Tory gave the ropes around Priscilla's ankles a final tug, then sat back on his haunches and surveyed the man before him through speculative eyes. "Why did you let her drug you this afternoon? You could have faked it easily enough."

The Colonel's slender fingers stroked Crater's head. "Perhaps, but only if I'd pretended to wake up first. No, I thought it best to take another calculated risk. You see, Priscilla needed me at that juncture. On the other hand, you were suspicious enough of my act. I knew if you thought there was a chance I hadn't been drugged, you would never have felt free to talk in front of me." With his gun, he motioned at Kristian. "I'm truly sorry, my dear," he said gently. "I'm going to have to ask Tory to tie you up, as well. I have to leave, you understand. Granted I do have a hologram running elsewhere, but unless it's absolutely necessary, I prefer not to rely too heavily on mechanical alibis."

The fearful tremors that slid through Kristian's body weren't dispelled by the Colonel's remorseful tone, or even by the touch of Tory's fingers on her legs. "What are you going to do to us?" she demanded with far more defiance than she felt.

A sigh escaped the Colonel's lips. "Do you really want to know?"

"She wouldn't have asked if she didn't," Tory said quietly.

"I suppose not." The Colonel's eyes shifted to the stack of crates where a gagged and bound Priscilla sat propped up and glowering poisonously. "However, I feel compelled to give credit where credit is due. This was my erstwhile partner's idea." He swept a graceful arm about the large storage area. "The location, the method of destruction—everything except the actual construction of the device. I realize it won't be of much comfort to you, but you'll be going out in a blaze of glory. Yes, it should be quite a spectacular show when my bomb goes off."

Bomb? For the second time that week, the baneful word sent Kristian's head into a tailspin. A controlled tailspin. She flatly refused to fall apart. From the fragments of her courge, she dredged up as much of her voice as she could and managed to croak, "Won't you also be killing a lot of innocent people?"

"Oh, I do hope not."

How could a heartless murderer infuse his voice with so much contrition, her bemused mind wondered as Tory, having bound her wrists behind her back, gave her fingers a reassuring squeeze.

"You'll now tie your own ankles," the Colonel instructed him. "Then, I'm very much afraid that Crater and I will have to depart. I have some very valuable information to extract from the NORStar computers."

"And after that?" Tory prodded.

"I'll mourn your deaths along with everyone else at the park, drop a few subtle hints here and there, create a few new inculpating holograms and before they know it, the authorities will think Telstar is dead once again." He twisted a strong rope around Tory's wrists, checked all the knots and rose smoothly to his feet. "Before I do anything else, however, I must ensure that those most incriminating holograms you and Kristian discovered this afternoon are destroyed. Yes, I must do that post haste."

Satisfied that all was well, he turned Crater for the door, pausing only briefly to pinch Priscilla's fury-mottled cheek. "Don't feel too badly," he consoled. "Some of your ideas were rather unique. I'd never thought to freeze a victim before. You've been a most intriguing partner. Perhaps we'll meet again in the realm of Pluto. Or as you here on Earth more commonly refer to it . . . hell."

Smiling serenely, he touched Crater's shiny back. And glided off, dissolving into the darkness without a sound.

"WHAT ARE WE GOING TO DO?" Kristian demanded in a whisper. She was already engaged in a heated battle with the ropes around her wrists, but it had to be one of the most futile fights she'd ever put up. "For God's sake, Tory, did you have to make the knots so tight?"

"No, but if I hadn't, Telstar would have."

A shudder of revulsion shimmered through her. "Please don't call him that. If I keep believing he's just the Colonel, I might be able to convince myself that we stand a one-in-a-thousand chance of surviving this."

"We do."

His matter-of-fact tone brought her struggles to an abrupt halt, her eyes up to his dispassionate features. As always, his calmness was notable. Irritating, but Tory through and through. And if he could be unflappable in the face of death, dammit, so could she. "What did you say?" she asked in a determinedly neutral voice.

Using the crates behind him as a brace, he climbed to his feet. "I said we stood a one-in-a-thousand chance of surviving."

"Those aren't great odds," she muttered, staring up from the filthy floor. "Do you have an idea?"

His eyes glittered in the dim light. "Come here."

The rein on her quaking nerves snapped. "Are you out of your mind?" she shot back, exasperation and unbridled terror making her throat raw. "This is no time for—" Quickly she clamped her mouth shut. What was he thinking? What was she accusing him of thinking? Out loud, she changed her reproach to a more sedate "Why?"

"Because I don't intend to die without first doing what this is no time to do several more times and under slightly more favorable conditions."

Despite their dire situation, that totally convoluted statement brought a reluctant smile to Kristian's lips. "I hope you get the chance. What's your plan?"

"If you stand up, I'll show you."

For once she didn't argue. Didn't even mutter under her breath as she levered herself to her feet. "All right, I'm up. Now what?"

"Turn around."

She sighed. "I feel like a puppet whose strings are all tangled."

"Just be thankful he didn't gag us."

Some inexorable force drew Kristian's eyes to Priscilla's motionless face. She was glaring at them, not making a sound, not moving a muscle, flaying them with those soulless brown eyes of hers.

Tory's deft fingers were performing some arcane ritual on her ropes and, dragging her eyes away from Priscilla's, Kristian pressed her lips together. A bout of hysteria wouldn't help and neither would looking at her nemesis. How had Priscilla become involved with Telstar? How long had he been planning this particular theft? He'd been working at the park since before it opened fifteen months ago. Doubtless he'd joined the staff with one goal in mind. And now that his goal was close to being realized...

She sank her teeth into her lower lip, rejecting the rest of that thought. She couldn't, wouldn't believe her life was over.

"Okay, that should do it." Tory's voice, composed as ever, interrupted her dark musings. "Move your wrists."

Somewhat mystified, Kristian complied. And felt a bolt of shock shoot through her when the ropes fell away.

"How did you do that?" she asked, staring in amazement at her former bonds.

"Military magic. I'll give you a lesson sometime. But first, let's get out of here."

Kristian's fingers worked feverishly at the ties on his hands. "What about the bomb? We don't know where it is or when it's set to go off."

Tory dispensed with the ropes on their ankles then crouched down beside Priscilla, an unpromising smile tilting the corners of his mouth as he appraised her venomous features. "You check the doors. I'll find the bomb—won't I, Priscilla?"

Shivering, Kristian turned her back on the woman and hastened to inspect the three doors this building boasted. Doors that were constructed along similar lines to those on high security bank vaults. No vandal stood a chance of breaking in and stealing any of NORStar's fireworks. By the same token, she realized, no one locked inside stood a chance of breaking out.

Giving the third door a frustrated kick, Kristian limped back to the storage area, trying desperately not to count the hundreds of crates she passed. The amount of explosive material contained in this building didn't bear close examination. Suffice to say, it was enough to blow away one full corner of the space park.

"You know what you can do with your questions, Tory," Priscilla was snarling when Kristian rejoined them.

At the negative shake of her head, he wrapped a thick strand of Priscilla's hair around his fingers and offered her a bland smile.

"You might want to reconsider your position," he said without so much as a hint of anger. "I'm not always as nice as you might think."

Priscilla's answering curse was loud and rude. "You don't scare me." Her chin jutted belligerently. "Why should I help you, anyway?"

"Think of it as helping yourself," he suggested, but she merely snorted her derision.

"Right. I'd be helping myself right into a prison cell. Besides, you two deserve to die."

Kristian refrained from taking a swing at the woman's stubborn jaw. "I hate to be the bearer of bad tidings," she said instead. "But if we die, you die."

"So?" Priscilla's chin jutted even more. "Maybe I'd rather die than be stuck in some jerkwater women's prison."

Tory's fingers tightened on the lock of hair he held. "Look at it this way," he said pleasantly. "There's always a chance you could break out of prison. I've never heard of anyone breaking out of hell."

Priscilla's nostrils flared, and Kristian thought she detected a small quaver in her rigidly set features. Going down on her knees, she made one last attempt at reasonableness. "If we die, Telstar walks away with exactly what he wanted."

"Whereas if we live, we'll nail him to the wall," Tory released her hair and trapped her chin. "Who knows, you might even be able to swing a deal with the federal prosecutors."

Pulling away, Priscilla sent them both a smoldering glare. "Top crate, second stack to your left," she growled at last. "The one marked 'Starburst.'"

It took five long minutes to remove the bomb from its hiding place. Five of the most excruciating minutes of Kristian's life. Her palms were sweaty, her mouth and throat dry, her heart pounding double time against her ribs.

"Which wire?" Tory demanded of a still-seething Priscilla.

"How the hell should I know?" she shouted. "I didn't make the stupid thing. Try the blue one."

"Are you sure?"

"No—yes. I think that's what he said."

"Pull the red one," Kristian whispered.

"Pull the blue one," Priscilla countered.

"The red one."

"The blue one!"

Fingers poised above the deadly mechanism, Tory gave Kristian a quick kiss. Then reached out and pulled the red one....

THINGS WERE GOING SPLENDIDLY, Telstar reflected, opening the door to his workshop. As far as anyone who mattered was concerned, he'd been in the Cosmic Theater control room from 7:00 until almost 10:00 p.m. Very soon the fireworks storage building would explode, taking Kristian and Tory and Priscilla with it, and he'd be alone as he'd always preferred to be.

"Footloose and fancy-free." He addressed Crater beside him, then pulled up short and blinked in surprise. "Well, now, what do we have here? A belated dose of Priscilla's handiwork, I expect."

He swept into George's area of the workshop, mildly annoyed with his ex-partner but confident that George was

engaged at the Planetarium. At least he couldn't be respon
sible for the twenty-five or more holograms that were cu
rently flitting about the black-walled room.

Although Telstar knew he shouldn't, it was hard not t
stop and watch the aliens play. They certainly were a d
verse lot, from the pixieish Venusian cloud drifters to Pe
erell in all his lethargic glory.

"I believe I'll miss these creatures, Crater," he co
fessed. "Peverell, Norres, even..." Again he stopped shor
and this time felt a prickle of unease crawl down his spin
"You!" he exclaimed, his voice little more than an asto
ished whisper. He stared in disbelief at the person befor
him. "What are you doing here? I thought you had to sta
in the dark... No! This isn't real. You're an illusion, a h
logram. You have to be."

Even as he uttered the words, he began to edge bac
ward. The figure followed, moving slowly, silently, its blac
robe fluttering in the nonexistent breeze.

Was this person real or not? "What do you want?" Te
star demanded, but the figure didn't speak. Nor did it a
pear to walk so much as float across the lacquered floor.

In a strangely hypnotic motion, one bony white hand ros
up, reaching for him. An illusion, he prayed, reaching f
him.

Telstar saw a flash of teeth, heard a soft, raspy chuck
and felt something tighten painfully in his chest. A fie
contraction that brought with it a sweeping surge of dar
ness, the acrid smell of brimstone. And the bitter taste
death.

"A MASSIVE CORONARY, that's what the doctors are callir
it." George shook his head in perplexity. "Damndest thir
I've ever heard, and I've heard a lot. Most of it in the pa
three hours." He glanced at Kristian, who was too bus
punching commands into her office computer to react to h
subtle gibe, then back at Tory who'd just wandered in aft
a long discussion with the FBI. "You want to run this stor
past me one more time?"

"It isn't a story," Kristian informed him distractedly. She apped a few more keys and frowned at Tory. "The information's not here. At least if it is, Southern Cross isn't the correct address code."

Tory rested his hip lightly against her shoulder. "Try the generic name."

"*Crux Australis*?" She shrugged and switched her attention back to the screen, leaving Tory to face another round of questions. Not that he minded when those questions came from George.

"Where would you like me to start?" he asked, stretching his arms out in front of him.

"How about with the Colonel's heart attack. Or should I call him Telstar?"

"Call him what you like. He's dead. As you said, the doctors are labeling it a coronary. They figure it hit him about fifteen minutes before Kristian and I found him, somewhere around ten o'clock."

"And you found him lying on the workshop floor, with a bunch of holograms swarming around him."

"Yup."

"Very strange," George mused. "What about Priscilla? Why did she get mixed up in this?"

"Pure greed," Tory said simply.

"Is she in custody?"

"Jon's taking her to the city now."

"You don't sound too sympathetic."

Kristian removed her eyes from the computer screen. "She killed three people and would have doubled that number if the Colonel hadn't thwarted her plan. It's hard to feel sorry for someone with the morals of a modern-day Maleficent. Tory, the information's not under *Crux Australis*, either."

He grinned and brushed the tangled blond hair from her cheeks, "Then try the simpler version of the name."

"Crux." She sighed and began striking the keys anew. "If this doesn't work, we're going to have to rethink Simon's entire message."

"Or assume that Telstar got to the information first." George regarded Tory shrewdly. "Do you have any idea how this unholy alliance between the Colonel and Priscilla was formed?"

"Jon figures it started five years ago in Las Vegas. Telstar heard about Morton's interest in backing the space park, saw an easy in through his goddaughter and slowly began to devise a new plan even as he was finishing up an old one."

"One involving Willard Barrows?"

"Jon insists that was Telstar's usual M.O. He always had another scheme lined up and waiting. To understate a point, he was a man of many talents."

"And a weak heart." George leaned on Kristian's desk. "Does anyone know how old he was?"

Tory shrugged. "Sixty, sixty-five. Nobody's really sure. I gather he was in impeccable health."

"With one notable exception," George drawled. "How's Morton taking the news about Priscilla?"

Tory glanced toward the Pallas Hotel. "Actually, very well. It was almost as if he knew before I told him."

"Yeah, I've heard he's like that sometimes. What did the bomb squad have to say?"

"That we were lucky to have pulled the right wire." Kristian gave her hair an impatient toss and the keyboard a disgruntled whack. "There's nothing here. I even tried the Latin name, *Crucis*."

"Then forget it." Leaning over, Tory switched off the computer. "Let the experts search."

She sat back in her chair, staring thoughtfully at the screen. "Maybe the Colonel did get to it first. He could have changed the code word again."

"In which case, the chances of finding it any time in the near future are slim," George informed them, moving aside as Crux wheeled into the office on his programmed route. He looked at his watch. "It's 1:05 a.m. I don't know about you two but I'm beat."

Kristian smiled wearily. "I think in my next life I want to come back as a robot. They never seem to get tired."

Tory chuckled. "No, they just run around threatening to blow people up in space pods."

"Only the nasty ones. I'll just make sure I come back as Crux instead of Crater."

Tory saw the small frown that creased her forehead as her eyes settled first on the computer screen, then on the robot who was completing his speedy tour of inspection. "What is it?" he asked and was nearly knocked off-balance when she suddenly shoved her chair back and jumped to her feet.

"Crux!" she exclaimed, grabbing his arm. "Tory, it's Crux! The constellation, the bar...the robot. Crux is the Southern Cross! Simon didn't change the access code; he copied the information."

"And gave it to Crux," Tory finished for her. "Damn."

The robot was already halfway across the office floor, but George, closest to the door, nabbed him before he could escape. "Not so fast," he said quietly. "Let's see if you're carrying around any excess baggage."

With Kristian hanging over his shoulder, Tory crouched down in front of Crux's barrel chest and flipped open the panel. "Anything?" she breathed while he poked at the wires and circuits.

"Not that I can—" He cut the sentence off as his fingers came up against a jutting edge. Thin, sharp and decidedly out of place.

"What is it?" Kristian demanded in his ear and, smiling slightly, he withdrew a black floppy disk from inside Crux's chest.

"Simon Juniper's version of the Southern Cross."

"DARTH VADER," Kristian murmured, leaning back against Tory's relaxed form on the porch lounge outside his ranch house. It was three in the morning, the stars were still glimmering overhead and the smell of pepperoni pizza was strong in the night air. "I wonder why the Colonel wanted us to believe he'd seen Morton in the Cosmic Theater the night Simon was killed? It really wasn't necessary. For all intents and purposes, his alibi was intact.''

Tory grinned and pulled her closer, running his lips along the side of her neck. "Maybe he had a *Star Wars* fetish."

She couldn't resist a smile. "You have a warped mind, you know that?"

"I know." His mouth slid lower to her shoulder. "That's what you love about me."

"You're sure about that?"

"Sure that's what you love about me?"

Eyes closed, she tipped her head back. "Sure that I love you at all. Maybe you're one of those passing things. Like malaria. Every eleven years I have a recurring attack."

Tory's fingers had no trouble dispensing with the buttons of her uniform. "Keep up the flattery," he murmured in lazy amusement, "and I'll start to think you care."

"You would." She bit back a gasp of pleasure as his knuckles slid lightly over her breast, grazing her nipple beneath the lace of her bra. Even so, she managed a dry "Remember, if it weren't for George, I'd be in Las Vegas right now rather than here with you on this porch, the near-victim of a mercenary secret-seller and his bloodthirsty ex-partner."

"Not quite true," he said, sliding his hand over her flat stomach, while his mouth attacked the pulse at the base of her throat.

She pushed at his wrist, but it was a token gesture at best. "You're a swing vote, Tory. Nothing more."

"Nice try, but no cigar this time."

"What do you mean?" Twisting in his arms she brought her lips against his, and Kristian immediately melted into him, forgetting all about conversation and denial and the pricks of her stubbornly resistant conscience that had long since begun to fade into oblivion.

His mouth came down on hers, but not before she heard the words that fell from his lips. "George was the swing vote."

He might as well have told her he was Telstar's apprentice. Dragging her mouth away, she stared at him. "What?"

Unperturbed, he ran his lips over her jaw. "You heard me. I'm the one who wanted you to manage to park."

"You?" Somehow she suppressed a smile of pure delight. "Why?"

"Why do you think?"

She twisted back around in his arms, letting her gaze roam the starry night sky. "Because you love me?"

"Good guess."

"Then that makes us even," she murmured, "because I love you very much. In fact, I love you more now than I did in…" Her half-closed lashes flew up as something streaked through the darkened heavens in a flash of green light. "What was that?"

Not removing his lips from her shoulder, Tory inquired, "What was what?"

She scanned the star-studded sky. "Didn't you see it? It seemed to come from the space park. I swear it looked like a—"

"Flying saucer?"

His teasing tone had Kristian relaxing against him; his relentless mouth soon had her dismissing the image in favor of a much more erotic thought. After all, she knew as well as anyone that there were no such things as flying saucers.

And certainly no such things as little green men from outer space.

HE STOOD in the darkness he'd come to know so well, staring at the distant trail of green light, his black robe fluttering around him. It was a strange world, he thought with a tiny smile. Not perfect, but a place he could call home.

For now.

From *New York Times* Bestselling author
Penny Jordan, a compelling novel of ruthless passion
that will mesmerize readers everywhere!

Penny Jordan

Silver

Real power, true power came from
Rothwell. And Charles vowed to have it,
the earldom and all that went with it.

Silver vowed to destroy Charles, just as surely and
uncaringly as he had destroyed her father; just as he had
intended to destroy her. She needed him to want her . . .
to desire her . . . until he'd do anything to have her.

But first she needed a tutor: a man who wanted no one.
He would help her bait the trap.

Played out on a glittering international stage,
Silver's story leads her from the luxurious comfort of
British aristocracy into the depths of adventure,
passion and danger.

AVAILABLE IN OCTOBER!

 HARLEQUIN

SILVER

Harlequin Intrigue®

REBECCA YORK

Labeled a "true master of intrigue" by *Rave Reviews*, bestselling author Rebecca York continues her Harlequin Intrigue ongoing series

It looks like a charming old building near the renovated Baltimore waterfront, but inside 43 Light Street lurks danger . . . and romance.

Don't miss the next book in the series when private detective Jo O'Malley finds herself being stalked by a serial killer. Chilling suspense and a fiery romance.

Look for #155 SHATTERED VOWS in February 1991. And watch for more 43 LIGHT STREET titles in the future.

HI-LS-1